THE ILLUMINATORS

THE ILLUMINATORS

Copyright © 2024 by Guadalupe Gonzalez.

Cover design and elements by: Canva and Shutterstock
Map and chart design created in: Canva
Chapter illustrations and breaks by: AnesayArt on Etsy
Other celestial illustrations by: SunnyAfternoonsJPG on Etsy

ISBN: 979-8-9921287-0-3 (paperback)

First Edition: December 2024
10 9 8 7 6 5 4 3 2 1

To those whose mind, heart, and soul
belong beyond the universe.

THE ILLUMINATORS

BOOK 1 OF THE ILLUMIVERSE SERIES

GUADALUPE GONZALEZ

Illuminators
Powerchart

EARTHKALAIS (ORDER OF ELEMENTS)

FIRE (Flamers) = Mercury
Manipulates fire
ICE (Flakers) = Venus
Manipulates ice
WATER (Liquis) = Earth
Manipulates water
AIR (Aires) = Mars
Manipulates air

JOVIANKALAIS (ORDER OF SCIENCE)

BIOLOGY (Bios) = Jupiter
Controls and manipulates biological matter
PHYSICS (Physicists) = Saturn
Controls and alters metal-related matter
CHEMISTRY (Chems) = Neptune
Controls and creates chemical matter
ARCHITECTURE (Archs) = Uranus
Controls and creates architecture techniques

CELESTIALKALAIS (ORDER OF THE MIND)

MEMORY (Eidetics) = Pluto
MIND HEALING (Menders) = Ceres
ILLUSIONS (Illusionaries) = Eris
PROTECTING (Protectors) = Make Make
INVISIBILITY (Invisibles) = Haumea

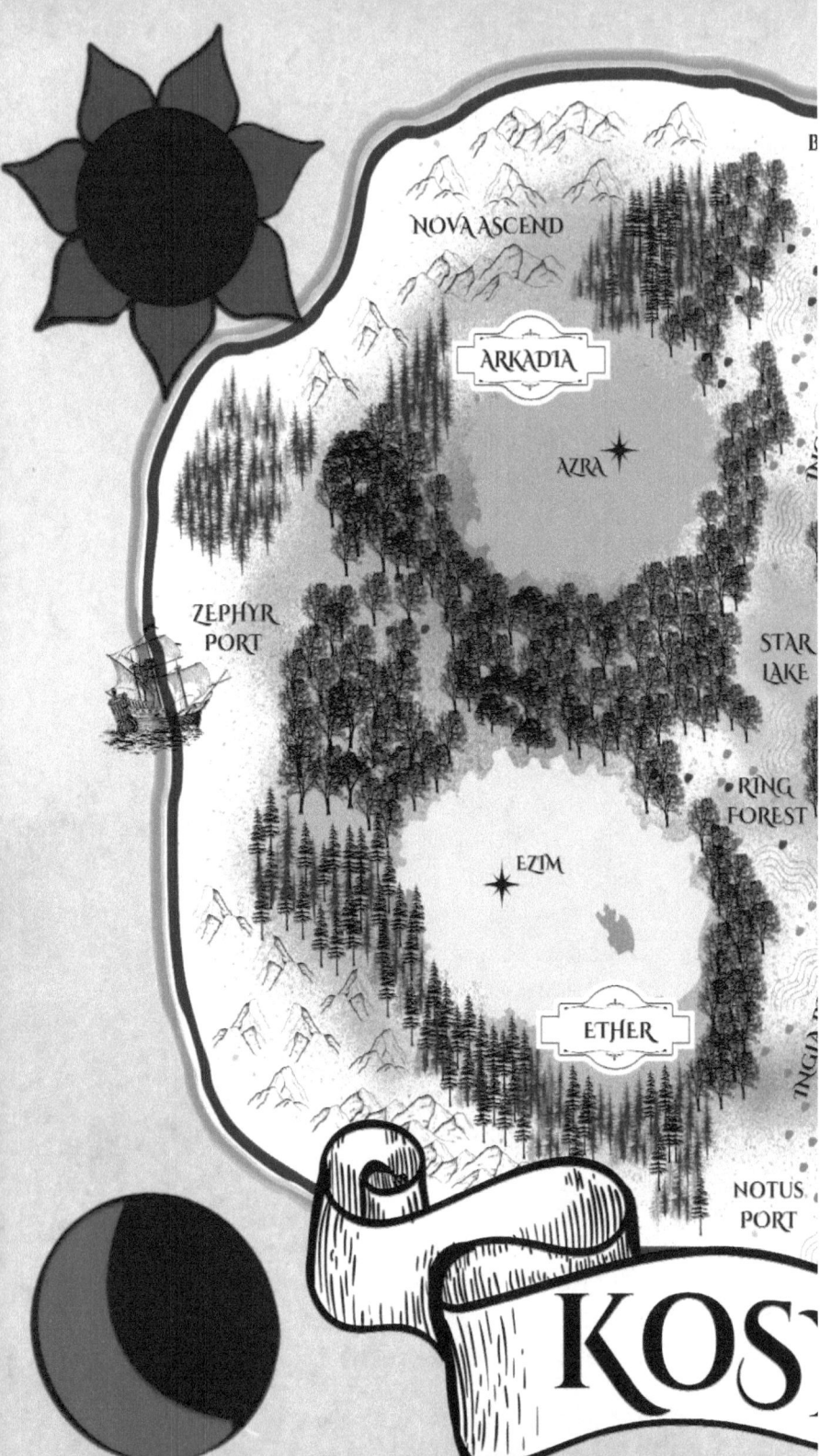

BOREAS
PORT

SOLAR CASTLE

STELLAR CASTLE

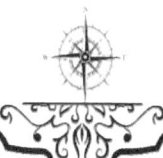

PLANETARIUM
CONSERVATORY
OBSERVATORY

LUNAR CASTLE

MOS

CHAPTER I
FOREST NIGHT

THE ONLY THING THAT STAYS WITH YOU WHEN YOU DIE ARE THE MEMORIES. A fine line between the mind, heart, and soul. With an impenetrable connection to emotions and feelings. As time passes, you try to hold on. To the good because of who you are and to the bad because of who you became. I tried to hold on, I really did. After all, memories were the only thing I had left.

Like an electric shock, my mind awoke. The bright light around the room ached my head. *Sunlight.* I could've sworn it felt like heaven for a second. *Only* for a second until I realized my pain. My legs hurt as if I had run for hours, and my head pounded like I hadn't eaten in days. Worst of all, I couldn't even remember if I had.

I tried to sit up, ignoring the excruciating pain in my entire body. Glancing at myself, I had scars on my arms and my clothes were ripped and covered with a mixture of mud and blood. *What the hell?* I tried accessing my memory but it was muddled in confusion. Fragments from my mind were missing, disappeared into thin air. Several of my memories were lost and jumbled away like I had been asleep for most of my recent time awake. I wasn't completely aware of it before. Not like right now as my thoughts became conscious and I could not remember how I got inside the two-story mid-size house. Not one I'd ever been to. I was confused about where I had been or what I had done last night. My mind was fifty percent blank.

I looked around the room, adjusting my eyes and trying to analyze my surroundings. The pastel green decorations were brighter than my green-grayish eyes. It created a peaceful atmosphere, especially the emerald green of the sofa I was sitting on. There were only three sofas in the middle of the living room, one to the right and one on the left, with a black center table in the middle. Almost like a thrust stage facing a wall and two open spaces, which appeared to be the dining room on the left and a hallway on the other side. A grand staircase took up most of the space on the wall at the right.

The walls were a light gray color and made the large house appear classy. There were paintings on the wall, a grand piano, and a few beige-brown decorations that all reminded me of my apartment back in Texas. I kind of wished I was home, where I wouldn't have to worry about the fact that something mysterious was going on. Yet I did like mystery and adventure, so it was my fault for jinxing it. Since I wasn't in some kind of dungeon or locked up in a room, I thought that I might not be in danger. Just in case, I kept my mind alert and ready for an attack.

My adrenaline slowly decreased as I saw a lady coming out of the dining room. She carried a mug, reminding me of my mother's abundant tea cups. Her warm aura brightened the interior of the house.

"Oh dear, you're awake," she said nicely, her reddish lipstick neatly put on. "I brought some herbal tea and medicine." She sat next to the sofa I was sitting on, looking concerned and put both items on the center table. Her over-the-waist brown hair moved slightly as she sat down, along with the end of her long black ruffled skirt.

"Thank you." I returned her half-smile but hesitated at the medicine. I couldn't be too careful.

"My husband, William, and I found you in the middle of the forest while going for our daily walk this morning," she explained slowly. I looked around me. Neither my purse nor my phone were anywhere to be found. With a jolt, I remembered having left them at the hotel for no exact reason. *Why would I leave them at the hotel?*

"Do you remember anything that led you there? Did someone hurt you?" The lady frowned, looking at my dirty clothes with curiosity and concern. "You have blood in your clothes, should I call the police or take you to the hospital?"

I, on the other hand, was more slightly curious than worried. I quickly responded, "I'm completely fine. I... can't remember anything anyway." *I can't remember.*

Nevertheless, I intended to figure it out. First, I had to get out of here as soon as possible. I had to figure out the truth just like my dad did whenever he worked on a case.

Truth is the value that matters the most, it connects you with people, and it connects you to who you truly are. No one wants to stay in the dark. That's what he always said. *There is no exception for telling the truth because no matter how hard it is, the truth has to be told.*

Sudden anger arose within me *and* for me. Not remembering what happened last night made my mind spin but that wasn't the only problem. Some fragments of my memory since I arrived in England were also unclear. The order of events leading up to yesterday night didn't make sense, like watching only parts of a movie and not knowing the whole story. There was a hole inside me that no matter how hard I wanted to fill, I couldn't. Memories that I had but were now missing.

The scars on my body mocked me for the reason that I, a semi-trained fighter and a good parkour runner, hadn't been able to prevent them; I didn't even have a clue of what the hell had happened. I thought about my parents being a bit disappointed after all the fighting sessions they took me to.

Still points to me for staying alive.

"Are you sure you're alright?" The lady spoke in a gently soothing voice, interrupting my train of thought.

A second after she spoke, the sound of a closing door filled the house, making us both turn towards the hallway on the right that I figured led to the main door. Seconds later, crashing sounds were coming from beyond the dining room. *Maybe whoever came into the house was going through the kitchen?*

My conclusions were right when the lady looked towards the dining room. "Hello, Gilbert," she said, her posture relaxing.

Sitting farther away, I was unable to see who "Gilbert" was. Until a pleasant young man with short curly brown hair walked into the room holding a small glass of water. He looked a little out of time with the brown vest he wore over his white shirt like he belonged at an old university.

"Aunt Mary—" he started to say but immediately stopped, realizing that I was there. "Gilbert, you came back so soon?" Mary smiled widely.

Except, Gilbert seemed distracted, looking at me with a mixture of confusion and curiosity just as Mary had. I looked back at him, noticing his jawline, not that that was important.

"Um, I see we have a guest," he said with furrowed brows, ignoring Mary's question.

Mary looked at me. "Oh right, we found her this morning lying unconscious in the forest, so William and I helped out... this is Gilbert, my nephew."

I smiled at him, nodding but not introducing myself. Gilbert made a slight side nod. "Nice to meet you as well."

For a moment, quiet and awkwardness filled the room. Gilbert looked at me, narrowing his eyes, so I decided to speak up.

"I need to get back home." Out of their kindness, I hoped I didn't sound too desperate to leave. "Thank you so much for your help, you basically saved my life."

"We did what was right to help," Mary responded kindly.

As I got up to leave, I started to feel dizzy and lightheaded. Gilbert quickly placed his glass of water on the table and came up beside me, holding my arm to keep me from falling. A tingling sensation went through my skin where our hands touched. Like I hadn't had human contact before. Like I was scared of it. I heard Mary's small gasp. Taking hold of the sofa, I looked up at him. "I can manage. I just feel a bit tired." He slowly nodded and moved away as I sat back down.

I hated feeling vulnerable and weak. My mind was full of energy, ready to get out of here, but my body failed to receive that same adrenaline. "What if you stay here today and spend the night, dear?" Mary suggested, looking back and forth between me and Gilbert, who then added, "I agree. You are welcome to stay here and rest until tomorrow."

I gave a strained smile, feeling a bit uneasy at their weirdly concerned glances. It was unexpected for them to care about someone they'd barely met, to want me to stay with them instead of just dropping me off at the nearest hospital. If someone else had found me, they might have just left me for dead. But these two were exactly the opposite.

"No, it's okay. Can I just stay here for a few minutes while I get more strength?"

"Of course, you can. I will go get some ice for that bruise on your neck." Mary nodded.

A bruise? No wonder my neck hurts. I wondered how I got that. It would have made sense for me to be running and falling in the forest since my clothes were awfully dirty. *My wounds must have been from the branches, but my neck is bruised.* It didn't make sense.

It was funny to think that it was a supernatural creature that caused it, yet my beliefs in the mystical faded after being obsessed with all those fictional shows back in middle school. If not, and surely not, supernaturals, then someone had probably attempted to hurt me.

Mary disappeared around the corner to get the bag of ice. Gilbert stood there, staring at me like I wouldn't notice.

"Can you stop staring?" I said sharply. "Just ask whatever you want to ask."

"I don't want to ask anything..." He crossed his arms, frowning. By his look, it was obvious he was lying, but he still wouldn't say anything.

"It's not like I remember anything, so it doesn't matter," I lied. Of course it mattered, especially since I wasn't just going to leave it at that. I was going to be the detective on my case, and I was going to solve it.

After a few seconds, Mary came back from the kitchen handing me a bag of ice. I placed it on my neck feeling the fresh coolness and wished I could take a cool shower and get out of my filthy clothes. She proceeded to ask Gilbert her earlier ignored question about why he had come early, forgetting my presence.

"Right, Uncle Will needed some papers for the payment of the bakery and other files regarding the deals with other businesses," Gilbert spoke in a very sudden professional tone. If only he wore an apron or a tie, he would have played the part.

Mary nodded, fixing her straight hair. "I have them in the study..." With that, she went up the brown stairs to get what Gilbert asked.

I put my head down and closed my eyes for a few seconds.

My head throbbed immensely, making me reconsider taking the painkillers Mary had set down on the table at once. I heard Gilbert's footsteps coming closer.

"May I?" He asked, sitting next to me and bringing his hand close to the ice bag to hold it.

"I can do it myself," I said, looking up and moving away from him. He noticed my uneasiness and moved inches away.

"It is strange for an accident to happen in the forest, people don't usually venture that far into it," he said after a few seconds of silence.

"Well, my situation says otherwise," I replied defensively.

He frowned at me.

"What?"

"I'm sorry..." He casted his brown eyes down.

"No offense, but you are strange."

He looked up, eyebrows raising in sync. "Is that so? You're straightforward and fiery-tempered."

"I'm not," I averted my gaze, which was promptly met with a pulse of pain in my head.

"Point taken," Gilbert whispered. I rolled my eyes trying to contain my self-control. We were arguing like we had been friends for a long time. *Really? I'm literally arguing with a stranger.*

I turned to look at the beautifully designed dark railings of the second floor, glancing at Mary coming down the grand stairs, holding a portfolio. She was about to step into the living room when a knock on the door was heard, echoing from the small hallway once again. I wondered who it was this time. Mary quickly went ahead to open it. The unlocking of the door filled the awkward silence yet again, until Mary exclaimed, "Killian, what a nice surprise?!"

Footsteps were heard coming towards the living room from the foyer. I looked up, curious about who Mary was excited to see. A young man, maybe a bit older than Gilbert, appeared from the hallway wearing all black: black pants, boots, a shirt, and even a black leather jacket. Not surprisingly, his straight hair was also black colored. *Cliche.* I thought, accidentally looking at him in the eye. Only his amber eyes stood out, making everything about him even more mysterious.

For a second, he looked at me with a slight shock. Almost matching Gilbert's facial expressions when he first saw me. He quickly hid his amazement, and I looked away, pretending I didn't notice. That's when Gilbert got up all of a sudden. By the confused back-and-forth stares between them, I sensed that something weird was going on. It was probably just a friend visiting a friend like normal, but I felt the negative and awkward energy. I clutched my hands. *Why am I still here?*

"Killian, I didn't know you were coming today?" Gilbert said, his posture stiffening but moving towards Killian.

"Yes, I was just coming to talk to you about something important," Killian responded, revealing his British accent. He observed me, finishing his last word.

Mary appeared from behind Killian. "Gilbert, can you come to the dining room, so I can explain to you about these files?" Gilbert inclined and followed Mary to the dining room, giving me a last look.

I looked away from Killian's gaze for a moment. Besides his obvious clothing choice, there was something about him that somehow alarmed me. He stood with such confidence and looked at me devilishly. "You look horrible, love. Hunting in the woods?"

I glanced back at him. "No offense, but it's none of your business."

"No, but I am curious."

"Then don't be."

He smirked and crossed his arms. "I'm Killian."

I looked up at him, straight into his eyes. "I'm someone who you don't need to know about."

He grinned, shaking his head. "And I'm someone who would want to know."

I glared at him. He was about to say something else, but Gilbert came to the room, holding the portfolio and interrupted. "Let's go outside." Killian looked at Gilbert, then at me, before they both turned away and walked into the entrance hallway.

I heard the door close and immediately tried to stand up. My body still felt a bit weak, but I had to go as soon as possible towards the crime scene where I was found. I hoped my mind would get triggered with memories of what happened last night.

I walked towards the hallway and glanced at the kitchen once I passed the arch doorway and saw Mary opening the oven. The smell of chocolate chip cookies filled the air, reminding me of how hungry I was. Ironically, I couldn't even remember the last time I had eaten either.

"Dear, you should be resting," she said, looking up at me after closing the oven. "I was about to prepare lunch. I am rather famous for my chicken pasta recipe." I imagined the delicious food.

"Thank you. But that's ok, I'm not that hungry. In fact, I wanted to ask you a quick question before I leave," I said, trying to ignore the smell of food.

Mary's eyes shone. "Yes, of course, what is it?"

"Where did you find me exactly? Is it far from here?"

"Mmm, by the right path in the forest, past a daisy and delightful landscape…"

I nodded. "Okay, thank you." She then looked at me with interest, and I sensed what she was thinking. "I'm not planning to go there or anything. I'm just curious, that's all."

"Gilbert will be glad to give you a ride home."

"Thank you so much for everything, Mrs. Mary…"

"*Gram* dear," Mary said. "Mary Gram."

"Thank you, Mrs. Gram," I repeated. "I appreciate everything, but I have to leave."

She walked towards me and gave me an unexpected hug. To not be rude, I returned it, feeling like I was in a field of flowers the second I smelled her sweet perfume. One of the two small black pearl pins, the one just above her left ear, shone through the small rays coming from the kitchen window. For a second, a sense of relief washed over me, making me not want to pull away. "I don't know how you ended up in the forest, but always be careful," she advised. I pulled away and turned around to leave.

I wanted to close my eyes at the warmth of the Sun on my face the moment I stepped outside. The house stood in the middle of a terrain, surrounded by woods, filled with autumn-colored trees. There were small fruit trees and flower pots that gave the outside a colorful view. *Flowers.* I thought. *No wonder.* I stepped closer to a white rose pot. Yet it seemed they didn't have their usual floral smell as I did and retreated from it. Gilbert and Killian were a few feet away talking about something I couldn't exactly hear. They immediately stopped their conversation and turned to look at me once the door behind me closed.

"Hey... I'm leaving now," I said, their stares burning more than the actual Sun. "Thank you for helping me."

"It was no problem. Do you want a ride home?" Gilbert asked.

"No thanks," I replied.

"Are you sure? There are cabs out of this area, but the path out of here to the city's motorway is about half of a mile long for you to walk." He looked at the slightly visible path in front of us.

"I'm sure, thanks," I reassured. Gilbert nodded, but Killian only grinned at me. I was starting my pace when Killian spoke.

"If something happens. Just scream..." He stopped to reconsider. "Or run. Whichever."

"Right," I responded. "Like fighting back isn't an option."

"Of course it is," He smiled. "But the other two give chances to protect you."

"He is right, you know," Gilbert added. "Are you sure you don't want a ride?"

"Thank you again, but I'm sure." I forced myself to smile. "And if something happens, I'll just scream, fight back, *and* run."

Finding myself with nothing else to say, I quickly looked at the path in front of me towards the highway to the city of London and then to the right path towards the forest Mary talked about. I walked steadily down the main path, not showing any hint of curiosity towards the forest, just in case I got followed. Gilbert and Killian's voices faded into birds chirping and branches moving the further I walked.

Only a few minutes passed when I was already halfway from the Grams' two-story house. I made my decision and walked fast out of the path and towards the woods without turning around. If I walked north and turned east, I would be able to find the path that would lead me to where I was found or so I hoped.

I didn't go deep into the woods to avoid getting lost on where I took the east turn, but I was far enough that no one would be able to see me through the branches once I turned direction and found the forest path. I started walking faster, taking notice of how badly my legs hurt. After a few minutes, I took the turn and started walking slowly since I could see the silhouette of Mary's artistic house. I walked towards the clear path in front of me, crossed it, and hid between the trees beside it. Luckily, the path was slightly curved, or else I would have been seen clearly from the house.

I walked fast for a few more minutes, stepping on soft-looking grass and avoiding twigs until I could no longer see the Grams' house. I slowed down, hearing low rustling noises behind me, yet nothing was in sight. Just in case, I started jogging. If I had been healthier and stronger at that moment, my running skills would have been better. I stopped to catch my breath, when someone grabbed my arm. My fighting instincts controlled me and punched the person in the face, taking them by surprise.

"What the hell!" I quickly said, completely confused. Gilbert slightly bent down rubbing his face.

"You just got punched by a girl mate, ouch." Killian, who was behind Gilbert, said mockingly. I glared at him. "A young lady." He smirked.

"What are you guys doing here? How did you find me in the first place?" I asked, looking at Killian.

Gilbert slowly stood up, half-smiling in shock with his face red from the punch, but no sign of blood. I guessed he was just surprised that a *young lady* would know how to fight in the *21st century*.

"Are you trying to get killed?" Gilbert asked.

"You didn't answer my question," I replied.

"We were taking a walk... and we *walked* pretty fast," he responded, nodding his head.

"Am I supposed to believe that?"

How was I supposed to believe that they had suddenly decided to take a walk in the forest? Wasn't Gilbert busy in the first place? How fast did they even walk?

"Gilbert, you should have told me that your friend here is a suicidal psychopath," Killian said, crossing his arms. Gilbert must have told him about what happened. I rolled my eyes at them.

"I'm joking..." Killian cracked a grin, holding his hands up at the lack of humor in the air.

"So, what exactly were you planning to do?" Gilbert asked afterward, raising his brows.

"It's none of your concern." I shook my head, annoyed.

"Alright... we are coming with you for whatever you're doing." He stood up straight.

I took a step back. "As you can tell I can handle myself. And how do I know you two weren't involved in whatever happened to me last night?"

"We didn't know you until today, love," Killian said. I shivered at the word *love*, no one had ever called me that. And he seemed to have a habit of it.

"We just want to help. Besides this is my family's property, therefore it is kind of my business. *Whatever* happens here we investigate it to make sure the property isn't vandalized, and you'll be kind of trespassing right now." Gilbert crossed his arms, matching my stance. I could tell he wasn't going to back down.

I surely didn't need their help, but he wasn't wrong. I couldn't compete with two taller guys in good condition against my weak state to fight and bolt. There was no other choice but to cancel my solo mystery trip. "You see, if you want something done perfect, you have to do it yourself. So, whatever happened to me, I'll deal with it. It's my problem. Check your property and that's it."

Gilbert nodded, Killian grinned, and I turned around to lead towards the 'Mystery Crime Scene.'

I walked ahead, while the two friends were a few feet away behind me talking in small whispers so I couldn't hear any of their conversation. Why would two strangers help me? I didn't trust them, especially not Killian, but Gilbert seemed nicer and didn't look like a cold-blooded mysterious murderer. Plus, he lived with his aunt Mary, who appeared gentle. I hadn't met his uncle but seeing as his family had saved my life, my trusting level in Gilbert had increased from zero to five percent.

Going away from my thoughts, I looked up at the sky. It looked as if it would rain soon. In no less than five minutes, it started to drizzle followed by calm winds. I turned around. "We should hurry."

I didn't dislike the rain at all, I thought it was rather peaceful, but some evidence from the scene could've been washed away. And I wasn't going to leave without a clue.

The duo walked faster, which they did walk rather fast, as it slowly drizzled. Gilbert walked, thankfully, between me and Killian.

"So, why don't you guys put fences around this place since it's your family's property?" I asked Gilbert, filling in the silence.

"My aunt wanted it to be a public place for the neighborhood, but we don't have lots of neighbors nowadays since most people live in the city now. We just kept this place as it is for the animals and Mary's love for the environment," Gilbert spoke proudly. My mom would've loved to see the great view. We kept walking and I was surprised by Killian's lack of jokes and sarcastic comments. Trying not to ruin the peaceful walk I decided not to speak about it.

Eventually, we came across a peaceful daisy landscape, which I guessed was the one that Mary had described. The white and yellow field was beyond anything I had ever seen. I could be lost in the silence for hours while it drizzled. We passed the landscape in less than five minutes and the further we walked the lonelier it seemed to be. I could no longer hear the birds singing or signs of wildlife. Only footprints stood on the mud path in front of us.

"I think we are getting close." I walked deep into the woods following the barely visible footprints ahead.

"Careful love, there could be monsters or worse supernatural creatures," Killian warned.

"You can't be serious." I walked slower and turned to Killian, shaking my head.

"You don't believe in supernatural identities?" asked Gilbert.

"I did... back in *middle school*." I half-laughed, turning around to keep walking at a faster pace. "This must be it." There was blood on the ground mixed with mud due to the rain and a bloodstained tree. *Too much blood.* I couldn't help but feel both disgusted and horrified at the sight of it. I tried to concentrate over the unpleasant smell, but no hint of memory seemed to emerge from inside. "What the hell happened here?"

"You can't remember anything at all?" Gilbert tilted his head.

"Nothing. I've never seen this place."

I kept looking around for more clues. I walked behind a nearby tree and stopped, squinting at some type of small purple and bluish object on the ground. I walked forward and grabbed it.

A crystal necklace. I turned it over, examining it. It was almost impossible to see it from afar, but at the bottom, the letters *R & W* were engraved on it.

"Did you find something?" Killian asked. I turned around to show him the necklace. He stood still. His eyes stared straight at the necklace.

"Have you seen it before?" I questioned. Gilbert stood next to me to inspect the necklace, then looked at Killian for a response.

"No, I haven't... it looks like one that an old friend had except it was different in size and color."

I looked back at the necklace. "It's not mine. I haven't seen it before or even had one like it." Whoever tried to hurt me must have left hurriedly, not realizing they left it. I looked around one last time to take a quick inspection, but there was nothing else to find.

"We should go back soon, it looks like a storm is about to take place," Gilbert said, looking up and walking in front of me along with Killian. I placed the necklace safely into my black jacket, making sure the pocket itself wasn't ripped.

"A friend?" Gilbert tried to whisper to Killian as they walked beside each other.

"Yes, a *friend* mate," fixed Killian, his steps in sync with his friend. "I'm not exactly the loner here. Am I?"

"Shut up," said Gilbert.

After minutes of walking, both of them had been quiet and it was starting to make me nervous.

"It has been silent. I'm not complaining or anything... just wondering why." I stopped in my tracks. Unless I was crazy, it was kind of obvious something else was going on. Maybe they were shocked... or not shocked at all that they didn't even wince at the sight of blood, like they were used to it.

"If you think we know something love, you are wrong," responded Killian, stopping to look at me.

"We are sorry. But we don't know anything," Gilbert added. There was no use in making them talk. Either way, I wouldn't have believed them. So I sighed, remained quiet, and kept walking.

Not remembering my memories was driving me insane. *How could I know that I'm missing memories but not actually remember them? Who would want to hurt me if I don't even have enemies?* I reconsidered. *At least not that I know of.*

The thought circled around my head over and over again. Trying to remember something. Anything. I thought of the people I knew or met throughout the trip, wondering if my friend Dani who stayed with me in the city hotel noticed something, or even if I had met Gilbert or Killian before. But with missing memories, nothing made sense. A cold chill went through my spine. I thought of Gilbert and Killian walking behind me. Watching me, probably wondering how I didn't die last night... or planning another demise against me. *If they wanted me dead, I would have been already. Maybe it's not them.* I hoped.

I had been way too deep in thought to realize we were more than halfway through the daisy landscape. A few more feet and we were finally in the forest path again. Feeling my heart palpitating in my chest, I noticed how out of breath I was. My face burnt hot and sweaty even though the breeze was fresh. In seconds, I started to feel dizzy, my head spinning, and a sensation of weakness in my whole body. *Not again.* I stopped walking, feeling my legs betray me. As I grabbed hold of the closest tree next to me, I saw Killian instantly coming towards me.

I guessed it took a while for Gilbert to realize what was happening because I heard him scream "I will go get the car!" after five seconds. His blurry silhouette rushed off, while Killian held me. He let me down slowly, put me down on the ground, and leaned my back on the cold trunk. My eyes failed to stay open like

I hadn't slept in days.

"Stay awake, love," he said softly, almost with worry. He touched my caramel-brown hair, pulling the strands out of my face. "Stay awake... stay awake, Clara. Gilbert will come soon." His voice had started to fade away, echoing in the air, leaving me with one thought. And one thought only.

He called me by my name.

CHAPTER 2
GOLDEN BLOOD

I WOKE UP TO THE SOUND of the television in the room. I didn't even have to ask where I was; the antiseptic smell gave it away

was completely. My whole body was still in pain, but I could handle it. Weakness started on my knees like I had gone for a morning run, which I technically had but more like a first-time morning run for a beginner.

"Hello, sunshine," Killian, who sitting in a chair beside me, said sarcastically.

This is great. I rolled my eyes at the sight of him and tried to show no uneasiness towards the fact that somehow, he knew who I was. I had to play dumb until I resolved who the hell Killian and Gilbert were or what they were hiding because I was sure I didn't hallucinate him saying my name.

"What time is it?" I asked steadily, slowly sitting up.

"It is about six in the afternoon," Killian responded. "Where is Gilbert?"

"He is at the front desk, paying for the hospital bill."

"What?!"

I looked at the logo that was on the wall that said *Florence London Hospital* and recognized the name from the time I was looking at a map of London, England.

"Are we downtown? This hospital must be super expensive." I sighed.

"You are most likely correct. Gilbert had a feeling you would deny and wanted to pay anyway."

"Well, that was not necessary. I just fainted, it isn't like I got stabbed." I had to talk to Gilbert about his generous yet unnecessary actions. Killian smiled mockingly.

I narrowed my eyes on him. "It's not funny."

"No, it's not but it is when you're angry at someone's help."

"Maybe I should've stayed sleeping." I glowered at him and then looked away, looking back only for a second to see him still smiling from the corner of my eye.

It wasn't long before I remembered that Dani must have become worried about me not showing up at the hotel early. I was so invested in the mystery that I had forgotten to even call. Danielle had been my closest friend for two years since meeting at the Art Institute in Texas. The institute had planned a Study Abroad London trip a year ago. Unfortunately, Dani and I were unable to attend because of the art internships we had both applied for. She was the life of the party. "You are invited" was the first thing she said as I was taking photographs of a painting made by one of her friends at the Institute. It was the first week and Dani, being herself, wanted to make more friends by having a small welcome party. We found out about each other's love for fashion and adventure that same week and became closer after that. Which eventually led to us planning the London trip weeks after college graduation.

"Do you have a phone I can borrow? I need to call someone," I asked Killian. He winked, reached into his leather jacket, got his cell phone out from the inside pocket, and handed it to me. I started dialing Dani's phone number. Amber eyes stared at me intently as I did.

"Hello?" Danielle's voice spoke.

"Hi, Dani," I said, avoiding looking at Killian.

"Clara! I've been worried! Where are you?!" Her voice squeaked slightly.

"I'm okay. I will be back at the hotel soon, so don't worry."

"Are you sure you're okay?"

"Yes, don't worry. Tell you everything later."

"Ok, be careful."

"Thank you, you too. Bye." I didn't know exactly what I was going to tell her or whether I should even tell her at all.

I gave Killian his phone back. "Thanks." He put it back in his pocket and turned to look at me again.

"Your boyfriend?" he asked, sitting up.

I half-smiled. "Your business?"

He slightly smirked at me, annoyed I hoped.

The television noise filled the awkward silence between us. I watched him from the corner of my eye every now and then as I looked at the TV that played a drama movie about a girl on trial for an uncommitted crime. His stare was creepier each second until someone knocked on the door softly. We both looked towards it. Gilbert. He peeped inside and walked slowly towards us.

"Hey... how are you feeling?" He spoke gently.

"Like I need to get out of here," I responded. "By the way, thank you, but you didn't need to pay for the bill. I'm not exactly poor you know, and no offense, but we aren't exactly friends..." Sure I was grateful but enough weirded out at them going above and beyond to help.

"You just don't like being helped, do you?" Killian said, turning around to look at Gilbert, but Gilbert just stood there smiling until he said, "You are welcome."

I glared at them. *Can this 'niceness' get any worse? Or should I be thankful?*

Another knock on the door was heard, and this time it was a nurse who came in holding a carton bag and a clipboard.

"Hello... gentlemen, can you please wait outside? The patient will change to new clothes, and we will give her more medication for the pain," she said kindly. *New clothes? What hospital gave patients new clothes?*

"Yes, of course... we will be going to the cafeteria. Would you like coffee or food? Both?" Gilbert asked me.

"Yes, please. Since you are so rich, just bring the whole menu," I joked. He smiled, watching Killian getting up from the chair. I hoped they would take an immense amount of time trying to figure out what to get.

When both friends left the room, the nurse came to my side and gave me the bag. I looked at the clothes, they seemed new and still had the price tag. "Who bought these clothes?"

"The gentleman that was sitting down beside you," she said, moving around wires and electronics behind the bed.

"Seriously..." I mumbled.

"Pardon?" she asked.

"Ooh... I was saying that I don't want the medication, since I don't feel pain anymore."

The nurse shook her head, pressing her lips together. "I'm sorry, but you are dehydrated, and it seems that you are diagnosed with medium levels of anemia. You need medication before we discharge you. It is the doctor's order." I got up from the bed to walk into the restroom, grunting under my breath. *Anemia... that's ironic and concerning.*

I quickly started taking off my filthy clothes and changed into the new ones. Black jeans, a black long-sleeved shirt, and a brown leather jacket. I was surprised that Killian got the correct sizes. The clothes were neither tight nor too loose. I had almost forgotten about the crystal necklace I had put in my pocket before I fainted. As I took the necklace out and into the pocket located inside the leather jacket, I saw a small microdevice with a red blinking light. A tracking device. Similar to the ones my dad had given me to '*Check up on me*', as he would say, during my college years. "What the hell?" *Do they think I am that stupid?* I took the device and put it in the sink vanity. I checked the pockets of my old clothes in case I found something valuable, remembering that I usually carried emergency money all the time. The inside of my jacket pocket had some pounds, enough for one or two cabs. Dani and I exchanged our American currency for the United Kingdom pounds the first day we got to London. I threw my dirty clothes away, seeing as they didn't have much value. Away from the restroom view, the nurse still organized the tubes and machines. I walked quietly towards the door, thankfully the loud sound of the television concealed the low creaky sounds and allowed me to delicately slip out of the room.

I wasn't sure how the UK hospitals and health system worked. During my London research, there was less than any probability that I would end up needing care. But now I walked through the hospital floor at a steady pace, looking for the reception area to obtain what information Gilbert gave about me. It was obvious that he must have given them my name to sign and pay the bill and I needed to have evidence to know I was not insane. I passed the double doors to get out of the hall and headed towards the waiting room and reception desk just ahead.

"Hi," I started with a smile. "I wanted to pay my bill. I'm Clara De Rose."

The receptionist nodded. "Alright, let me check," he said, switching papers and looking closely at the files on the desk. I slightly noted his British accent, his voice clearer than Killian's.

"Room 1216?" he asked.

"Yes."

"I remember you. Here it is." He shuffled the first page, putting it close to his face. I glanced at the pages quickly, catching only *Clara* in bold letters. "*Ms. De Rose* it appears that a man named Gilbert Gram has paid your bill and the doctor signed your discharge papers earlier." *I knew it! I'm not crazy!*

"However, he stated he didn't know your last name, therefore we will need it for our records and to provide you with future medication. Is your full name Clara De Rose?" he asked. "And you sign here." I nodded without thinking. Gilbert only knew my first name just like Killian, but how and why?

"Yes, can I have a copy of all the papers?" I asked after I signed my name under the dotted line.

I waited anxiously for the doors to open as I read the map directions of the hospital on the poster wall. My jacket pocket was somewhat heavy from the folded copied papers. I was on the second floor, and the cafeteria was on the fourth floor. The doors opened showing a crowded family seeking to quickly get out of the incommodious platform. In a matter of seconds, I was heading towards the ground floor and out of the hospital. I turned back at least three times for possible stalkers, but it seemed like no one was paying attention to me or following me.

The evening Sun was really lovely. I wished I had my camera with me to photograph the amazing view, but I didn't have time to ponder about that in the middle of a vanishing act. Being in London for a month didn't exactly made me an expert at memorizing all the London streets, also given the fact that I didn't remember fifty percent of memories since I had been here lowered me down to an amateur at memorization.

There was an intersection to the right of the hospital, along with a lot of traffic and people trying to cross the streets. I walked rapidly towards the other side of the street with a group of very fashionable people. In an attempt to fit in the crowd, I said cheerfully, "I love the red coat, may I ask where you bought it from?"

The young woman with blond hair to my left answered, "Thank you! I bought it from Tree's Thrift Shop, it's east of the city by the way."

"I'm residing east of the city, but I haven't been here long enough which is probably why I never saw it." Dani and I had gone to more well-known places like museums, parks, and famous restaurants. We had made a list of the most famous places in London we wanted to go to, so we didn't walk into random stores that weren't on the list. Our budget fitted in with the plan, leaving us with limited places to visit.

"In that case, we could meet up sometime and talk about fashion in London," the lady said excitedly. She handed me her business card, which read *Rosie Val, Manager at Tree's Thrift Shop* with a phone number underneath. I smiled at her before we parted ways on the sidewalk. She headed west and I headed east. I looked towards a clock on the wall of a restaurant next to me. Seven minutes had passed, at this point by now Killian and Gilbert would have realized I wasn't in the hospital room. Unless Gilbert's generosity had made him buy more food than needed.

I quickly walked towards a cab that stood by the sidewalk before people came to get a ride.

"Hi, can you drive east of London? I need to stop at a restaurant. I don't know the street names, but I might know the way," I said kindly, getting inside the cab.

"Yes, ma'am," the driver assented.

I told him the directions towards the 'restaurant' that in reality I wasn't exactly going to. Instead, my plan involved getting into two cabs to avoid being followed by the duo or the unknown forest enemies. I told the driver to stop at the restaurant around the corner I had seen before with Dani. Immediately, I paid with some of the emergency money I had and got out, taking a glance around me for any suspicious activity. Another cab drove closer to the street, I took my chance and signaled for a ride.

This time the driver was a lady. During the entire ride, she spent time talking politely on the phone with her friend about their holiday plans. I had already planned with my family for all of us to see each other in Texas for the holidays and came to London with the intention of buying their presents. Now, I was only missing my older sister, Aurora's, present.

Waiting for a small quick pause in her conversation to interrupt, I said, "Excuse me. Can you stop in this street?" The street we stopped at was close to the hotel Dani and I were staying at. I just needed to walk two more streets. I paid her and got out of the cab. "Thanks." She went back to her conversation.

I passed the coffee shop, the bookstore, and the pretty garden with tree lights. Until I saw the brown building standing between two other buildings that sold London souvenirs. The front of the hotel was surrounded by a black gate, along with a sign at the top that read, *Lovely Hotel*, it sure suited the place accurately. I took a look around again, at least three more times.

The hotel was beautiful and cozy from the inside and was surprisingly not that expensive. Obviously, I had done full research on where to stay. This was one of the nicest hotels in London that was affordable for new tourists. When entering, there was a staircase with a red carpet that led towards the front desk, where the hotel receptionist named Clark stood to greet guests. To the right, there was a cafeteria, tables beside the beige wall, and windows to see the people and cars pass by. Eye-catching decorations, especially the warm lights hanging from the ceiling were beautifully arranged. I walked by the front desk, and Clark waved. I waved back and quickly walked down the hallway that led to the elevator before he started asking me questions about Dani. He had a crush on her, but she didn't do well with long-distance relationships, so she tried to stay away from him to not give the wrong impression.

Not a lot of people were out. I was the only one in the elevator. The hotel only had five floors, including the ground floor, and four rooms on each floor. I pressed the button number '4' where our room was and waited anxiously to head rapidly to safety. Our room was at the end of the hallway to the left. I knocked on the door and waited.

Dani opened the door slowly. "It's me, Dani... not *Mr. Blue Eyes*," I said, half-laughing.

"Clara!" Dani exclaimed, hugging me once I walked in. The smell of her strong cherry perfume surrounded me.

"Where have you been? Are you okay? You don't look great," she said, her dark shiny hair placed in a neat ponytail. I grimaced, deciding where to even start.

"I'm okay, really. And I've been to a stranger's house, a mystery forest, an expensive hospital, and all-around London," I rambled.

She gave me a blank look. "Okay... what?"

"That's what *I* said." I almost sat down at the edge of the bed for a few seconds. Then, choosing to just stand up, I reevaluated the unfortunate and mysterious events in my mind.

"Ok, what happened? I was worried," she said, sitting by the window sofa at once. I decided to tell her everything that had happened since the morning, from the Grams' house to the holiday planning cab driver. As well as the two nerve-racking mysterious friends that have saved my life for no apparent reason.

"Are you sure you didn't dream it?" Dani asked as I reminisced about my tragic unbelievable experience.

"I'm positive," I said. "I mean what the hell is this? We haven't even been in London long enough to have enemies... unless you count the time that I bumped into that girl at the bar intentionally because she started humiliating you."

"I agree that was crazy, and thanks again. I was too drunk to even remember most of it." She laughed. I remembered the wild night. "So, what are you going to do about this weird situation? I would tell you to stay away, but I know you well enough to know you won't be able to walk away from a mystery."

"Exactly. But I have to keep a low profile, for now, to figure out the truth. I only remember times of us together, touring, and times when I went by myself to buy books or coffee but others I don't. Did anything seem off to you?"

Dani sighed. "I'll tell you, but promise me that you'll update me if anything happens, and don't go crazy alone on a trip..."

I listened. "Okay."

About twenty minutes were spent on question after question,

analyzing my actions. Based on what Dani said, I had a huge change of attitude for days after we came to London, which was the same day that I found her at the bar. I was happier and more excited to do stuff than I usually was. She explained I kept things to myself and wouldn't tell her anything regarding where I went throughout the days, completely unlike myself.

I listened closely while she continued. "At some point, I thought you were going out with a mystery boyfriend." Dani grinned.

"Me? No. I'm currently at the point of *Independence at Its Finest*," I said, half-laughing. "Do you remember anything about yesterday? Weren't we supposed to be packed all ready to leave tomorrow?" Dani and I arrived in London on September 30th. Initially, we had planned to stay for a month and go back to Texas to plan for the holidays to refrain from utilizing more money than necessary. Except that London bakery shops were astonishing, and having self-control not to buy all pastries was challenging. Clothing shops were also incredible, yet nothing can succeed at making one happier than food.

"Yesterday, we hung around like usual each morning to eat breakfast. Then I had to go on another date with the cute British guy we met earlier, and you said you had to go search for Aurora's present," she continued. I nodded remembering the last conversation we had.

"Well, apparently I didn't find anything."

"I came back to the hotel to change clothes. Minutes later, you enter the room thrilled. You gave me a whole speech about how you wanted to stay longer in London, I agreed even though you were out of the plan, then you said you had made an appointment to dye your hair or something."

I looked at my wavy caramel hair and wondered where I even got the idea to dye it.

"Are you serious? I said a thousand times before we came, that I was certain to leave here in a month," I asked, confused. "What could have possibly changed my mind?" Luckily, I had bought plane tickets that were available to use for the entire week, I just needed to send an email beforehand so they could reserve the seats as quickly as possible.

Dani nodded, starting to unfold the bed sheets to go to sleep. "And then you left again, leaving your purse and phone. I was going to call you but then I realized..."

I started to pace for a bit, not believing I hadn't taken my purse or phone for no reason at all. Or a reason I didn't exactly remember.

"Honestly, you were just your really sunshine self to the max... no one except me would have noticed your craziness." She chuckled.

"Hey!" I laughed and threw her a pillow from the white bed, even though she was right. She threw it back playfully.

"Still... everything that happened was so weird. They were so generous," I said, referring to the mystery duo and walking towards my suitcase, which stood on the floor close to the foot of my bed.

"Maybe you are overthinking it? Or it could have been luck?"

"Maybe." I placed the suitcase on the bed, getting clean clothes to take a cold shower. "Let's just get some rest. Be ready to run some final errands tomorrow and pack to go home." I let out a breath and picked out my pajamas.

"You look horrible by the way," Dani said. I looked at her from the sudden memory of déjà vu.

I shook my head at her. "If only I knew why." And disappeared into the restroom.

Thirty minutes. The time I had spent in the restroom making sure no mark of weakness showed. Yet it was impossible. Scars and bruises showed everywhere including my eyebrow. I had to untangle my hair and spray perfume to remove the smell of humidity. Dani was still awake in her bed, her nails tapping her phone, probably texting another potential date.

"Goodnight." I yawned, going straight to bed. She placed her phone screen upside down on the pillow next to her, the pink and white case sparkling in the light.

"Goodnight." She turned off the light of her lamp as I did the same.

My brown purse and phone sat neatly on the nightstand. I went through the phone calls and messages, but everything seemed normal. The last person I called and messaged was Dani, two days ago. I sighed, lying back on my bed and watching the light through the window.

After a few minutes, Dani fell soundly asleep, but I couldn't help thinking about past events, and how in the world they could be connected to me. I didn't have many friends and kept everything to myself. Maybe Dani had been right, and I was overreacting to this whole situation, yet I didn't think that everything happened for no reason. It was easier for me to write everything down. I decided to get my bullet journal, the one I used for daily planning, and write every important event with details in chronological order just in case I had another memory loss.

The Mysterious Events

- *Arrived in London on September 30th*
- *Acted weird days after arriving, starting October 4th. Dates after that are blurry and most memories are gone.*
- *The night I don't remember at all is October 30th/31st depending on the time (Dani clarified the events and my weird actions). October 31st is the morning that Mary and William Gram found me in the mystery forest by their house.*
- *Acted really, super happy. Heightened emotions?*
- *Somehow I wanted to dye my hair...*
- *Didn't want to leave London... doesn't make sense with any previous perfect planning and budget.*
- *The only memories I remember are with Dani. Other memories of being by myself are mostly gone.*
- *No indication of contacting anyone else through cell phone.*

Meeting Killian and Gilbert at Gram's house on October 31st in the morning where I found an "R & W" crystal necklace at the crime scene. I was taken to Florence London Hospital, but I ran away. Killian and Gilbert know my first name only. Told Dani the truth. (The day I'm writing about these events).

- *Planned to leave on October 31st (which would have been today).*
- *Tomorrow's packing day will be November 1st and we actually leave London on November 2nd.*
- *DON'T FORGET!*

I laid awake, reading my notes, trying to remember everything until exhaustion took control of me and fell straight to sleep.

The alarm clock on my phone beeped loudly, waking me from the peacefulness. My neck still hurt from the bruise. Even so, I got up and changed into comfortable clothes. The day was chilly, so I decided to wear a black long-sleeved shirt, jeans, ankle boots, along with a long bluish coat.

"Come on Dani, it's our last day! Wake up!" I exclaimed cheerfully, as Dani's alarm beeped ten minutes after. Dani lazily got up and frowned at me, to which I smiled compassionately. As she changed in the restroom, I started to send the email for the plane seats and put the crystal necklace in my brown leather purse for safekeeping, as well as the hospital forms. Dani got out of the restroom revealing her more fashionable clothes, she would have easily fitted in with some of the people I had stumbled upon the day before. She had the energy to always wear trendy fashionable outfits, on the other hand, I wore classy outfits with a touch of both modern and vintage auras. Mostly coats—maybe lots of coats.

"What do you think?" Dani asked. She wore black leather pants, a crop top, and high-knee boots. "I like your boots?... I adore your outfit. Not my style. But you look amazing as always!" I beamed. "You should consider wearing a jacket though, it might be cold."

"It will ruin my outfit." Dani pouted, opening back up her suitcase to get a white leather jacket with feathers in the sleeves.

Clark was the first person we stumbled upon after getting out of the elevator. "Good morning, ladies!" He greeted, taking a step back until his back touched the counter.

"Good morning, Clark!" I said, noticing Danielle's rapid walking pace, glancing briefly at Clark. We both headed out of the hotel and towards a cafe for our last breakfast meal in London.

"Hey!" I said catching up to Dani the moment we got out of the hotel. "I know you told me to not intervene, but there was no reason to ignore or be mean to Clark. You can be a bit nice."

"Are you judging me?" Dani said, frustrated.

"No... I'm just giving constructive advice." Dani looked at me annoyingly. "I know I can be judgy sometimes, and I'm trying to be nicer now. But... there is a difference between judging and the truth. This would *factually* be the truth." She raised her eyebrows. "Okay! I will try not to say anything anymore but remember how you felt in college with the whole 'Mason phase'," I reminded her, sighing.

Back in the Art Institute, a few months ago Dani had met Mason Presley, who was a total jerk. She had a huge crush on him, but he turned her down saying "College it's almost over and there is no point in going out", which made no total sense. Overall, Dani was completely crushed and refused to ever seriously date anyone again.

"Can you check the location of the cafe again?" Dani asked,

ignoring my last statement. During our London planning, we both had decided to walk when going to breakfast each morning. We went from hot chocolate stores to macarons. The cafe we were going to was the last from the list of 'Places to Visit for Brunch' and the most far from the hotel yet being a five-star cafe made the trip worth it.

I checked the location, which consisted of a lot of turns in unknown streets. We took up about twelve minutes of walking until we took the last turn and saw a sign that said *Francesca's Cafe*. The coffee shop took place around the corner of a street, allowing people to sit outside and view every street surrounding it. We sat outside at the table with the best view, where we could see the sunrise from afar. Classical music played inside the shop, making the early morning more peaceful than it already was. After sitting down at the rustic table, a waiter came to give us the menu of coffee drinks, breakfast meals, and pastries.

"Everything looks so amazing! I want to order everything. I'm starving," I said, flipping through the menu.

"You are right, but I don't know what to order." Dani flipped through the menu from the start again. The waiter came back to take our order after a few minutes of food dilemmas.

"I will get a black hot coffee with vanilla syrup, a chocolate muffin, and a grilled cheese sandwich with ham," Dani said, looking back and forth between the menu list and the waiter.

"And I will get one omelet, two chocolate muffins, an orange juice, a mini pancake bowl, and a medium caramel iced coffee." I handed the waiter the menu. "Can you bring water bottles as well? Seems that I haven't drank much water lately." He looked at me puzzled, telling me I was crazy to order a lot of food.

"I will eat everything," I stated. He grabbed the menus with furrowing eyebrows and left.

"That's a lot of food." Dani raised her brows and shook her head at me.

"I haven't eaten in about two days... I think, and it is our last day in London so we might as well enjoy it."

She slightly frowned. "You can't even remember if you ate?"

I shook my head, thinking about how weird it was to not remember something so simple.

"I don't want to worry you Clara, but maybe you should go see a doctor," Dani advised. And she was right, a sane person would have gone to the doctor straight away. But an inner feeling told me it was something else, something that I needed to figure out for myself.

"I should," I agreed, still believing that there was no way I could have suddenly forgotten due to something wrong in my brain. Or at least that's what I hoped.

"What do we do after eating?" Dani asked, after a few seconds.

"Maybe we can go to a few stores and buy souvenirs..." I replied. "Also, if we have time, I need to go to the bank to pay back the money to the strangers who helped me at the hospital. Then go to the hotel and start packing." I exhaled, relieved to have our last day planned.

"Sounds great," she said while nodding. "Also, that bruise looks bad."

"It hurts more not knowing why I have it." I sighed.

For the rest of breakfast, we sat in silence enjoying the awesome food.

"How do you eat that fast?" Dani said, shocked to see me taking the last sip of the iced coffee. I waited for her to finish her sandwich. After we were done, we paid the bill and got ready to take a small tour around before walking back to the hotel, staying close enough to be there in time to finish packing our suitcases.

We walked at a steady pace watching the inside of the stores through the glass windows as we passed by. Our morning peace was suddenly broken when a bicyclist came at full speed by my side causing me to stumble and fall, hurting my hand at the silver pole on the floor. Almost losing balance from the bicycle, the blonde-haired guy kept riding anyway without even stopping to say sorry.

"That jerk!" I started to get up with Dani's help, my left hand began to pound and hurt from the fall.

"Should I go after him?" Dani scoffed angrily, watching the bicyclist disappear around the corner.

I shook my head. "I would say yes and go with you, but there is no point wasting our time. Karma will strike him before we do." Dani let go of my right hand. She was about to speak until someone else behind me spoke first.

"That cut on your palm doesn't look that great." I turned around to see Gilbert semi-smile at me, eyebrows squishing together at my arm.

Without trying to look shocked, I faked a smile. "What a huge coincidence seeing you here. Trying to stalk me again."

"I work at a bakery nearby." He frowned, pointing down the street.

"Hi, I'm Danielle!" Dani greeted him out of nowhere. I glanced at the palm of my right hand, the pain increasing. I examined the cut closely, at the strange realization that some parts of the blood changed from red to gold when it surfaced from the cut.

"Nice to meet you. I'm Gilbert Gram," Gilbert said. I looked up quickly and saw Gilbert looking at my palm, tilting his head with a curious expression on his face. The same expression he had when he was analyzing the necklace and when we first met. Confusion seemed to be his automatic watermark. I hid my arm behind me. Dani looked at me, realizing that Gilbert was one of the strangers I told her about.

"Dani, we should go now. We have a lot of things to do," I said. She nodded accordingly. I was about to turn around, but Gilbert spoke gently, "That cut could get infected, there are first aid kits at the bakery." Dani looked at the cut, then at me shrugging as if saying *He is right*.

"Thank you, but I don't want your help. Ok," I quickly said. "By the way, I'm returning the money you paid at the hospital, so you should expect a check to be delivered to your house."

"You don't know my address." He slightly shook his head.

"I'm rather good at memorizing and analyzing places. I can do online research."

Dani raised her brows at me but didn't speak.

"Right... of course," he responded, crossing his arms.

With that, I started to walk forward quickly with Danielle by my side. She turned around to glance at Gilbert until she saw me, eyebrow-raising at her, and then fell back on track.

Once we turned the corner, Dani said, "Online research, huh? What happened to 'being nice'?"

"I'll find a way to pay him back somehow and even if he did help me yesterday, I'm not going to be fully nice to a stranger that I barely met close to a forest where I could have died."

"A really *cute* stranger... and a baker too." Dani beamed widely. I shook my head at her. "He is right though, that cut does look bad. I'll look for a pharmacy nearby to buy supplies and patch it up."

"Thank you. That would really be *nice*," I said, looking back at my palm and turning my head to make sure I was seeing clearly.

The wound slowly pulsed faster, but I was more worried about the fact that my blood still seemed gold. And somehow based on his facial expression, Gilbert noticed.

"Dani, does the blood look gold to you?" I asked, interrupting her from the pharmacy search on her phone.

"What?" She looked closely at the cut and blinked. "No. Why?"

"Never mind..." I responded. We proceeded to walk to our next destination. "I think I'm hallucinating."

CHAPTER 3
UNEXPECTED

DANI SQUINTED AS SHE helped me bandage the wound in my palm. We sat on a bench outside the green pharmacy building. People walked by, eyeing us curiously. Some frowned or looked away at the sight of blood. "Terminado," Dani said, happily in her native language. I learned a lot of Spanish from her and my practice. It was now easier to understand, especially since it was personally similar to Italian.

"Thanks, I appreciate it," I said, wincing as I tried to move my hand. "Okay, let's go!" I stood up at once, not wanting to waste any more time.

"Where are we going?" Dani said, hand on her waist.

"It's actually a surprise I had been planning." I twinkled and started walking to find a cab.

Dani followed me. "Please say we're going to a party. I want to meet new people before we leave."

The traffic increased as we turned onto the next street. The driver, Jamie, had introduced herself to us rather enthusiastically the moment we entered the cab. I had shown her the location on my phone, saying she knew London like the palm of her hand. "You guys have great fashion," she stated, looking from the rearview mirror. She seemed around Dani's age, only two years older than me.

"Thank you!" Dani and I said in unison.

I spoke without thinking right after, "Dani is opening her new business soon! Her fashion designing abilities are to die for."

"Really! That's great. Congrats! I haven't found my 'aesthetic' fashion *yet*..." Jamie mumbled. She wore normal skinny jeans and a plain gray shirt with a logo that said *Dreaming Forever* in white. Dani looked at her and then quickly rummaged through her purse.

"Here," Dani started, her professional look on her face. "This is my business card in case you want to talk for advice."

For the remaining fifteen minutes of the ride, Dani and Jamie talked all about fashion and how to match clothing by color. I watched them while they shared information, but my mind kept replaying the events from the morning, trying to find clues that I may have missed. I looked at my wound, the bandage was a little stained, and I could still see spots of golden blood. I had two problems now, but I was sticking with the main one first.

"We are here," Jamie informed. I looked at the tinted window beside Dani and towards the average-sized store next to the two other large stores on each side. One of them had a clearance sign and the other had 'Closing Soon' and 'Sales' signs in bright yellow and red colors. It wasn't until I got out of the cab that I could see the gleaming lights of the thrift shop. Even the sign at the top that said: *Tree's Thrift Shop: Modern and Vintage Clothing* gleamed up radiantly overshadowing both stores. "Bye!" I heard Dani say to Jamie before she closed the backseat door.

"Wow," Dani exclaimed, looking exactly as shocked as I was.

"I know. Do you still want to go to a party?" I raised my brows at her. She laughed and walked towards the entrance, pushing the hazelnut elegant doors that one day she dreamed of owning.

She hurriedly grabbed my arm to lead me towards the 'Modern Dresses', but I stopped walking before she led me farther.

"What's wrong?" she asked.

"Nothing! You go ahead, okay? I just have to use the restroom really quick, so I will go and ask…"

"Don't take long." She beamed as she turned around to follow her path.

I turned back around and pretended I was looking for the restrooms, but what I was looking for was not a thing but a very lively person. The store was semi-huge, and the clutter of clothes blinded my view a bit. I searched through my purse, bumping into the person I had been looking for.

"I'm sorry," I blurted. "Rosie?"

"Hello! You're here!" Rosie exclaimed, giving me a hug. She wore a brown jumpsuit with a white lace blouse underneath, along with blue diamond hoop earrings.

"I was actually about to call you." I swung my phone in my hand.

"Ooh, I'm sorry! I was in such a hurry. A client wants to make a complaint about the fabric of this sweater... she says it itches," Rosie said, annoyed, showing me the soft-looking sweater.

"That is not accurate." I touched the cuff of it. We both shook our heads at the weird complaint. "Maybe they are allergic to the fabric."

"Yes, that is what I thought." She folded the sweater and placed it over her shoulder. "Anyhow, what can I help you with? Looking for a specific type of clothing?"

"No, not clothing. A necklace actually." I took out the *R & W* crystal necklace from my pocket and showed it to her.

"Wow!" she marveled, looking at the necklace closely. "This seems expensive!"

"I know. Do you happen to know where they sell this type of jewelry?"

"I don't know much about jewelry stores, my specialty is clothing, but I can call my boss for information."

"That would be great." I nodded, taking back the necklace.

"I will be right back." Rosie left in a hurry.

I walked around for a while until I stood by the entrance, deciding to text Dani after two minutes.

I'm looking for something at the front of the store:)

She replied. **Okay, take your time. I'm busy trying on dresses anyway.**

I looked up at the sound of heels on the wooden floor. Rosie and a medium-sized lady in a dark blue dress walked towards me. The woman was tall, and her skin matched the chestnut shade of the elegant doors behind me. She walked confidently, smiling widely at me.

"Hello!" she said, hugging me like Rosie had done.

"Hi!" I stumbled at the sudden hug. "Are people in London always this happy and generous?"

"Maybe that's just us," burst Rosie.

"Especially today!" the lady exclaimed.

"Right! I saw the closing sign at the other store, which means you will have more clients or have already stolen all of them."

"About time!" She stretched her hand with cheerfulness. "By the way, I'm Tree. Nice to meet you."

"Clara. Nice to meet you too," I shook her hand. "You must be super busy."

"It's alright. No worries," Tree said kindly.

I quickly got the necklace out and showed it to her. She inspected it, frowning the way Gilbert had that day in the forest, she raised her brows and said, "I believe this was bought from *Bellives Pendants.*"

We suddenly heard a bell ring, which made me almost jump. I turned at the sound of it, towards the cashier. Dani stood at the register beaming at the pile of clothing on the counter that she had chosen to buy.

"That is my cue," Rosie said, quickly walking towards the register to help the cashier out with Dani's purchases.

"Thank you so much. I have been trying to figure it out," I told Tree.

"Special present for someone?" she asked.

"Something like that..."

Tree left quickly at the shout of someone at the back of the store, hugging me again before she turned on her heels. I smiled at her and then looked at Dani walking happily towards me with a full bag of clothes. Rosie shouted, "See you soon!" and waved goodbye.

"Come again!" added Tree before Dani and I stepped back out of the store and into the cold.

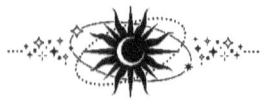

"So, chicken sandwiches?" Dani asked. We'd come to the apartment to start packing for tomorrow.

"Yes, please!" My stomach had started to grumble the moment we had gotten out of the thrift store. Dani nodded, soon leaving to pick up lunch at the cafe downstairs, while I started packing my self-care essentials. I looked at the address that Tree gave me for Bellives Pendants. It turned out it was close to London Bridge, just a few streets away. I didn't know if I had enough time to get there, yet there was no option of not going. I packed faster, trying to keep everything organized and making sure not to leave my flat and curling iron behind.

Soon, Dani came back, her eyes wide in thought. I closed my luggage, looking up at her in wonder. "Why do you have that look?"

"What look?" Dani said, quickly glancing at me.

"The 'something happened, but I'm going to act normal' look."

"Nothing..."

I raised my brows. "Come on. Spill."

She hesitated. "Clark asked me out in the morning... and the date is tonight."

I looked at her in shock. "What? Are you serious? And you didn't tell me?!"

"I didn't say anything because I knew what you would say," she blurted, putting the bag of food on her unmade bed and crossing her arms.

"I haven't said anything."

"You are thinking about it." Dani sighed. And I was thinking about it. I knew I was right; Dani and Clark would make a nice couple. He was nice, and Dani needed someone who would be honest with her.

"Are you going out with Mr. Blue Eyes then?" I questioned, trying to convince her to give it another chance to date someone that was not like Mason.

"I don't know..." she frowned, starting to sit on the bed end to unwrap her sandwich.

The elevator doors opened to the ground floor. Clark stood by a wall wearing a black tuxedo that brought out his blue ocean eyes. In the end, I managed to convince Dani to go out with him, and give new relationships a try.

"Wow, so professional," I whispered to her as we walked towards him. She raised her shoulders, and I stayed behind her.

"You look beautiful," Clark said, his eyes widening at Dani's approach.

"Thank you," she responded. She looked beautiful indeed. The red strapless dress with the black fuzzy sweater, and glittery heels made her look like royalty. She had always been surrounded by people who admired her and her high-class fashion.

"You look good too," Dani said kindly. Awkward glances were shared between the two of them.

"You guys should go before it gets too late," I blurted, breaking the awkwardness.

"Right," Clark turned to me, then said, "I like your camera and purse..."

I glanced at my camera that hung around my neck and smiled back. Unlike Dani, I wore a red long-sleeved shirt, burgundy pants, and a coat. The brown purse and camera made the outfit stand out.

"Thanks," I responded. He stood next to Dani, offering his arm to walk her outside. I walked behind them towards the fresh air, kind of feeling the third-wheel effects until they entered the car to leave.

Goosebumps rose in my skin from the chilly night. I walked fast, passing the slow people in front of me. I had passed about three streets, following the directions on my phone. Finally, coming to a halt at the entrance of Bellives Pendants. The windows of the white elegant store showcased exquisite necklaces. Pearls, diamonds, crystals, and gold necklaces illuminated under the fluorescent lights. I slowly entered the store taking in the bright light.

"Hello, welcome!" An elderly man, who was standing behind a jewelry display, greeted me kindly.

"Hello," I said, walking towards him. A lady stood in front of him across the counter as he typed something into the computer, wrote a paper receipt, and handed a copy to her. The lady looked down at the shining item in her hand, heading to the exit door.

"What can I help you with?" the elderly man asked, walking

towards me and placing the copied receipt in his denim overall pocket.

"I would like to know who bought this crystal necklace." I took out the necklace from my purse. He reached out to inspect it.

"Who could forget a crystal like this? It's an original and most rare," the man informed, standing on the other side of the counter. *It must've cost a fortune.*

"Do you remember who bought it?"

"I remember selling it recently but to whom I do not remember. I only have copies of the receipts, but I'm afraid that is personal information."

"Please. I just need the name, that's all."

I was afraid he would ask why. Instead, he walked to a small room at the back of the store, holding a set of keys in his hand. He disappeared coming back after five minutes and started to open the receipt dated black box. *November-December.*

"The receipt is somewhere here." He fixed his glasses into place, handing me half of the receipt stack to revise and search the other half himself.

I started to go through the recent receipts. First the lady's receipt and others from the recent days. There were no actual names on the receipt, only initials, prices, and date of purchase. The prices shown on each receipt were completely unbelievable. Halfway through the stack nothing had appeared, but I couldn't give up. It could have been possible for the buyer to have come back and taken the receipt in secret. I flipped through each piece of paper, my eyes reading at a faster but careful pace. Until I saw it. A purchase was made the day before I was found. The initials shown were *O.W.* Only the *W* matched the letter written in the crystal. With no exact name or clues, besides the *W*, I was back to square one.

"You must have security cameras?" I asked the man.

"I'm sorry, miss, unfortunately, they stopped working five days ago," he shook his head, handing me back the necklace. *What a coincidence!*

"That's great, thank you." I gave a strained smile, walking out of the store frustrated.

Finding out who bought the necklace was the only clue I had to move forward. I was going home with an unsolved mystery. Frustrating over it wasn't worth it anymore, but I couldn't help it. I kept on walking down the lonely street, looking at the necklace, putting it back in my pocket, and then trying to figure out what to do during the last hours in London. A cold breeze flowed through my coat and onto my skin, and it suddenly reminded me of that night. I was cold, so cold as I ran through the woods. Icy wind had touched my face. Was that snow or rain? I was running, but why?

I turned around, hearing close laughs behind me. Two men, one clearly with a cap, walked a few feet away from me conversing in whispers. I quickened my pace hoping that they would enter a store or turn around the corner, yet I could still hear them whispering and their steps quickened with mine. Fatigue circulated through my body at the thought of running or fighting. I kept on walking hoping to see a busy restaurant or groups of people in the next street, but nothing and no one appeared. All of a sudden, someone grabbed my arm. I turned to see Killian smiling at me. His amber eyes turned a darker shade of brown in the dark.

"Hello, my love! Long time no see," he spoke cheerfully. I stopped for a second, recognized what he was doing, and followed his lead.

"Hi, how are you?" I exclaimed, a wide grin on my face. He started walking next to me.

"Wonderful, really..." he said loudly. I turned around and the two men had curved around the street I just walked by. It annoyed me how little power people thought I had.

"What the hell, Killian?" I said, moving away from him, as soon as the two men were out of sight.

"Hello, gorgeous." He grinned widely, making me shiver.

"You were following, weren't you? Why? Came to figure out why your little microdevice didn't work?"

"Don't flatter yourself, love. I wasn't following you. I was taking a walk down this depressing street until I saw that *they* were following you."

"Whatever. I don't have time for this." I quickly walked away from him brushing past his shoulder. For a few seconds, everything stopped. Images and voices filled my mind.

Where are we going? No answer. Killian held out a jewelry box to me. I opened the box and looked at the beautiful crystal necklace it contained. "Forget about all of this," he said.

The images stopped, and I was back to reality. *What the hell was that?* I didn't know how I knew, but the memory had happened the night before I had been found in the Gram's forest. It took me only a few seconds until I had the urge to run. But I didn't. *Breathe.* I tried not to look amazed as questions flowed through me like an interrogation. *Don't fear.* I proceeded to walk until Killian stood in front of me. *Stay calm.* For a moment, I thought he had noticed my eyes bulging, but he just said, "We need to talk to you."

I looked at him, unmoving, keeping my expression steady. "By 'We' I'm guessing you and Gilbert?"

He nodded and walked away to a nearby dark alley. I hesitated to follow. Whether I would die of curiosity or be involved in something dangerous, I didn't know. One thing I did know was that Killian knew me before we met at the Grams' house. Maybe he was the reason why I didn't remember. Maybe there was more to the story. Either way, I was going to figure out the truth.

Two lamp posts lit up the small alley. Gilbert stood in the middle of it, and Killian stood next to him, their expressions almost unseeable in the dark. I wondered if they could hear my heartbeat palpitating with fear. I stood away from them but close enough to hear what they had to say. Gilbert only seemed to half-smile at me.

"So, what happened to 'Hey, Clara? Do you want to go to dinner so that we can talk about something important?'" I said, keeping my composure. Gilbert's smiling expression suddenly disappeared from his face. I heard two footsteps coming from behind me. I turned quickly to see the two men from earlier standing close to me, enough to touch me. They stared at me unpleasantly. I stepped back at once.

"Are we missing a party, mates?" The man with the cap said, looking at Gilbert and Killian. I stood frozen, afraid to look away or walk to either side.

"This is not a party *mate*," Killian responded coldly, walking towards me.

"We don't want any trouble, you should go back," Gilbert warned them, following behind Killian. *Really? Now I'm a damsel in distress... again?* I rolled my eyes. Adrenaline coursed through me once again, and my brain started to function, acting at the current dilemma.

The moment I decided to move back to the mystery duo, the other man moved his hand onto his jacket and got out what appeared to be a small gun. I shrunk for a bit, watching the man pointing the gun at me.

"We'll leave with the girl..." he said, staring at me. I sighed, frustrated. I looked at Killian and hoped he understood what I was going to do as I slightly shook the camera I carried around my neck. "About that... I don't think so."

Killian nodded. I pressed the shutter button on it, releasing bright light, blinding the men's faces. I moved aside, closer to where Gilbert stood, looking at everyone's irritated appearance. In a flash, Killian moved towards the man with the gun, grabbed him by the neck, and took his gun. He pointed the gun at the other man, who stood away in shock.

"I'll give you two options, *mates*. One, walk away alive, or two, walk away as ghosts..." Killian threatened, his eyes turned into a glowing shiny gold.

"Killian," Gilbert warned. He shook his head at him.

"We'll leave..." the man that stood frozen whispered, while the man around Killian's arm nodded. He slowly let go of him.

"I will be keeping this if you don't mind." Killian shook the gun. The two men nodded, stared stunned at Killian, then quickly disappeared onto the street. Killian smirked at me, proceeding to put the gun in his pocket.

"What was that?" It was all I managed to say, looking at Gilbert and Killian back and forth.

"Clara, we—" Gilbert started slowly.

"Let's get this over with. We are vampires. Surprise!" Killian confessed with almost no emotion in his voice. "Well, Gil is half-vampire." Gilbert glared at him.

"I'm sorry... what? You can't possibly be serious." I started to chuckle, denying the possibility. But Killian and Gilbert stood still, looking at me, waiting. Realization hit me. Both suddenly and slowly. The forest. The blood. The crystal. It was all them.

Breathe. Don't fear. Stay calm.

"Oh my god," I said, stepping away from them. I didn't know whether to feel fear or anger. *Always expect the unexpected.* Another quote my dad used to say every time he took me to a training session. But what if the unexpected seemed impossible?

"It wasn't us who hurt you in the forest, and we won't hurt you ever. We just need your help," Gilbert spoke. But his words went through my ears like inaudible whispers, trying to make sense of it.

"I don't believe you," I murmured, shaking my head and containing tears of anger in my eyes. I looked at the ground, behind them, at the darkness of the alley. Anywhere but them. "I want nothing to do with you or anything supernatural."

After everything that I had read growing up, I couldn't believe the words that came out of me. Especially, how much I actually meant them. Slightly shaking, I walked past them both without stopping. All I wanted to do was go home and hope that this was all a dream.

"You're an Illuminator," Gilbert said before I left the alley. "I saw the golden blood too, you *are* supernatural."

I didn't turn around. I couldn't, even if I wanted to know more. No matter how much curiosity killed me, I had to manage to walk away from all of it. My younger self, the one who was obsessed with fictional characters, would've said to stay. I remembered reading the books and watching the shows. So obsessed with vampires and supernatural things that I pretended they were watching me outside, waiting to turn me or show me the world. But there was one thing I hadn't taken into consideration at that time. Anyone that was close to them or befriended them died. It was getting killed, turned, or losing someone special. And I wasn't going to let that happen.

Neither Killian nor Gilbert stopped me.

With no sight of the duo and the two creepy men, I got to the hotel as quickly as possible in a cab. Avoiding my thoughts, denying them, and vice versa. No one was in the lobby. Clark and Dani were not back. I changed into my purple silk pajamas and finished packing the rest of my stuff, huffing when it didn't look well organized. *Stay focused. Please, stay focused.* Dani's empty hot pink luggage lay on the corner mocking me. Anxiety rushed through me. I didn't want to think about what had happened, but it was hopeless. Who could ever forget that vampires exist?

Gilbert had said something about being an "Illuminator" and

that it was connected to the golden blood. *What in the world is an Illuminator?* I got my phone to check online for the word, but as I expected, nothing showed up. I wondered whether my parents knew about this and whether it was a genetic situation. But they never showed any signs of abnormal or magic abilities. I looked at my memory journal, hesitating whether I should write it all down or leave it hidden in my mind.

The sound of the door shuffling interrupted my thoughts.

"Hey, Cinderella..." I said. Dani entered the room. She looked at me with her brown, drowning eyes, yawning in complete exhaustion.

"Are you okay?" I asked, but instead, she went straight to the restroom and came back two minutes later wearing her red plaid pajamas, flopping in her bed.

"Dani... you do realize that we are leaving tomorrow morning, right? And your luggage is literally zero percent full?"

"Can you shut up? I want to fall asleep..." She groaned.

"Oof, really?" She didn't pay attention to me, so I decided to let it go, and let her sleep. Whatever happened was between her and Clark. I was glad she seemed to at least have a nice date with Clark to the point of drowsiness.

I put all my items in the corner of the room, darting a gaze at Dani's stuff all around the room. And I restrained myself from thinking about her messiness. I walked towards my bed, noticing the unbelievable silver diamond ring on Dani's finger. It shined bright in the light. I couldn't believe I missed a hint of it when she walked in. Based on the pattern on the surface and the huge diamond, the ring must've cost the same or way more than the jewelry from Bellives Pendants. I couldn't even imagine how Clark gifted an expensive ring for a date gift. He must really like her a lot, sadly I didn't think Dani felt the same.

The 6:30 am alarm rang furiously, causing Dani to toss and turn the same way I had done every single minute of the night. The alley memory played like a broken record over and over again, making my head hurt. The words "We are vampires" and "You are supernatural" repeated second after second.

"Turn it off already. It makes my head explode," Dani said, putting a blanket over her head to refrain the sunlight from striking her face. I shook my head and stood up quickly.

"Get up! You haven't even packed yet!" I sighed, confused at her sudden change of attitude while I headed to the restroom. I couldn't manage to look at my neck in the mirror. And I kept avoiding it. But the hurt of it as the warm water hit my neck, resurfaced the negative thoughts. Gilbert had said that it wasn't them who hurt me, but it was impossible to actually trust him or Killian after everything. Yet, I had to go back home, and what happened in London was staying in London. And I was never coming back. *Well, maybe not for a few years.*

When I got out, Dani was already halfway through packing her stuff chaotically.

"I'm going downstairs to get breakfast. Do you want anything?" I asked.

"No, thanks," she responded.

A joyful cleaning lady got out of the elevator at the same time I headed in. On the ground floor, Clark was occupied showing another worker how to use the computer. I guessed he was a new arrival.

The delicious smell of cinnamon traveled from the warm brown bag to my nose seconds before the employee handed it to me. There were a lot of options to buy for breakfast, but I got a cinnamon roll and hot coffee. I headed towards Clark, who was now standing reading an article.

"Good morning, Ms. De Rose." He looked up at me.

"Good morning," I responded nicely. "So? How did everything go..."

His eyes shone. "It went pretty great actually. We went to the Fashion Museum, and it was quite fun."

"That's great!" I said, still curious. "See you later!"

He nodded. "Of course." I walked away and held back from asking about the ring, reminding myself that their relationship was none of my business.

Throughout the entire airplane ride, Dani didn't speak to me. I tried to think of reasons she might be mad at me. Although it might have been a long list of annoyances, none of it was serious enough for her not to speak to me. Or I hoped not. She went to sleep while listening to music, so I decided to write in my journal. I wrote all the information I knew about the 'Mystery Scene' and the 'Supernatural Duo', yet I didn't know where to start. A lot of pieces of information were missing. *What is an Illuminator? What can vampires do? Aside from drinking blood obviously.*

The sound of people moving brought me back to reality. Dani got up and so did I. She walked ahead of me as we entered the inside of the San Antonio, Texas airport.

"I'm going to the restroom," she said tiredly, after getting our luggage.

"Okay, I'll wait here." She moved her luggage closer to mine and headed to the restroom.

"Hey, wait..." I blurted. "Are you okay?"

She gave a nod. "Just fine." And walked away.

I waited, looking around the airport still anxious until she came out of the restroom. She smiled at me when she got out. I replied to her with a quick smile but didn't say anything. We walked out of the airport in silence.

"Over here!" I immediately recognized the voice. I turned around to see Johnny waving at us. I quickly walked towards him and hugged his slim body.

"Hey, Johnny," Dani only said, walking past us towards the airport parking lot.

"What's wrong with her?" Johnny said, curious.

"I have no idea." I shrugged.

The morning weather was much colder in San Antonio than in London. At least that's what it felt like when my muscles quivered nonstop. Johnny and I followed Dani towards Johnny's red car in the parking lot.

"So, how was London?" he asked.

"It was gorgeous," I answered, still worried about Dani's weird attitude.

"London or the guys in London." Johnny grinned.

"*London*." I fixed my response, trying not to think about

Killian or Gilbert. "How was studying?"

He sighed. "What do you think? I study better when you help me." Johnny was currently in his junior year of college. Soon, he would have earned his bachelor's degree in English literature. We had actually met at a coffee shop he worked at by the Art Institute, became friends, then I introduced him to Dani. Until we became coworkers at the Daily Planner.

Johnny helped us put our luggage in the trunk. I sat in the passenger seat and Dani in the back seat.

"Did London change y'all into completely different people?" he said, after the awkward seconds of driving in silence.

"No. We're just really tired," I explained, from my perspective. "The airplane was filled with very lousy and unorganized people."

Dani yawned about three times throughout the ride to her home. *Maybe she is just really tired.* I thought. "Bye! See you at the Daily Planner tomorrow." I watched her walk to her building. She waved goodbye.

Now it was my time to return home. I watched the recognizable streets, feeling stressed about returning to my busy life. As Johnny kept on driving, I could see on his face that he wanted to tell me something.

"What is going on?" I asked.

"I don't want to say anything yet because the morning mood is not exactly positive." He frowned.

"What do you mean? I am in a good mood, so tell me."

"Later..."

"You can't just tell me you have to tell me something and not tell me right away..."

He hesitated only for a second. "I'm going out with some-one..." he paused. "Actually, I've been going out with him for about a while now. I just wasn't sure it was going to last."

"Really? That is so great! I'm so happy for you!" I said in shock, giving him a quick hug once he stopped at the red light. He had seemed lonely for the past weeks; I was starting to worry.

"You will meet him... hopefully soon."

I beamed at him. He really deserved to be happy with someone.

"Are you sure you don't need help?" Johnny screamed from his car seat. I shook my head. "I'm fine, thanks! See you tomorrow!" I waved at him, entering the black and brown apartment building unit. Johnny drove away into the sunset. I sighed, looking around the organized and clean area, which was one of the reasons I had chosen to live there. The four buildings were neatly together, and the two pools were always crystal clear. People didn't usually speak to each other unless there was an emergency. My apartment was located in the second building, on the third floor, number 306.

Dust greeted me as I opened the door of my apartment. The first thing I saw was the amazing comfortable beige and yellow couch. I walked slowly around the still-organized apartment, looking exactly how I left it. The beige-colored walls made it seem more professional and cleaner. I frowned standing between the white kitchen and the peaceful living room, deciding whether I should rest or clean. But the smell of dust teased me. "Who am I kidding," I said out loud, feeling anxious at the sight of dust on the center table. *At least, the plants on the balcony still seem alive.* I put my luggage in my room and headed towards the kitchen first, realizing I needed to go grocery shopping. Then moved onto the living room, bookshelf, and cozy bedroom. I tried to clean as much as I could until the Sun no longer hit my window, and no dust was visible in human sight.

CHAPTER 4
MEMORIES

N OTHING THAT I DID throughout the week made me forget about Killian and Gilbert. Even Johnny had started asking if I was ok because I looked "worried". And I was. I had researched the libraries nearby for clues about vampires or Illuminators, yet nothing appeared unless you counted the fictional books about vampires that I remember reading when I was young. Of course, completely useless.

Business at the Daily Planner ran low. The only times I heard the sound of the door opening was when Johnny, Dani, and I entered the office. We only had about three parties to organize: two weddings and one quinceañera. Johnny and I worked on one of the weddings that was happening in two weeks, while Dani worked on the quinceañera. We all took care of the reception, invitations, catering, fashion advice, and much more since our boss ran other similar businesses around the city. Dani worked more on fashion by helping people decide what was best to wear and where they could get what they wanted while I took care of the organization of the party. Johnny wasn't an organizer or knew much about fashion, yet he needed the job and had learned a lot since.

"Ok, so we have a problem," Johnny said, coming out of his office frowning. I sat at the reception desk, looking at a picture of the wedding venue and deciding where to display the food tables.

"What's wrong?" I asked, hoping it wasn't about the food.

"Um, turns out that there was a fire incident at the catering company, and it is currently closed down."

"What?!"

Joanna, the bride, was strict about food choices, and we couldn't afford to lose another customer. Johnny frowned slightly while I got ready to go to the meeting room.

About three times a week, we had meetings at a certain time. The purpose of the meetings was to give each other updates about our planning and ideas and today's updates didn't seem very good. Johnny and I entered the meeting room and waited for Dani, who later came in, twisting her ponytail back and forth.

I sighed. "What's going on? Please, tell me the news are not that bad."

She sat down before she spoke, making me nervous. "Worse actually. Joanna called. She canceled the wedding."

I panicked for a second then reconsidered the events. "That is fitting, considering the company that was catering the wedding had an incident yesterday."

Dani bit her lip. "I know."

"So, what do we do now?" said Johnny, looking at me and Dani for an answer. "We can't afford to lose more customers."

I huffed, shaking my head. "Don't give up? We need a way to advertise the business. We already have a website and business cards. We can do more... like put flyers on receptions and signs on billboards."

"That's a good idea, but we are on a budget. How are you going to plan all that?" Dani wondered, doubting me.

"Leave it to me. I can be very persuasive."

We left early that day since the wedding was canceled. Our priority was saving the business and then getting worried about the other wedding. Dani stayed at the Daily Planner, while Johnny invited me for a coffee at his part-time job. He told me to meet him there, so I drove by my apartment to quickly change into more casual clothes. A white long-sleeved shirt and a gray coat with black heeled boots.

The cafe Johnny worked at was by his university. *The Coffee House.* In most circumstances, he would usually go study at a public library closer to the Art Institute instead. That's how we met. The quietness of the public library was way better than either of our universities. We were both shocked to find out we had both graduated early from high school and worked towards a college degree. He needed a math tutor for a required class and as an overachiever student, studying till late at the library, I was there to help. The high school notes I had saved were most certainly useful.

"Ooh, look who is here to see me!" said Santiago annoyingly the second I entered the coffee shop. I shook my head at his remark.

He was one of Johnny's coworkers, and the most annoying of his coworkers, who had been bothering me about dating him since I met him. I tried to ignore him to a great extent in order to not send him mixed signals. Yet, it was impossible for him not to talk to me.

"What makes you think I would waste my time to see *you*?"

"You are so cruel," he said, shaking his head. I was about to say something else until Johnny appeared from the storage room.

Johnny looked at Santiago. "Man, you never get tired, do you?"

"Never." Santiago smirked, walking away to help a customer. I rolled my eyes at him and turned to look at Johnny.

"It's never going to happen. He is completely crazy."

"He is obsessed with you. Every day he asks me if you are coming. Can't you give him a chance?"

"Whose side are you on Johnny?"

"You are going to be mad at me if I tell you I am on both," he said as a matter of fact.

I glared at him. "Anyway, what did you want to talk about?"

"I want to ask if you can come with me downtown. I have to meet with my writing partner for a class project," he informed me.

"Obviously, I'll go with you." I nodded, smiling. "I need to do research for something too and pass out the Daily Planner flyers."

He hugged me. "Thank you. You're the best." Then he let go. "I'll go get your coffee and we can leave."

"Don't worry. It's done." Santiago stood behind Johnny; he passed the cup to him. "Enjoy." And walked away.

I shook my head. "I was going to order something else."

Johnny narrowed his eyes. "No, you weren't. You always

order the same thing." He handed the cup to me, quickly walking away, and disappearing behind the supply room after Santiago.

The business flyers rested safely under my arm while I tried to convince the hairstylist to let me leave a small stack of them at the register counter. Based on online reviews, the four-star hair salon was crowded on weekends. At last, I persuaded the man by offering a discount at the Daily Planner whenever he or his family members needed help with planning an event. I walked around leaving more flyers at different event-related places until there were none left. Looking at my watch, I still had about an hour to research. Only an hour had passed since Johnny and his partner worked on the writing project. I checked the list on my phone of nearby libraries. Two libraries were five minutes away, so I chose whichever seemed pleasing and headed that way. I tried to increase my pace, but the people in front of me walked so slowly.

"Excuse me," I urged, passing between the group of people.

A sudden peaceful silence greeted me the moment I walked into the vintage-looking library. Colorful books laid on the brown shelves, and the spiral staircases had an alluring leaves design on the handrail. A sudden memory materialized in my head. I was at a library but not the one I was currently standing in.

"Watch your step, Clara," a voice said in a serious tone. I turned around to smile at Killian as I walked up the stairs.

"It's fine! See I'm not even holding the rail!" I said, laughing happily and without care.

Killian sighed and grabbed my hand. "Come on. Let's get out of here. We don't want to disturb people."

"What? You're the one that said, 'Stop being so serious and have fun'. So, that is what I'm doing!" I imitated Killian's accent. He grabbed my arm more tightly, making me wince.

"What are you doing? Let go of me!" I said once we were out of the library. "It hurts!"

He led me into an alleyway that was close by. It was still daytime, but no people passed the dirty alley.

"Stay silent, this won't hurt as much." I obeyed him, it was as if I was hypnotized. He moved my wavy hair and bit me on my neck. He finally pulled away, there was a hint of gold in his amber eyes similar to the red-golden blood on his lips. It was my blood, yet I didn't know why I wasn't that scared. Killian got out a flask from his pocket in his jacket and handed it to me. "Drink this. It will heal you." I grabbed the flask and drank whatever there was in it. The pain in my neck decreased.

"Thank you, love... again," he said. I handed him back the flask. I couldn't think straight. I couldn't speak. I just stood there, frozen.

He stared mischievously and looked straight into my eyes. "Now, tomorrow, meet me at the museum just like today. Don't bring your phone either, less distractions. Go rest and forget this ever happened." In a blinking of an eye, he was gone, and I headed home to rest just as he said.

"Hello, ma'am? Are you okay?" I was almost out of breath, standing back in the vintage-looking library and in the same spot. A woman stared at me puzzled. My hands trembled at the dizziness.

Pain passed through my neck, but I wasn't sure if it was because of the memory or the bruise I actually had. It took me a second to speak.

"Um... how long have I been standing here?" I asked.

"A minute or so... are you alright? You seem frightened..."

I nodded at her and slowly walked away, feeling her curious stares behind my back. She probably thought I was crazy, but what could I say, maybe I was. I walked up the staircases, trying to focus on the research rather than the memory I had. It was obviously no use.

There was no way the memories I had been seeing were real, they just couldn't be. *But if they aren't, why do they feel like a part of me?* I shook my head, avoiding the thought.

Time passed as I searched each mysterious shelf that I could. Some books were copies I'd seen before at other libraries, and I was getting frustrated. The clock on the wall showed I still had a few minutes left until Johnny's meeting was over. I walked past the aisles, rechecking the shelves. I was so focused on the books, but I couldn't help but think about the memory. Killian's face when he pulled away from my neck. He seemed out of control, like a complete monster. That Killian was not the Killian I met at Gilbert's house unless he was faking it.

I turned around the corner of the aisle that I was walking through again, still thinking. And jolted, bumping into a book cart. "Oh my god... I'm sorry!" I said, looking at the guy in a black hat and mask, who was pushing the cart.

"It's okay. My fault." I could barely see his face, but his eyes showed a hint of curiosity. "Do you need help finding a book?" he asked, his voice rasped and low almost like a whisper.

"No, I'm—" I started to say until I looked at the glittery letters of a book in the book cart. The shining gold letters of the black book in the cart read the word *Illuminated*. The book was medium-sized, leather-bound, and had no written author or publisher. I focused my eyes again, making sure I was seeing correctly.

"That book is actually for free," the guy said, noticing my interest. He nodded at the 'Free Donated Books' sign that hung in the cart.

"Really?"

He nodded again. I didn't hesitate and quickly took the book. "Do you happen to know who wrote this book?"

"No, sorry. I work here, but ironically, I don't read many books."

I moved out of the way. "Thanks."

His eyes squinted to a smile and walked away. As he did, I noticed a blue streak of hair peeking out of his black hat. It reminded me of one of my mom's paintings of a blue oleander flower.

A second after getting out of the library, I flipped through the pages of the book, wanting to know what was hidden within. I clutched it, examining each of them. A problem arose. The whole book was blank, except for the first two pages that contained two quotes. *Light and Darkness need a balance. Are you the one to secure it?* The quote on the first page stated. While the second page said,

As your true bloodline drops on the square, the book must open and ignite.

I looked at the drawing of the tiny square at the bottom of the page. It was the size of a quarter coin. I guessed only Illuminators were able to open the book. Whoever created the book must have been pretty smart. I frowned, realizing the people walking by.

Downtown became more crowded. I walked through the crowds of people, closing the book, and deciding to go home to thoroughly inspect it. And continued towards my car, calling Johnny to let him know that I was going home because "something urgent came up". He didn't mind, saying that he would be working on the project longer than expected.

I almost bumped into my neighbor by my apartment door, anxious to figure out the truth. I quickly entered my home, got a needle from my thread box in the closet, and sat down on the couch. Both excited but nervous. "Okay, this is crazy. But the fact that vampires are real is crazier." I spoke to myself.

Taking a deep breath, I pricked my finger. Letting red-golden blood appear from within, shining in the sunlight that peaked through the window. And fingerprinted the small, squared drawing like the ink fingerprints on the cases my dad used to solve.

The blood soon absorbed itself into the paper; leaving it clean as it was before. Suddenly, something shone on the front cover of the book. I turned it to the front. The golden letters from the word *Illuminated*, actually lit my face more than the sunlight did. My eyes had become warm and still. The light slowly decreased. I started to flip through the pages. Words, pictures, and signs slowly appeared on each page like magic. Killian and Gilbert were right. I knew it. Warmth and adrenaline. The energy coursed through me, as I touched every inch of the illuminated book. There was no doubt that I was an Illuminator.

I had no idea whether I should be concerned or excited about the revelation. I had too many questions but no idea how to get the answers. Was I an Illuminator due to genetics? If so, why didn't my parents say anything? Would I have found out if I hadn't met the mysterious duo? Frustrated, I flipped back to the beginning of the book. More words appeared at the bottom, next to the square. *You have five hours to read the information in this book. For protection, more blood will be necessary after hours are over.*

The Sun shone brightly when I walked to the door of my childhood home. It warmed up my face even though the cold breeze turned it back, counteracting the temperature. The neighborhood still looked the same way it had been a while since I had visited. My childhood home stood so apart from other houses. The large autumn trees almost covered the front of the two-story Spanish villa. Like always, the flowers were perfectly organized, colorful, and healthy. Mom took care of them like her own life. She had inherited the beige rustic house from my grandparents. She had told me and Aurora the story of how she promised her dad to take care of the house and of course, she kept her promise. I knocked at the brown door twice and waited with my camera around my neck. But no one opened and there was no sound coming from inside. I knocked again... still nothing. Anxiously, I turned the knob over in case it was open and it was. I entered slowly, but only complete silence welcomed me.

"Surprise!" Everyone screamed, coming out of their hiding spots.

"Oh my god..." I said, startled. I thought somebody might have broken in or something worse. This was the first time they had done something like this.

"Happy Birthday!" Everyone exclaimed in sync.

I opened my arms. "I missed you guys!" My parents were the first ones to approach me from the living room. My dad hugged me, then Mom, Aurora, and Johnny.

My mom pouted. "You are growing up so fast."

"We missed you too," my dad said, putting an arm around Mom. I laughed, feeling a tear running down my cheek and wiping it away swiftly.

"Mom... I think the cake is burning!" said Aurora.

"Oh, yes. The cake!" My mom walked hurriedly to the kitchen.

"I better go help or she will kill me again... I don't even know how I've survived this long," Dad joked out of my mom's earshot. I laughed at his comment. He walked to the kitchen right after.

"You haven't forgotten about me? Have you, sister?" Aurora said sarcastically, giving me another hug.

"About my totally disorganized sister? Of course not," I smiled back, handing her the camera. "London had great views."

"I don't doubt it." She took it at once, hanging the camera on her neck and putting her curly hair out of the way.

"Be careful," I demanded.

She turned the camera on to go over some of the photographs, then put it back down in hesitation. "I'll go help mom instead before she goes crazy. But I'll be back!"

I huffed, watching her shadow become replaced by a beaming Johnny. "So, don't get mad at me," he started.

"Did you plan the surprise party?" I asked, not entirely shocked that he came up with the idea.

"Yes. After all, you are turning nineteen," he began. "But that is not the reason why I told you to not be mad..." He stayed quiet for a few seconds as if deciding what to say.

I sighed, knowing the only thing that Johnny knew could get me somewhat irritated.

"Did you invite Santiago?"

His silent stare gave me the answer.

"Really Johnny!? First, you pretended that you forgot my birthday this morning when I passed by the cafe, which totally did not work. You disappear, leaving me alone with Santiago, whom I'm not interested in. And you invite him here!"

"Look, he genuinely likes you. He basically begged me to invite him after I accidentally spilled the idea of a surprise party. What was I supposed to do?"

"I don't know... Decline!"

"He literally kneeled down." I looked at him seriously. "Okay, he didn't exactly kneel, but you should have seen him."

I rolled my eyes at him, taking in that Santiago was already invited and that it would be rude of me to disinvite him after arriving cheerfully. I wondered whether Dani was going to come, and I started asking, "Is Dani—"

I couldn't finish my sentence. An immense sharp pain went through my stomach and the feeling of throwing up rose to my chest. I hadn't gotten sick in a very long time.

"Clara, are you okay?" I heard Johnny say as I ran to the restroom. My whole body became warm like I was slowly burning from the inside. I started to throw up in the toilet. A second later, I would've ruined my mom's perfectly cleaned lime green mat in the hall. My head throbbed excruciatingly. Johnny came to hold my hair while my body released whatever toxic things it had inside until I was finally able to breathe.

"Thank you," I whispered to him, flushing the toilet. With water in my eyes, I could still see Aurora walking fast from the hall and into the restroom.

"What happened?" Aurora asked worriedly from the doorway.

"She just started feeling sick," Johnny answered.

I got up slowly with the help of Johnny. "I'm okay. It's probably food poisoning." Both turned to look at me concerned. "I'm fine." I half-lied, supporting myself with the sink cabinet to avoid falling. *Best Birthday Ever!* "I look horrible... I'm going to clean up."

"We will wait for you in the kitchen, okay?" Aurora half-smiled. I nodded. She and Johnny got out of the bathroom, giving me one last glance, so I could fix myself for the family birthday party. I started to run warm water on the sink to wash my face, but I was no longer in the restroom.

"I'm surprised. You are late," Killian said. He stood, leaning

against the wall of what seemed to be The British Museum in London. A water fountain stood behind me, freshwater ran smoothly through the cement. I didn't speak to him, feeling confused about why a complete stranger was talking to me and why I wasn't slightly scared. He sighed and walked towards me until he stood inches away.

"Remember yesterday," he said as he looked straight into my eyes. And I did. I remembered the last time we met when he bit me. A realization came to me, I wanted to run. But before I could take action, he grabbed my arm tightly, just as he had last time. His cold skin passed through my thin gray sweater.

"Don't be scared, darling. I'm your friend so loosen up," he said. I could still feel it, a small dust of fear. I knew why I was scared, yet I stood still. He grinned at me and started walking. I followed behind him like a lost puppy.

We walked for a while as he talked on the phone. A rush of happiness, and adrenaline seemed to rise out of me, taking the fear into my subconscious.

"Can we go to the mall?" I said. He hung up, paying no curiosity to his phone call.

"Why not?" he responded, smiling.

He drove to the mall in this modern car. I was amazed by the design. The mall was not as crowded as I had expected it to be. In less than five minutes, I had chosen a pile of clothes, which were mostly coats, to try on. Killian stood there smirking and watching me choosing some outfits.

"What? You are the one who told me to loosen up, remember?" I reminded him. He agreed, nodding his head. Hours after, I was exhausted, completely tired, but my mind kept rushing.

"Let's go," Killian said. We walked out of the store.

"It's too early," I grunted.

"Sorry, love."

We got out of the mall. Deep inside I had no idea what was happening, but I kept following orders.

"Where are we going?" I asked once we were inside the car.

He drove silently for a few more minutes. I kept trying to figure out where we were heading, but I couldn't recognize anything anymore. We stopped at a red light, I looked around and found myself deeply staring at one specific store. The jewelry store reminded me of Aurora and her present for the holidays. All of a sudden, Killian drove towards that exact store and parked beside it.

"Wait here," he said, getting out and walking inside Bellives Pendants. I hated waiting inside the car, so I got out and waited outside instead, pacing in circles until Killian finally came. He held a tiny jewelry box. For a second his face softened and handed me the box. I opened it in confusion, raising my eyebrows at the delightful crystal necklace it contained.

"Why would you buy this for me? We don't even know each other?"

"Put it on," he insisted, smiling.

I smiled back and did what I was told.

My reflection in the mirror reflected exactly what I felt. Anger, fear, and disgust. I clutched the vanity, closing my eyes and looking away from the mirror. *How could I have been compelled?* I was being forced and manipulated to do things and act differently. I couldn't help but follow Killian. Like a puppet being pulled from its strings. I wanted to scream. Negative energy filled up inside like nothing else. *I let myself fall for it. Why wasn't I strong enough to fight him off my mind?* I hadn't had a memory since that time at the library. This memory didn't seem like it was the first one. *How many times have I been manipulated?*

The feeling of throwing up went away, replaced completely by negative feelings. I opened the door to get out of the restroom and headed towards the kitchen. Everyone, except my mom and dad, was sitting at the kitchen table. They looked so happy; I didn't want to worry them. All I could do was muster a smile.

"We are about to serve the food, Clara. Go ahead and sit down," my mom said. I passed her, savoring the smell of the food.

"It smells amazing, Mrs. De Rose." Johnny grinned from the dining room. I went and sat down next to him and my sister.

"How was Italy?" I asked, looking at my mom, who had gone to visit our distant family members. She had tried to persuade me to go since I hadn't gone to Italy since I was a child, but I had already planned the London trip with Dani.

"It was really great!" my dad responded smiling; my mom's parents loved him so much. Their conversations always turned into funny stories and jokes.

"I regret not going," Aurora frowned, expressing my exact thought.

"I would love to—" Johnny got cut off by the sound of someone knocking at the door. "Maybe it's Danielle or... Santiago?"

My dad grimaced at the name of Santiago. "I'll go check," he said half-confidently. I shook my head at Johnny, who held a lopsided smile and whispered, "Please, don't tell your dad."

The dining room wasn't far away from the entrance of the house. I tried to concentrate on the sound of my dad opening the door over the frying noise of the pan. Wondering what my dad's reaction would be if it was Santiago. He opened the door. I didn't hear a sound until...

"Hello, good afternoon. I'm Gilbert. A friend of Clara's."

"And I'm Killian."

CHAPTER 5
ZATARA SUNSET

F EAR AND ANGER ROSE THROUGH MY BODY. Johnny looked at me, eyes furrowing to the voice of two guys at the doorstep of my childhood home... on the day of my birthday. My dad turned to look at me, eyebrows raising about what was happening.

"Clara, my *daughter*, you have some visitors," my dad said steadily. He had a firm look on his face, the look of a detective in action. I got up and walked towards the door, standing next to my dad. Gilbert looked at me with a beam on his face, and Killian just smirked. I couldn't help but remember the memories I had minutes ago and wished I could take off that smirk from his face with a slap.

"Hi! I see you finally decided to come to Texas for the wedding!" I stared at Gilbert. It was the only idea that came into mind as an excuse for why they were at my family's doorstep.

Everyone looked wide-eyed at what I just said.

"Wedding?" My dad asked, stupefied. "What wedding?"

"Ooh, sorry..." I said, pretending that I had forgotten about telling everyone about the situation. "Gilbert and Killian are a couple. And I'm helping them plan their wedding."

I turned to Mom. "They explained they wanted a portrait. But I didn't know they would be here *today*..." I stared at Gilbert and Killian's faces in full confusion and shock. Gilbert made a slight nod, putting one hand on his hip. I could have burst out laughing if I wasn't angry at them. My dad's shoulders seemed to become more relaxed.

Gilbert cleared his throat. "Yes... we met Clara in London. We found out she was from here and a wedding planner... told her we wanted to visit here on the weekend to find a setting for the... um wedding."

I quickly turned to my dad. "Sorry, I gave them the address. You know... work is work." My dad inclined and said, "Right, work is work."

He left back to the kitchen, and I stood at the door with the awkward pair.

"Ok, we should talk outside," I said, feeling the stares of the people in the kitchen. Both began to turn around.

As soon as I closed the door, I looked at them sharply. If looks could kill, they would've been dead. Or at least Killian.

"What the hell are y'all doing here? And how did you find me?" I said, walking further from the house.

"Nice to see you too, Clara *Valerie* De Rose," Killian smirked. I couldn't even manage to look at him for more than five seconds.

The more I saw him, the more the memories reappeared along with the anger. *Try to stay focused, Clara.* Keeping my feelings in check was the only way I would be able to overcome the supernatural. Besides, if I told them that I knew what they did, it wouldn't have been an advantage for me. Better to stay quiet than let them figure out what I knew and about my powers.

"Finding you was... a long online process, and we are here because we need your help, Clara," Gilbert informed.

"For what? The wedding?" I crossed my arms.

He smirked. "Funny."

"What exactly makes you think I would help two *vampires*, who somehow creepily followed me across countries for *help*." I sighed and turned around to walk by the edge of the stony road.

"We can't tell you everything now," Gilbert said, continuing to walk next to me. "Meet us tomorrow, and we will help you figure out everything." He handed me a sticky note. It had an address written on it and a reminder to 'ask for us'. I put it in my pocket. He seemed to know curiosity was my weakness and used that to persuade me. *Quid Pro Quo.* So far, the book *Illuminated* hadn't helped as much as I thought it would, some pages still remained blank. I may have needed them, but I didn't trust them, especially not Killian.

I stayed quiet for a few seconds deciding what to do. My head started pounding immensely at the stressful dilemma over right or wrong. A decision of whether I wanted to get involved in something dangerous or walk away towards safety. Warmth spread throughout my entire body, exactly the way it had done earlier when I got sick.

"I don't feel—" I said, facing Gilbert.

"What's wrong?" Gilbert wondered. My head burned up again. I hated the feeling, but I couldn't fight the science or the exhaustion in my legs. Like the first time we met, Gilbert held me by my arm to stop me from falling to the ground. It was no surprise; at that moment I was no longer standing in the neighborhood.

"Don't even think about doing anything," Gilbert said, looking straight into Killian's eyes. They stood in the middle of a street in what appeared to be London, a place I hadn't seen during my visit there.

"I won't," Killian said in a serious tone. It seemed like that wasn't the only time that Gilbert had to tell him to control himself. "Ironic, isn't it? I was the one who helped during your turning, and yet here we are, you telling me to control myself."

"You only helped me because you needed a murderous partner... to which you successfully failed."

"Instead, you turned out to be an 'awful sober instructor'. Good for me." Killian grinned.

Gilbert did the same. "It's not 'awful' if I can tell when my 'patient' is thinking about getting out of control."

"No, it isn't... it's irritating."

"You do know we have to keep a low profile, especially with the witches around." Gilbert lowered his voice. "They would do anything to see vampires fail in human society." Killian only nodded.

They kept on walking towards a small coffee shop. Gilbert walked first before Killian. They looked like brothers, who were hanging out for the first time in a very long time. He was a few feet away from the entrance. A young lady was walking in the same direction, her hair covered her face. She was about to bump into Gilbert. But he stopped and waited for her to get ahead, then he opened the door for her like a gentleman. The young lady turned around to reveal her face. It was me.

For a few seconds, I came back to reality.

"Clara?" I heard Killian's voice say, but I shifted back into my hidden memory.

"Thanks," I said. Gilbert opened the door for me to enter the cafe. I half-smiled at him and then at Killian, going inside and sitting on one of the black stools by the counter. I was making my first shopping trip for holiday presents, while Dani went out on a date with a guy she had barely met the day after we arrived in London. The cafe was cozy, the walls dark-colored, but the mixed light-dark decorations made it feel odd. People were talking quietly and others reading. It almost looked like a coffee-themed bar which I thought was really creative.

"Can I get a hot coffee with five pumps of caramel syrup and a chocolate brownie to go?" I ordered when the waiter with the blue hat and black mask came by. He only nodded, grabbing the money from my hand and walking away. I found myself staring at the white and black marble floor tiles.

"Light or darkness, Caramel?" Someone had interrupted my peacefulness. I turned around to see Killian smiling at me, his eyes full of curiosity.

"What?" I said, confused. "What kind of question is that?"

"Have you stared around?" He smirked, glancing at the floor for a second. "And why not?"

I sighed a bit irritated. "Where is your friend, the one who was a gentleman and held the entrance door? Don't you have to keep him company or something..."

"He decided to go across the street to buy a book to read, as always."

"Or... maybe he just got tired of your comments."

"British humor, love. No one gets tired of that." He stared at me, not a flinch in his eyes from my remark. We stayed quiet, waiting for the waiter to hand me the change, a hot coffee, and the brownie bag. Then, he gave Killian a slice of strawberry pie on a white glass plate and a fork.

After a while of silence and avoided looks, I decided to answer. "Light. I would choose light. And I'm guessing you will choose... darkness?"

He gazed at me. "Do I look that negative to you?"

"I am naturally a positive person." He raised his eyebrows, taking a bite of the pie with a fork. "But not with people like you."

I took some sips of my coffee and stood up to leave. "It was not so nice meeting you..."

"Killian Walker," he added.

I wondered whether I should say my whole name.

"Clara."

He grinned and I walked away towards the exit as Gilbert entered the coffee shop again, holding a book in his hands. He gave me a quick look before I passed by him.

It had been a few minutes after the conversation in the cafe. It *was getting late, so I headed towards the address that Dani gave me to meet her there and go to dinner. She had seen some luxury clothing that she thought was my style. I walked in the silence of my mind, deciding that I would buy presents for my parents first, then Aurora, my friends, and me. People walked in and out of shops, smiling, laughing, hugging, getting mad, or telling weird jokes. I thought about my own family and friends until someone pulled me into the darkness of an alley.*

I didn't need to finish the memory to know what happened. I avoided the other three memories I had of him, it always ended in me being a blood bag. Everything made sense now. All the memories had come out of order, but I was able to put the pieces together. Meeting Killian, being a blood bag, forced to forget, again and again, and then the crystal necklace. The time after he gave me the necklace to the morning I was found by Mary and William was the only part I didn't remember. The 'R & W' meant 'Rose and Walker'. *But what did the necklace mean? Why don't I remember anything about what happened later that night? What did Killian do?*

"Clara? Are you okay?" Gilbert held my arm. His voice was now loud and clear. I bounced back. I knew it wasn't him who hurt me. It was his best friend. The physical pain had left entirely. All that was left was the emotional pain that the memories had caused. I never knew it was possible to hate someone, but at that moment my chest was heavy. I took a breath, pushing back the angry tears. *Nothing is impossible.* The pain turned to hatred towards Killian. I couldn't even begin to explain what he had done. It felt like a dream. *No. Not a dream. A nightmare.* Yet I had to look at him with no emotions at all. I wanted to yell or punch him straight in the face and demand to know the truth. But I couldn't... at least not at that moment. I needed to figure out more, and Gilbert was the only one who could give me answers. I didn't think he knew about what Killian did. I hoped not. After all, he was the one who told him not to do anything stupid. As expected, Killian ignored him.

"I'm okay," I said, trying to stand straight and act normal.

"Maybe you should take a seat?" Killian suggested. Gilbert nodded at the bench just by.

I shook my head, looking at Gilbert. "I'm alright."

"Are you sure?"

"Yes. Completely," I reassured him.

He took a step back. "You were having a party, weren't you? Is it your birthday?"

"Yes."

I knew why he was asking. One of the pages that I was able to read of the *Illuminated* stated that the day of an Illuminator's 19th birthday was the day they would get side effects. The side effects included headaches, fainting, throwing up, etc. It was also the day that Illuminators would ignite their powers. Mine being memory powers, of course, I had seen memories a few weeks ago. The powers would start showing one month before the Illuminator's birthday, but until the actual birthday, the powers wouldn't be strong enough. Same with the golden blood, nothing could be revealed or seen clearly to an Illuminator until close to their birthday. Everything was created for the safety of Illuminators.

"You are officially an Illuminator," Killian said with no emotion in his voice.

"Which means you have your powers already," said Gilbert.

"I know," I replied, looking at him. He looked at me confused, probably wondering why I wasn't as shocked as I should be.

"I... found a book called *Illuminated*," I confessed, hoping he could explain more about it.

"What?" Gilbert shook his head. "Supernaturals have been trying to get that book for years."

I frowned. "Seriously?" More mysteries piled up over each other, making it hard to not stress.

Gilbert was about to say something else until someone came our way and stood a few feet away from us. I turned around to see Santiago smiling at me and then frowning when looking at Gilbert and Killian.

"What's up, Clara?" Santiago said getting closer to me. *When things couldn't get any worse.* I shifted a bit to the right before he stood close to me.

"Hey," I said, sourly.

"Hey," he said, pulling out his arm to shake hands with Gilbert first, then Killian. "I'm Santiago... Clara's um..."

"Friend," I explained. "He is my friend." Gilbert squinted his eyes at me. As for Killian, I didn't even want to think of him. An awkward silence filled the space between all of us.

"Well, um... I'm glad you decided to come to visit Texas. If you ever change your mind about the wedding, I will be glad to help you guys out." I looked at Gilbert.

"Thank you. We will stay here for a few days to check it out and we will contact you if we change our minds," he answered happily, looking back and forth between Santiago and me. And with that, they walked away. Killian's silhouette had turned around. I was long gone, safe, and out of his orbit.

Instead, I turned to Santiago, who looked bewildered about what just had happened.

"What wedding?" he asked. And even though he annoyed me sometimes, I couldn't help but laugh. Whether Killian was still looking or not, I did not care. At least I tried not to.

The cake smelled like a mixture of sweet vanilla and chocolate. After taking millions of photographs, we all sat down in the kitchen talking to one another about our future plans. My parents were talking with Aurora. It was more like giving her life lessons. They asked her something about a job opportunity, but she shrugged and repeated that she could figure it out. Santiago just kept flirting with Dani, which was not surprising. She had come a few minutes after Santiago. I stared at her hand, but the ring was no longer there.

"I don't believe it... *them* a couple?" Johnny said, pulling me out of my thoughts.

"Yes... a couple who wants to get married... later on."

"What couple? Do we have a new client?" asked Dani. Before Johnny could speak up, I responded, "No, not for now." She knew Gilbert. I didn't want her or others to think there was something wrong.

"Ok," she said, going back to her conversation with Santiago.

Johnny frowned at me, but I only got up to get more cake. No questions were asked and no answers were given. For my sake and theirs, I wished they never got involved.

At sunset, everybody had left the party. Dani and Aurora were the first to leave. Then, Johnny had to convince Santiago to leave at the same time. I was helping my mom clean up the kitchen, while my dad went outside to take out the trash. Once we were done, my parents sat in the living room. Pictures of my happy family hung from the camel-colored wall along with a few of my photographs that mom liked to keep. One of my top favorites was my parent's wedding picture, it hung in the middle with their names *Vivienne and Arthur De Rose* written at the bottom. My mom's nervous smile and dad's cheerful one remained. They hadn't changed much. Then, there was me and Aurora when we were kids. Aurora and I during her senior prom, our first arcade, and when we went to the zoo. For a while, I had forgotten all those happy memories. Time had certainly gone by quickly. I sat down on the white sofa, on the opposite side of my parents.

"Clara, we need to talk to you about something deeply important," my dad started to say.

"I know... about the Illuminators." I broke the ice rather quickly than I expected. "I found out from another Illuminator when she saw my blood. It's rather a long story..." I couldn't exactly tell them that I had found out I was an Illuminator by two vampires. They looked at each other, their worried faces slipping away by the slightest. I guessed they were relieved that I knew the truth.

"We weren't sure who was going to be chosen, until two years ago after Aurora's nineteen birthday," my mom said softly. *When two light-bloods merge, only one descendant is chosen to follow the illuminated path.* That was what the quote from the book meant.

"So, you two are light-bloods, right?"

"Yes... but how did you know?" my dad asked, now sitting straighter than before. "Did the Illuminator inform you?"

"No, I actually found a book—"

"A book?"

I nodded.

"Where did you find it?"

"At a library," I said, "it was titled *Illuminated*, so it was obvious."

They both looked concerned for a second, the same way that Gilbert was, and I knew why. Finding that book was not a coincidence. My dad shook his head. "It was rumored among the supernatural that there was a book among Illuminators, but as light-bloods, we don't know much about it."

"How much do you know?" My mom sat up, her soft brown hair shifting.

"Less than half? Some pages were blank. I know that a human and a light-blood create a light-blood, two light-bloods create an Illuminator, but—"

"An Illuminator cannot have children at all." I never had thought about the future or whether I wanted a family, but knowing that I wouldn't be able to have children somehow pained me.

I nodded. "The price to pay for our powers." I spent only

about ten minutes telling them what I knew based on what I had read in the book so far. Starting with my powers. Illuminators got their powers depending on their traumatized events. In my case, I guessed that the night I didn't remember triggered my powers. I was forced to forget my memories, therefore triggering my ability to see others' memories or something similar. The book also mentioned how vampires benefited from both Illuminators and light-bloods, it didn't exactly state how but warned everyone to be careful. That is why no one, especially vampires, could see the golden blood of Illuminators or the silver-colored blood of light-bloods. Only light-bloods and Illuminators could see each other's blood, to know who to ally with.

"Your mother and I don't know much about the Illuminator world or anything supernatural. Everything that you just told us is mostly known by light-bloods," my dad said right after I finished explaining.

"Clara, you are just like your father," my mom glanced at Dad. "Curiosity drives you. But we tried to stay careful for your safety."

"You might be nineteen and living on your own, but you must understand that safety is of the utmost importance," my dad continued. "No matter what, Clara. Don't go looking for trouble."

I nodded slightly. *Well, it is a little too late for that.*

I couldn't sleep. It had not hit me until the night of my 19th birthday that I was now involved in the unbelievable. As the night hours passed by, I kept thinking over and over about all the information I still needed to know. About who I would become after knowing. Or if I should know at all. Yes, I was curious. But my parents' advice suffocated me. Because just like them, I knew they were right. And they trusted me so much as not to put myself or anyone else in danger. My head hurt from overthinking, so I got up and started cleaning up my apartment instead, avoiding the drawer in which I had shoved the *Illuminated* days ago.

By the afternoon and a thousand back-and-forth paces later, it had started drizzling. I wondered if the weather had some connection to my feelings. My not-so-developed powers decided to disappear on me, I hadn't had a memory ever since the morning before. I still wasn't sure how they worked or what else I could actually do with them.

The colored lights reflected from the Riverwalk right at sundown. It reminded me a lot of London. Row houses on each side of the river and small alleys. If it wasn't row houses, then it was restaurant after restaurant. Happy-looking couples were starting to get on boats for a romantic, peaceful ride. I moved out of the way before bumping into a waiter who was bringing lunch for the people under the red patio umbrella. I kept walking, passing more people sitting outside at the tables, looking for the restaurant I was expected to be at. Finally, I saw the yellow sign. It read *Zatara Sunset*. I had to walk up some stairs to get to the patio of the restaurant, then walk a few feet to enter the building.

From where I stood, the restaurant looked somewhat crowded. I clenched my hand tight on my black satchel bag, where the book *Illuminated* sat. A voice deep inside me screamed to turn around. To forget about it all and go home where I could be safer.

"Hello, ma'am," the man behind the yellow counter greeted kindly. Bottles of whiskey and beer stood neatly on the pastel orange wall behind him. I could hear dishes clashing and voices talking in the room, only a few feet behind the counter.

I greeted. "Hello, I am looking for two young men..."

"Ah, yes." He clasped his hands. "They are waiting on the balcony of the second floor."

"Thank you." I walked down the aisle that led towards the stairs to the floor above, a little far inside the room. The restrooms were to the left, feet away from the stairs. Different pleasant smells of different types of meals surrounded me. My stomach quickly grumbled. The stairs were next to a wall; I walked up without grabbing the black handrail on the right. More light brightened the smaller room on the second floor, fewer tables were filled with people. I guessed that the second floor was for private gatherings as some tables had a 'reserved' sign on them. I looked around and saw the door that led to the balcony. I could feel my heartbeat pumping faster as I took every step towards the outside. The duo vampires sat at the very rounded back table, talking in small whispers. My hands started to sweat. I headed their way. All the other tables were empty; we were the only ones there.

They turned around. Gilbert sat at the left side of the table and Killian at the right.

"Hello, princess," Killian said. I sat down in the chair that faced both of them. I was tired and didn't bother to remark, so I looked at Gilbert instead.

"Hi, Clara." He smiled.

I half-smiled back. "I brought the book... but before you see it, I need to know everything about what you are." Gilbert nodded. After the unnatural help that Gilbert and his family had given me, to some extent, I believed his actions were genuine and hoped he would at least tell me his truth.

"Ok—" he cleared his throat, getting straight to the point, "—we are vampires, as you know. We have immortality, strength, speed, semi-fast healing, hearing people's heartbeats, and compulsion. Compulsion works on anyone, including other supernaturals. But somehow Illuminators found a way to counteract the compulsion or make us weak."

Of course, they did, I thought. "Healing people or superpowers?"

"We only get some powers when we kill one of your kind," Killian said.

I glanced at the balcony behind him, shifting in my chair. "What do you mean?"

Gilbert continued, "Killing an Illuminator is the only way that a vampire can walk in the sun. When an Illuminator dies at the hands of a vampire, part of their powers transfers to the vampire along with the ability to walk in the sun. But light blood doesn't do anything, it is exactly like human blood."

"The *only* difference is that it tastes slightly better and helps with the existence of Illuminators," Killian added. Gilbert raised his brows at him.

"You guys have killed an Illuminator to walk in the sun?"

"Killian... did, but I didn't have to. I am half-light-blood and half-vampire. I concluded that light-blood deleted half of my vampire side. I was able to automatically walk in the sun, but I still age only a rate slower than a human being."

I wasn't surprised that Killian had to kill someone, it took one look to know that he would do anything to survive. But I wondered what Gilbert would have done if he needed to kill someone.

He finished his sentence, and I tried to make sense of all of it.

"So, I'm guessing Killian has powers?"

"Yes, I do." Killian gloated, uncrossing his arms and leaning forward. "Want to see them?"

I was about to say yes, but Gilbert shook his head at him. I agreed it wasn't the appropriate time to joke around. Killian sunk back in his chair, mischief leaving his face.

"Is that it? What about Illuminators?" I asked Gilbert.

"Illuminators are completely rare, more than light-bloods. Besides the Illuminator that Killian met years ago, neither he nor I have stumbled upon an Illuminator, until you." The book was right, but I wondered how many exact Illuminators existed.

"What do you know about Illuminators?" asked Killian.

I told them exactly what I had told my parents. About how I found the book, the creation of Illuminators, and how the powers manifest slowly.

"What are your powers?" Killian asked right after I finished explaining.

"You can stay guessing," I said, taking the book out of my bag. The golden letters from the title stood out against the black book. He crossed his arms.

"Fancy cover. Why would they create an obvious title for a

book that is supposed to contain secrets of Illuminators?" Killian asked, leaning forward as Gilbert had. I turned to the second page to ignite the book with my blood.

"I need something sharp..." I started to say, but Killian quickly pulled a tiny knife out of his jacket pocket. I grabbed it, ready to make a small cut on my fingertip. But I stopped and looked at the duo.

Gilbert nodded. "It's okay. We can control it." I somewhat, maybe less than *somewhat*, trusted Gilbert, and I didn't think Killian would act foolish with him around. I prickled an unhurt finger and red-golden blood appeared like the last time I wanted to open the book. Sure enough, they seemed unaffected by the blood. I continued and pressed my finger against the tiny square sketch, leaving a blood fingerprint. The blood disappeared, the title began to illuminate, and words appeared slowly throughout the page. The first page read *Congratulations, Clara Valerie De Rose. You are officially one of the Illuminated.*

"Is something supposed to happen?" Gilbert asked.

I blinked at him, thinking he was being sarcastic. "What do you mean?"

"I don't see anything."

"Same here," Killian said. But I was able to see the words, drawings, and symbols. *Clever*, I thought.

"There's your answer." I looked at them. "Vampires and lightbloods can't see the book, only Illuminators can, it's that obvious." I turned over to the pages I wasn't able to see last time, expecting to find them blank. But they weren't. All the pages were now filled with ink.

"You said that you weren't able to see the entire book? Is that still true?" Gilbert asked.

"Yes," I lied, trying to hide my amazement, seeing more words appear. I couldn't tell them the truth. At least not yet. I knew it was selfish because I wanted the truth as much as they did. But I thought there must be a reason that vampires couldn't see the book or hidden information that only Illuminators should know. I checked my watch. Half an hour had passed, it was 9 pm.

"It is getting late..."

"Right," said Gilbert. "You must be tired." *And hungry.* The smell of the food around us was killing me.

There was still so much more that I wanted to ask, so many questions. *How did they turn?* But it seemed to me like a confidential question that involved talking to them individually, and I didn't think that was ever happening, not with Killian. My head was already exploding, trying to fit all the pieces together. "I want to find the truth about everything. About who or what attacked me that night and about who I am..." I ranted. Gilbert nodded in understanding.

"We can talk about it tomorrow, love," Killian said. "However, I am curious about one thing. Why weren't you scared of us?" He squinted, leaning forward with his gaze straight into my eyes. "After you learned that we were vampires, it was clear you wanted to leave for safety... not out of fear. Why?"

I sat up in my chair, letting out a sigh. A question I was actually glad to answer. "Because vampires are overrated."

CHAPTER 6
MURDEROUS CREATURES

G ROWING UP, EVERY BOOK OR NOVEL I had read involved them. *The vampire phase.* Everyone seemed obsessed with the idea of these supernaturals. Including me, even if I disliked admitting it. At this point, the question "What is a vampire?" was an understatement.

Gilbert half-chuckled at my comment. Then, he suddenly got up. "I will get coffee."

The imaginary smell of coffee eased my stomach. I was starving, but I didn't want to be left alone with Killian.

"I can go—" I started to say.

"No, it's alright. I will just ask..." He walked away. I hoped for silence after Gilbert left the balcony, but with Killian, there was no way.

"You were one of those girls obsessed with those *bad actors* in supernatural movies." Killian smirked. "Am I who you expected?"

He stared at me. "I'm sure, I'm way better than you expected." I shrunk in on myself, wanting to hide even though there were no shadows for me to do so. *Can't Gilbert hurry up?*

I sat up as soon as I heard the footsteps of someone behind me, Killian's face turned to confusion, and I turned around.

"I'm here to bring coffee," the waiter said with a smile.

I frowned. "What?"

"I was told to bring coffee here..." He took a glance at the table number, nodding.

Killian's phone rang. He got it out of his pocket and answered. "Have fun!" I could hear the voice say before hanging up. *Gilbert's voice.* Killian stood up. I followed quickly and walked towards the balcony, standing next to him. Gilbert stood down below, next to the Riverwalk, smiling widely at us. He showed goodbye using the two-finger salute, turned, and walked away from the restaurant. *Are you kidding me?* I shook my head.

Killian looked at me, both eyebrows raised and a cocky smile on his face. His black coat slightly swung from the wind. I hadn't realized my palms were sweating until I grabbed my cold bag and hurried away. I could hear Killian's footsteps behind me, but I kept walking until I was out of the restaurant and next to the Riverwalk.

"You can't run away, Clara. We found you literally across countries," Killian reminded, continuing behind me.

I turned around. "That doesn't mean I can't stay as far away from you."

He walked towards the white boat that was a few feet away from me to the right. "We can take a ride and talk." His request brought chills down my spine. He made it sound like we were friends ready for tea time.

Since my family and I moved to San Antonio, we had never gotten into the famous Riverwalk boat rides. I was sure I didn't want to start now.

"I'm sorry. But what makes you think I want to talk to you?" I said, crossing my arms. I remembered the memories he compelled me to forget, the fear that I had. The feeling of being vulnerable. But I had powers he didn't know about and that is what gave me strength. Even so, a part of me knew he wouldn't kill me.

"Curiosity is written all over your face," he teased. "You have questions, Clara... and I have answers." I sighed and walked towards the boat. Killian got inside first, holding his arm out to help me get on. His wrist showed a black beaded bracelet in the light. I ignored him and got on the boat without losing my balance. The boat was large with a table in the middle. Snack baskets and a candle on each of the four corners.

A few months ago, Johnny and I had come to speak with a restaurant owner about catering for a wedding. After doing business, we walked for a while. A crowd stood close to the river, cheering happily. If I didn't have double sole shoes, I wouldn't have been able to see the happy couple getting engaged. Johnny and I had joked about how romantic it would be if it happened to us. However, that wasn't the case anymore. Because I was an Illuminator sitting next to a vampire, who I truly disliked, in a similar scenario.

I took a turn around the table and sat on the right side of the boat, almost towards the edge. Killian stood in front of the boat conductor. "It's only us for right now, mate."

The man nodded and started the boat. Killian came to sit about five feet away from me.

"You always use compulsion to get what you want?" I said, almost disgusted.

"Only when necessary."

"This boat ride seems *unnecessary*, we could've just walked."

"We walk every day. Boat riding isn't done daily."

"You're a *vampire*, I'm sure you have done boat rides a lot of times in many different places." Two of the perks of being a vampire: Immortality and never-ending adventures.

The view from where I was sitting looked the same as I had imagined it with Johnny. Lights reflected from the water and aromas of food passed by. If only I had been here under happier circumstances.

"I haven't, not since my family died drowning," he responded, almost carelessly as if it was an insensitive topic.

"What?" I said, stunned by the sudden confession.

"I was twenty-two years old. My parents and I were at a family party. We were heading back home at night, driving down a bridge when a drunk driver collided with us right at that moment causing the car to fall over. I was the only one left alive."

"I'm so sorry," I murmured. He looked down for a few seconds, his face a bit somber. Somehow, I could tell he was trying to hide the pain.

"No need to be sorry, sunshine. It happened years ago."

"It doesn't mean it still doesn't hurt," I looked at him. "I don't need to know..."

He shook his head and continued, "A month later after their death, I lost it and became an alcoholic. That is when I was turned into a vampire." I stayed quiet, unsure of what to say.

He sat up and composed himself. "I was walking home from a bar in the middle of the night. Ironically, I wasn't drunk that time, and I didn't hesitate to run." He stopped for a second, then looked at me and added, "A vampire has to force you to drink their blood, say 'I turn you' in Latin, and kill you, for you to turn into one."

"How long have you been a vampire?"

"Since 1984," he said. I shouldn't have been shocked about all of it, but I never thought that something so supernatural could ever happen. Imagining something was never the same as hearing it in reality. I let out a breath and looked around. For a moment, I had forgotten we were on the boat. I was so focused on Killian and his story.

"You're shivering, Goldenrose," he mumbled.

"I'm cold... not scared," I assured.

"I didn't think you were." He winked and got up to the conductor. "Drop us off here."

I got right off the boat after it stopped on the side. I wasn't expecting Killian to follow me but he did.

"I can go by myself," I said.

"I'm aware you can, gorgeous. My truck is this way too."

I rolled my eyes at him. We walked silently through the Riverwalk. I was surprised that I lasted this long. Having a normal conversation with Killian. But that still didn't make me forget about everything else. He was still Killian, a murderous vampire stranger. It made me wonder why I trusted Gilbert more than him.

Even before I knew they were vampires. There was something that made Gilbert look more trustworthy. His happier and approachable stance made him have a more positive aura than Killian. The way he acted was more understanding than Killian's.

We continued walking in silence. Some owners were already closing their restaurants. It was getting colder with a bit of a breeze, so I put my hands in my pockets. I didn't know what to say to Killian and that bothered me. I always had something to say, a remark, or at least questions. But here, I had nothing. His silence made it worse.

I could hear laughter ahead of us. The alley was getting darker. Only the lights that hung from the other side of the Riverwalk lit up the path in front of us. I didn't see to whom the laughter belonged until we walked closer to a group of young men. Three of them sat on the steps of a small house that was surrounded by two other small houses, while the other two sat on the floor on the edge of the Riverwalk. The sound of glass breaking made me realize that they were probably drunk. I was walking on the left side, so I moved closer to the middle, slightly touching Killian's shoulder. He shifted in sync, without looking at the foolish guys.

"That's a nice girlfriend you got there," one of the guys said. My hands immediately formed into fists underneath my pockets, but I ignored them and kept walking. Killian looked at me as if trying to ignore them too.

"Mind if you share," another voice said but this time it was closer. I turned around, feeling a hand touching my arm before I fully spun.

"Leave them alone," a lady cried. Two kids ran around the house scared and crying. Red-blue lights shone behind the curtains. The sirens of a police car.

It was a memory of the guy. A very cruel one.

Before I could punch the guy in the face, Killian had already done it. He grabbed him by the collar of his blue shirt and punched him twice. Two of the guys proceeded to run away, stumbling in their steps while two stayed ready for a fight. As soon as the blue shirt guy fell to the floor, the other two guys who had stayed ran away too. The blue guy shirt slowly stood up. I moved farther away from him. I thought Killian was going to pass by him and leave him, but he didn't. He punched him again.

"Killian! Stop it!" I screamed. He stopped and let the guy fall again. I looked at Killian. Only his face showed slight rage. I wasn't sure if I was shocked, scared, grateful, or angry. He walked away without saying a word.

"You could have killed him!" I said once I caught up to him. We were almost out of the Riverwalk path and closer to where the cars were parked.

"Were we supposed to leave and ignore him?" he said, shaking his head slightly.

"No... I would have punched him too," I said, glancing at his reddish-marked hand. *Especially after seeing his memories.* "But you would have killed him. You hurt yourself for no reason."

"Is that a hint of concern I detect in your voice?"

I looked up at him, eyes blazing. "You're a vampire. I would be more concerned about the people you've hurt."

"You're welcome, darling." Killian winked, ignoring my remark and walking away, heading towards the other side of the street where a black suburban truck was parked.

My fingers had started to hurt again. "You're off the charts, Clara," Julien said in a bitter but jeering tone, the corners of his lips mocking me. I woke up Monday morning, deciding to practice boxing and fighting at Julien's gym. I punched the boxing bag, while Julien watched my moves carefully. I tried to ignore the pain from my recently prickled fingers from what I called the 'Blood Book Sacrifice'. Thankfully the homemade herbs I made, mentioned in the *Illuminated*, cured them faster than usual. They were bandaged for hours earlier, now they were numb to the touch.

"I still know how to punch," I answered. "I don't forget things easily."

"Yes, but it has been months since you haven't practiced, and your technique is *devastating*." I had known Julien since I was eight years old, he was thirteen at the time. Our dads knew each other in the Utah Police Department when we lived there. My dad had taken me and Aurora to train at a gym that Julien's dad recommended. That's where we both met Julien. We became friends, then we moved and to our surprise, Julien's family did too. Julien found his love for boxing and bought his gym place. I trained there while in college, but I got distracted with work and the London trip.

"That's not true and I've been busy," I said, stopping to drink water from my flask. My whole face burned, just as my whole body throbbed. Symptoms of being out of practice. The gym was semi-empty since it was early. It was divided into three sections: workout machines and weights to the left where the entrance was, boxing bags at the right, and fighting rings in the middle back. The restrooms were close to where we stood. Only a group of people were exercising and doing weights. Two others were getting ready to fight each other in the ring.

"I'm sure I am better at fighting than you now since you haven't practiced. Your dad will be disappointed." He mocked.

"Give her a break, Ankara," said Milana, walking towards us from the restroom. She was Julien's best friend, but I think she had a crush on him. Milana was the only one that called Julien by his last name, and she always seemed more composed around him.

"Hey," she said, it had been a while since we'd spoken. She was about to hug me.

"I am completely disgusting..." I took a small step back, but she hugged me anyway.

"You will never win me," Julien challenged. He stood in front of me, signaling me to punch him. Milana stood where he had been. I tried punching him in the face, but he ducked. I didn't move fast enough, and he punched me in the stomach. It hurt, but I was more focused on winning.

"Are you sure about that? I'm a fast learner, Julien. I will rise back in the ranks." I moved quickly to punch him back, missing and giving him a chance to punch me in the shoulder. The noises of the people around us faded, only to bring past ones.

"We know it's her, Julien." Julien's father spoke to him. "You take care of her when you can." They stood in their living room. A place I had been to twice.

"Of course, Dad," Julien responded. His voice sounded only slightly softer than his actual rough voice.

Now, he laughed. As the person in front of me had changed. "I will still be a better fighter than you." Of age maybe he'd change. He was always the same Julien to me. Funny, confident, and competitive. Yet the memory showed me the only part I hadn't seen. It took me a few seconds to shift back to reality. I focused on my breath. *Inhale. Exhale.* Julien smirked at me, probably waiting for me to back down, but he wasn't the only competitive one. Between us, one had to rise or fall.

"No, you *think* you are a better fighter." I took his comment and smirk as a challenge. I moved quickly, remembering how I had done months ago and punched him straight in the face. He sighed painfully at first.

"There it is!" he screamed. He and Milana high-fived each other, smiling at me.

"You fight better when you're angry," Milana added. "You needed a booster."

"Thanks." I smiled at them and took my gloves off. I missed the adrenaline that came whenever I fought. I headed towards the restroom to change and left home to take a shower.

The *Illuminated* stood on the nightstand calling me to be opened. I was so exhausted the day before that I didn't even want to think about it. I wanted to open it once my mind was clear. Checking the clock, I still had about two hours before heading to the Daily Planner. I grabbed the book, sat in the living room, and began to read. *Here we go again.*

Some of the pages already looked familiar. The structure and images of most of them were already integrated into my mind after re-reading them a million times. I skipped over the pages I had read, which was half of the book. The first half was all about basics, the most important information that an Illuminator needed to know before becoming fully 'Illuminated'. I was now in the *History of Illuminators with Other Supernaturals.*

No one really knew how Illuminators were created or who the first one was. Of course, light-bloods must have existed first to make an Illuminator, but other than that it remained a mystery. Later, as Illuminators evolved, it was discovered that they maintained the balance between supernaturals. After the creation of witches, vampires, and werewolves everything was chaos. Illuminators could maintain order. They could help or destroy the other groups, but weren't allies to either. Throughout time witches and vampires became enemies, making Illuminators both powerful and powerless. Both groups wanted to ally with Illuminators, but vampires, specifically, wanted their power. To kill them, walk in the Sun, and get their powers. That is when a secret society of vampire hunters arose to help protect Illuminators, including normal humans, in exchange for aid when they needed it. And that was it. Of course, the wording wasn't simple. It took me a while to fully understand what the cursive and old English phrases meant.

I moved forward to the *Vampires* chapter. The information

that Gilbert had told me was written. Like how vampires could walk in the Sun and the powers they had. I got to the *How to Stop Compulsion* part. An *allium* mixture: sunflower petals, garlic powder (not surprising), and salt; all mixed in water. The mixture needed to be placed on the main entrance door and windows to not let a vampire inside a residence. If the mixture was already placed, then the only way a vampire could get in is by getting invited to enter. In addition, the mixture needed to be drunk, by the potential victim, three times a day to avoid compulsion. Apparently, it was completely necessary to be on schedule.

The more I kept reading, the more questions I had. I thought about my parents, they were light-bloods and deserved to know about everything I was learning from the book. All light-bloods deserved it, it bothered me that they weren't able to read the book. Maybe some Illuminators informed light-bloods about all of it. But how about the ones that didn't know, especially the ones that isolated themselves from the supernaturals, like my parents?

I finally got to the last page of the section. There was a drawing of a wooden stake on the side with blood around it, and I knew what it meant. However, I wasn't prepared for what I read next. Turned out that in order to kill vampires, a wooden stake had to be covered with both light-blood and Illuminator blood. Then, it had to be staked into the vampire's heart. That was the only way to kill a vampire. Illuminators gave vampires advantages, but they were also the key to their deaths.

The next page was different from the others, it had drawings all over. Random symbols and universe-related pictures. The title in the middle glimmered, similarly to how the title of the book glowed when it opened. It read *The Illuminators: Power Chart*. My eyes lit up, reading the word *power*. The next pages mentioned all the powers, their abilities, their connection to planets, and their main symbol. There were three groups in which an Illuminator fell in based on the power they got. The three groups were also attached to groups of planets.

Earthkalais were Illuminators with pure elemental powers and connected with the inner planets. Fire belonged to Mercury, Ice to Venus, Water to Earth, and Air to Mars. Earthkalais' color was green.

Joviankalais were Illuminators with pure science powers and connected with the outer planets. Biology belonged to Jupiter. Biology powers included controlling plants and making herbs. Physics belonged to Saturn. Physics powers included controlling momentum, such as controlling the way objects traveled or stopping them. Chemistry belonged to Uranus. Chemistry powers made people experts in potions and chemicals. Architecture belonged to Neptune. Architect powers helped with great mathematics, measurements, creativity, and drawing. Joviankalais' color was orange.

Celestialkalais were Illuminators with pure mind powers and were connected with the dwarf planets: Ceres, Eris, Makemake, Haumea, and Pluto. Ceres were mind healers, they made someone feel at peace or safe. Eris were illusionaries, making someone see something that is not real. Makemake were protectors, protecting people with an electric or mind shield. Haumea belonged to the power of invisibility, the power to trick the mind into not noticing you. Pluto contained both the power of memory and the power of forgetfulness. Celestialkalais' color was purple.

All powers worked differently based on the practice of the chosen Illuminator. One could do a specific trick, control their powers better, or do the basics. After all, the powers came from the potential inside oneself or connected with the matter around us. Earthkalais and Joviankalais could manipulate natural elements, while Celestialkalais mostly used their minds. It was a lot of information to take in. A chart was drawn on the next page explaining the powers again.

My powers were connected to the dwarf planet, Pluto. I didn't understand why the powers were connected to the solar system planets and the book didn't fully explain. But it seemed nice knowing that somehow the universe was involved in the world of Illuminators.

I finally understood what the book meant about creating balance. About why both witches and vampires wanted to be allied with Illuminators for so long. Both groups had advantages *and* disadvantages when becoming allies with Illuminators. Vampires could either get killed by an Illuminator or gain what they have. As well as witches, considering that they already had magic of their own.

There were no pages to turn anymore. I had finished reading the book that contained everything regarding Illuminators and their connection to supernaturals and the universe. I rested my drained eyes, their energy slipping away as if I had read a book filled with math and science. I closed the book and stayed sitting, thinking about everything I had known. Connecting the pieces and creating more questions. I was an Illuminator in a world where the greatest and most iconic supernatural species existed. Somehow, I wasn't shocked enough, at least not how I expected it to be. I knew I wasn't exactly excited either to be involved, but I was curious. Or maybe just completely confused.

My phone rang and I lost my train of thought. Dani video-called me with Johnny. I answered.

"Hello, ladies!" Johnny exclaimed.

"Hey!" Dani said. They both looked happy.

"Hi!" I greeted. Dani seemed to be at the Daily Planner, while Johnny looked ready to go out.

"What's up?" he asked.

"So, I have good and great news," Dani shined.

"Spill!" I said.

"We aren't working today… because we have two meetings with two clients tomorrow!"

Johnny and I raised our brows.

"Really? That's great! But aren't we supposed to work to get *more* clients?"

"Clara," Johnny sighed, "stop being an overachiever for once and let our boss give us a day off." Dani laughed.

"Okay, fine." I rolled my eyes at them. "It was a suggestion…"

"I have other stuff to do later anyway," Dani said, semi-smiling. I knew that hidden smile so well. The expression of a pre-date or pre-party.

"Well, since we are free now… I wanted to invite y'all to the parade happening downtown in two hours. Gray and I are going. It would be great if you guys could come and meet him," Johnny beamed, his cheeks flushing pink just like Dani's.

"Of course." I grinned. Johnny had been talking to me about Hector Grayson non-stop. We hadn't had time to meet each other, but finally, I was going to.

"I'm not sure if I will be able to go—" Dani frowned, "—but I'll try." She winked.

The parade was a reminder that love was an extraordinary feeling. My camera swung back and forth in my hand. I had gone for a walk earlier, taking photographs of the holiday decorations hung around the streets. I viewed the location Johnny had sent me. I had called a taxi to take me downtown earlier, instead of bringing my car because of the huge traffic. Johnny was waiting for me at a nearby street where the parade was going to take place. The closer I got, the larger groups of people there were. Chatter and music increased. I finally saw Johnny waving at me on the other side of the street. A tall guy, about the same height, stood next to him. He wore gray pants, a red shirt, and a red hat. He waved as I walked to the other side. The closer I approached, I could see the bright smile on his face as he looked at Johnny.

"Hi!" I said before it got awkward. I noticed Johnny kept swinging his arm, which he usually did when he was getting a bit nervous. In fact, there was no need to notice his arms because I could see it all over his face.

"Hey! I'm glad you could make it!" he said.

I tilted my head. "Obviously."

"So, this is Hector..."

"Hi, so nice to finally meet you!"

Hector smiled. "Nice to meet you too!" We shook hands.

"I've been so busy, I haven't had time to hang out..."

"Yeah, with the Daily Planner and all," Johnny added. I nodded.

"Johnny told me you guys met in college?" asked Hector. He didn't waste time with random questions. *Now, I understand my responders.*

"At a coffee shop by the college," I responded. "There are actually great interesting stories about..."

Johnny quickly shook his head, biting his lip.

"About what?" Hector's eyes widened at Johnny. "Come on, I need to know if there are embarrassing stories."

"We aren't talking about my past." Johnny met my gaze at once. "What happened in the past stays in the past!" He tried to look serious but ended up smiling anyway. After a few seconds of awkward standing, Hector decided to go get water bottles from a nearby store. An announcement had been made that the parade was starting in ten minutes.

"Please, don't embarrass me," Johnny whispered the moment Hector walked away.

"I *won't*, I was kidding..."

"Or judge."

"I *won't* judge," I assured. Johnny glared at me and let out a breath.

"Anyway, I need your help. It is almost the holidays and Hector's family is having dinner, but I am not sure what to give him," he said worriedly.

"Is that why you are so nervous?"

"Is it that noticeable?"

I nodded. "Well..." He started shaking his arms. "Hey, you'll be great. What were you planning?"

"I was thinking of giving him a cologne set..."

"A cologne set?" I replied, giving him a small smile. "Johnny, you are completely bad at gift-giving."

"I'm sixty percent good..."

"You gave me a 'But First Coffee' keychain for my birthday... which I really do appreciate—" I turned sideways to show him the keychain dangling from my brown purse, "—but you need creative ideas, especially since it's for holidays."

"I'm going to die."

"No. Don't say that. I will help you."

Johnny shook his head, thinking until Hector had finally come back with the water bottles. He side-eyed me, but at least his arms had stopped swinging.

A huge crowd started surrounding us as the three of us moved towards the center of the street. It wasn't crowded to the point that people would bump into each other yet. People held out posters and screamed excitedly. Johnny and Hector walked next to one another. Besides the nerve-racking, I had never seen Johnny look so happy and peaceful at the same time. I remembered the yearning looks and raising heart pulses when caring for someone that much. The last time I liked someone was in high school. A tall, nice-looking, smart guy. We never really got serious, and we drifted apart during the transition to college. I decided to focus on my studies anyway. Since then, loving someone had never been my priority.

We had been walking for at least five minutes. I walked beside Johnny, taking photographs every three minutes. Now and then, some people would smile or stop to talk to us. It rapidly got more crowded. I don't know how it happened, but at some point, I lost track of where Johnny and Hector had gone. They had disappeared into the crowd. My heart palpitated faster than usual, and I wasn't sure why. I was never exactly bothered by a huge crowd since I was a party planner and all. But this time it was different, a negative energy flew through me. Deep energy I hadn't been consumed by before. And it wasn't until people bumped into me that I realized why.

Screams, happiness, sadness, hurt, pain, etc. People bumped into me and their memories appeared, along with an abundance of feelings. More hurtful memories rather than positive ones, rushed non-stop in my mind. In an attempt to remain calm, I closed my eyes and tried to control my shallow breaths. It wasn't helping. Inside the darkness, I could see and feel it all. I was still in the parade, but my mind was in a memory loop, and it hurt. Actual emotional pain. My head spun agonizingly, like pulses of electricity.

"Clara!" someone called. I got pulled out of the crowd. The moment I was out of everyone's reach, the memories stopped. I still remembered them, but they were now far away. They didn't belong to me anymore but to strangers. I slowly stood up straight. Dani stood a few inches away.

"Are you okay?" she asked, looking at me with worry.

"I'm okay..." I said, trying to give a half-smile but failing miserably.

"What do you mean, you are okay? I just saw you *crouched* in the middle of a parade, looking like you were hurting... and you are *okay*?" She looked both worried and angry. "You've been different lately, since London. Did something else happen?"

I looked away and sighed. I couldn't tell her, not even a thing. It wasn't because I didn't trust her, but because I wanted to keep her safe. Keep everyone safe. Keeping everything a secret, especially an unbelievable one, was the price to keep everyone alive. I didn't need to watch supernatural movies on repeat to learn that. *Truth has to be said.* My dad's words repeated in my mind. *But I love you and I will keep you safe at all costs.*

I looked her straight in the eye. "Nothing happened. Everything is okay. No big deal. I have just been physically tired or something. I'm pretty sure that affects my emotional state or whatever." Her frown slowly disappeared. *I'm sorry.*

"Okay... in that case. I think you need to party and get drunk... soon."

I beamed. "You know I love you right? You are like a sister to me."

"Aww, of course, I know. I love you too!" She hugged me, and not surprisingly, the memory of her breakup with Mason came up for five seconds.

CHAPTER 7
MYSTERIOUS BUYER

T HE FOUR OF US MET AT THE COFFEE HOUSE. Once Dani had found me, Johnny invited us to hang out for a while. Dani had also gotten downtown in a taxi. So, Hector drove us all to the shop.

"Santiago won't be there. Don't worry," Johnny said as we walked to the car. I only nodded, thinking about what had happened minutes ago. On the way there, Dani started talking about a party she was hosting that night. I shrugged and said "Maybe" when she asked if I would go.

We finally entered the shop. The smell of coffee flew around me. Yet my appetite had lowered to zero since the parade.

"By the way, what happened to you?" Johnny asked. He sat down next to Hector at the small table.

"What? Nothing, I got stuck in the crowd..." I said, smiling.

Dani eyed me suspiciously, her expression fading at the looks of Johnny. Luckily, she didn't say anything, I didn't want anyone to worry.

"Okay..." he responded. Changing the conversation, Dani talked about her plans for the soon-to-be party.

"Today at 8 pm," she informed us. "At the saloon by my apartment." I drifted out of the conversation and looked at the people coming in and out of the cafe, hoping that it wouldn't get crowded fast. The vibration and the classical ringtone pulled me out of my head. Dani was still talking, so I walked away to answer my phone. It was Max from the art gallery.

"Hi, Max," I said.

"Clara! Hey! I got great news!" I already imagined him walking back and forth like he always did. "Can you come to the gallery in an hour?"

"Sure, okay." I held my breath, hoping that the news was exactly what I was thinking. Max hung up and I headed to my friends' table.

"I have to go to the gallery. Urgent news! I'll see you guys later. It was nice meeting you, Hector."

"Okay, bye." Dani waved.

"See you, Clara. Good luck!" said Johnny with Hector waving beside him. I waved at them and left the cafe making sure I didn't bump into anyone.

With his dry "hello", the taxi driver didn't seem to be in a good mood either. He drove silently in the direction of the art gallery. A tear dropped from my face, then another. I rested my face at the car door to block the view of the driver. My life was great, I had hobbies I loved, an adventurous job, a great family, and friends. *Why am I crying?* The sad music that the taxi driver played on the radio concealed the small sniffling sounds. It seemed to make me want to cry more.

After a few minutes, I recognized the streets where the art gallery was close by. I quickly wiped my face with my hand and blinked a couple of times while looking up. *Okay, stay positive. Everything will be okay.*

"We are here," the driver said. I paid and thanked him with a slight smile.

The tall colorful building ignited my positive spirits. The art gallery was my peaceful place. I always loved nature. The ability to feel free. The fresh air, the bright flowers, the movement of the plants, and the warmth of the Sun on my face. I wanted every experience to stay with me like a memory. Photography enabled me to do so. My creative instincts arose when I started working at the Daily Planner around graduation. Then my mom suggested I should start selling my photographs. We went to the art gallery together for the first time. It took a while for my photographs to sell, eventually, they did. The ones that didn't always had a space to stay in. My mom kept them safely at home.

I entered the gallery and looked around for the man in a blue pastel suit. Max stood talking to another person who was looking at someone else's art. As soon as he saw me, he walked rather fast towards me, flapping his arms to the side.

"Clara!" he exclaimed, giving me a quick hug.

"Hey Max, so what are the news?!" I asked, anxiously.

"Your photographs..." He paused. "Completely sold for *more* than the price that you demanded!"

I looked at him in complete shock. "What? Really?"

"Yes, really! There's something else..." he continued, shaking his head. "The buyer said he will buy any future photographs that you sell... literally any of them!"

"Oh my god..." I couldn't believe it. This was the first time I got a good buyer. "Must have been a really rich person to buy all my photographs."

"I'm not sure, it was a call-in purchase. But you are so lucky! The money will be deposited into your account in about twenty-four hours after transferring the photographs," he said happily.

"Thank you, Max!" I exclaimed.

"Certainly, honey." He sighed, looking at the entrance. I grinned at him before he turned away to assist other people who were coming in.

Max was right. He had sent an email with all the details regarding the purchase, except the name of the purchaser. My account balance would increase immensely, even after the payment made to Max and the gallery. I tried to shake off the curiosity of who had bought the photographs and decided that maybe I was just lucky. The money would stay safe and sound in case of emergencies. I headed to an ice cream shop to celebrate and walked around for a while, stepping aside when people walked by me. It had been around thirty minutes of walking around until I received a message from Gilbert. He hadn't called or messaged since he left me alone with his annoying friend. Great time to spoil my happy mood.

Can we meet in the same place? There is more information about you know what.

Dealing with my memory powers had ironically made me forget about the deal with the vampires and witches. I still didn't know why the vampire duo even needed my help since we didn't get to finish the conversation the other night. I got in a taxi and headed downtown again.

When I arrived at the Riverwalk the sunset was slowly decreasing. People started to fill the small sidewalks. I walked fast, looking for empty spaces and groaning when people got in the way. Gilbert stood by the first-floor railing of Zatara Sunset, folding one of his arms while the other held a book, making him look studious. He wore a gray button shirt with khaki pants. His short hair was messy and a bit curly. When he looked up and saw me, he radiated and walked downstairs. I stood by the wall next to the stairs and waited for him with arms crossed.

"I see you're still mad?" he said, smiling mockingly after I glared at him.

"No, Gilbert. I'm not mad at the fact that you left me with your murderous vampire friend. In fact, I was so *excited* and *truthfully* waiting to be killed," I ranted.

"He is a good person. He wouldn't hurt you. And he won't hurt you as long as I'm alive," he assured. "We've been friends since

I turned, and I would trust him with my life."

I sighed. "I'm sorry, but I just don't... and actually, I am really curious as to how you guys became friends in the first place?"

I turned around to start walking and Gilbert followed next to me. He laughed softly and gazed at the river. "When I turned, a year ago, he was the one that found me and helped me survive."

"By what? Killing people?"

"Surprisingly no. At first, he did try to get me to drink human blood, but I was a light-blood and unlike new vampires, I didn't need much blood. I did drink from a blood bag the first week then slowly switched to animal blood." He looked at me, waiting for a response. It was still hard to think of Gilbert being friends with a person like Killian. An unexpected memory came to my mind as if I had manifested it.

"You are a vampire. You have to drink human blood, or you'll die within a week, mate," Killian said as he stood next to Gilbert who was holding himself from a tree trunk. They stood in the middle of a grove. I could see lights not so far away and a silhouette of buildings. It wasn't that late at night, so I could see the red and silver-colored blood in the grass and on Gilbert's neck, which had a small bite mark.

"No, I can't. And I don't think I need to." Gilbert breathed heavily, sweat falling from his forehead.

"I don't think you understand..." Killian half-laughed.

"I'm... a light-blood... was a light-blood. I don't know how to explain, but I can feel my body slowly rejecting the vampire side. My blood is counteracting it or something."

"That's a very, completely rare condition. But you still need blood..."

"A blood bag, bring me a blood bag."

"Human blood is better," Killian responded.

"No. A blood bag, please."

Killian sighed and ran before I could even flinch again.

The memory flashed forward to when Killian came back, holding a blood bag in his hand. He inspected it weirdly at first and handed it to Gilbert. He drank from it slowly, a relieved but disgusted look on his face. Killian crossed his arms and watched him, a bit surprised. Gilbert got up and stood straight. Color was rushing through his face, and he was no longer sweating. He gave Killian half a smile after he folded the empty bag and shoved it in his pocket.

"Thank you for finding me, I would have been dead," Gilbert said.

"Technically mate, you are dead..."

Gilbert nodded. "Right."

"I'm Killian..." Killian said, putting his arm out.

"Gilbert." They shook hands.

"Gil, you could be my new murderous buddy," Killian joked, trying to convince him.

"No, thank you. I got the impression you drink human blood, and I don't agree with your tactics. I could be your friend, but I won't murder anyone."

"You'll change your mind eventually, Gilbert."

"I don't think so."

I saw small flashes of their friendship. Talking about their past, always visiting each other or calling, drinking together (mostly Killian drinking), and many other genuine memories.

I stayed silent for a while, unsure of what to say. I no longer had the sick feeling I would get when I saw someone's memory. But it was replaced by a weird feeling that I could not explain. I understood why vampires lived the way they did, but I couldn't help but feel somewhat disgusted. Vampirism did not justify someone's personality, however, the way someone decided how to survive did. Gilbert was half-vampire; he didn't need much blood and even if he did I didn't think he would hurt someone. But Killian, I believed, was another completely different story.

"Weren't you shocked about the blood?" I asked. He shook his head, his smile not reaching his eyes. I nodded, deciding to move on from the topic. "Why do you need me? Must be very important if you came across the world to find me?" I said, wanting to know exactly what was going on.

"There are *rumors* among vampires."

I frowned at him.

"Killian's vampire friends think that witches are planning another war against us," he informed. "After the Supernatural War, there were a lot of deaths among vampires. But now it is different, witches have been quiet for years, and with the recent increase of vampires, I believe they could strike anyone at any time."

"Okay, but what do we do? We can't just go on a mission looking for witches when they don't want to be found." The word *We* echoed in my mind.

"You are the first Illuminator we've come across, *well for me considering Killian's encounter with one after he turned*, and we thought you might have information about it all," Gilbert said furrowing his brows.

"So, you came here for your benefit to help out your *vampire friends?*"

"*Killian's* vampire friends," Gilbert corrected. He stopped in his tracks and turned to me. "I don't want to leave my family alone. I can't leave them alone... or leave Killian alone," he explained slowly. I understood that Gilbert cared about the survival of people because he cared too much about others, even for people he didn't exactly know. But the fact that he had come to find me across countries didn't make sense.

"That's not the only reason, is it?" I questioned, turning to him.

"No." He looked back at the river, deep in thought as he continued walking. "It's about my parents."

I frowned, following his pace. "Your parents?"

He nodded. "A few years ago, when I was fifteen, they realized the danger between supernaturals was increasing. Of course, no one except Illuminators could see the silver blood, but the moment the vampires taste it, some can never stop. My parents wanted to keep me safe so they went to look for light-bloods for more information on how to keep us safe from vampires or any supernatural in general, who would want to ally or threaten. They never came back. They were found dead on a hiking trail close to a cabin where they were supposed to meet the others."

"Oh my god..." I whispered, shaking my head. "I'm so sorry."

"It's not your fault," he said, shaking his head. We stayed

silent for a few seconds.

"You think witches have something to do with that?" I asked. "You want revenge?"

"No. I want the truth," he answered. "The case concluded that they had fallen, but I believe otherwise. My parents loved hiking, they were basically experts at it and it just..."

"Doesn't make sense," I said, finishing his sentence. Of course, it didn't make sense. Some witches hated vampires, and viceversa, because *both* groups were fighting for more power. What would they do for it? What would they do to have more light-bloods and Illuminators that could help kill their enemy? Who would the witches *and* vampires blame for all the innocent deaths?

I understood Gilbert. I would have at least wanted to know the truth. Who would I be if I didn't? I looked at him and nodded. We walked silently down the Riverwalk, hearing the different types of music as we passed each restaurant, mostly Spanish music from what I could hear.

"Do you like books?" I asked him when I nodded towards the book he was reading earlier. He glanced at the book, showing me its blue cover.

"I have a business degree, but I'm currently studying to be a doctor," he said. "I'm a medical student." *The irony*. But then again it made sense.

"Of course you are."

"It seems someone forgot to send me an invite." Someone suddenly said behind us, the voice clear and compelling like fire. Gilbert and I turned around to Killian smirking. His eyes shifted from Gilbert to me and back again.

"I just informed Clara about the rumor," said Gilbert.

"Right, Miss Wants-To-Know-It-All is curious." Killian mocked.

"Says the Stalker," I added defensively.

"And you are wondering, why didn't you get an invite?" Gilbert grinned at Killian. They looked at each other, and I wondered whether they could read each other's minds.

I moved away from them. "Okay... it's clearly my time to leave."

"Killian could take you?" Gilbert suggested quickly.

"I don't think so, a taxi sounds more pleasing."

"You walked here?"

"Is that a problem?"

"No, it's dangerous," Killian crossed his arms. I rolled my eyes at them and turned around to leave. In a matter of seconds, Killian was already walking by me, his footsteps matching mine. I tried to walk even faster and give him a hint, but he always caught up to me. A scent greeted my nose sweetly. It was his cologne that spread through the gentle breeze. Almost like a fresh windy field with humid rain and plants. The smell of wintergreen.

"Glad you care, but I'm perfectly capable of getting home on my own," I said, hoping he would just leave me alone.

"I know, Goldenrose. But I have a dare to accomplish," he answered. I walked faster towards the street ahead of us, way too fast without looking around me. I didn't see the bicyclist that was about to pass by. We would have collided pretty brutally if it weren't for Killian. He grabbed me by the arm and pushed me back quicker than the speed of the bicyclist. Killian's face was four inches apart from mine, I could feel his breath in my face.

"The universe has proved you wrong," Killian whispered in my ear. I heard the bicyclist scream "Sorry", but I didn't turn around to see him. Time stopped for a moment. I stood there making eye contact with Killian, but looking straight into his eyes, I couldn't help but see the bad and brutal memories. I pulled away from his firm grip, he sighed and let me go. "Come on, I'll take you home."

I looked at him. "Fine." *Let's figure out exactly who you are, Killian Walker.* My heart rushed out of fear, letting the anger keep winning.

We walked in sync, heading towards a black truck that was parked down the street. He opened the door to the passenger's seat, so I could go in. The smell inside his truck was the opposite of the sweet scent I had smelled earlier. It wasn't bitter or sweet. More like a clean, icy fresh smell. I had to admit that just like Killian, his truck smelled nice.

Music played on the radio softly. I had given Killian the address of the apartment complex. I tried to avoid eye contact by looking out the window. But I couldn't help but look at him, calmly driving, and the way his eyes would narrow when he would focus. He had rolled up the sleeves of his blue shirt, revealing the black string bracelet with black and colorful beads on his wrist. When he moved his hand, I realized that it resembled the planets, there were six beaded stars, and a yellow bead had a ring around it representing Saturn. Killian turned quickly to look at me, but I turned around before he saw I was looking at him.

"Are you hungry?" he asked.

"No, not really," I said.

"Yes, you are."

"No, I'm not."

I was extremely hungry. I had been stressed for days and being stressed made me hungry at least most of the time. I had eaten some light snacks the entire day. Without proper food, my stomach grumbled every now and then. I just hoped it wouldn't while I was in Killian's truck.

Instead of going straight, Killian made a turn towards the left and then another turn heading to a plaza shopping center. "I'm really not hungry," I repeated, but he ignored me. He parked at the parking lot and said, "Be right back", then went quickly into a donut shop.

"What? Are you serious?" I said to myself, shocked that Killian had literally gone to buy food. I sat there in disbelief.

He came back four minutes later, holding a medium-sized bag. He entered the truck and placed the bag in the center console. When he closed the door, he turned to look at me.

"I ordered chocolate donuts and got you a hot coffee," he said casually.

"You didn't have to," I said, confused. "But thanks." He furrowed his brows.

"I'm hungry too," he said. I glowered at him. "For donuts, not what you were thinking of."

Of course, he was hungry too. I couldn't tell what was more annoying: the fact that for a second I thought he was being considerate or the fact that he was going to eat like an actual human being.

When he handed me the hot coffee, our fingers touched lightly. I shivered even though the cup warmed my cold fingers. Killian placed his coffee in the cup holder and put the bag in the backseat. He started driving without saying another word throughout the ride. I didn't take a sip of the coffee, placing it in the cup holder before he took the turn towards my apartment building. He had parked in the visitors' parking lot. I got out rather quickly. Killian got out a second after, getting the bag from the back seat.

"These are for you," he said, holding out the bag containing the other box of dozen chocolate donuts and the coffee cup. "So was the coffee."

I turned to look at him. "Thank you, but I can't take that. Give it to Gilbert. I'm sure he loves donuts." With no other words to say, I turned back around, imagining the quietness of my apartment.

"You don't trust me, but you trust Gilbert. Why?" Killian started to say the second I was a few feet away from him. I stopped and turned to face him.

"You are seriously asking?" I sighed.

He nodded, standing there with his hands full and a look on his face I couldn't comprehend. No one would ever guess he was not exactly a normal human.

"Because... he is half-human and you're..."

"A vampire."

"Yes," I half-lied, my memories intact.

"You said vampires didn't scare you, that they were *over-*

rated..." He shook his head, not believing me.

"Okay, then. Here is the truth. It's not about what you are. It's about *who* you are. You want to be friends? To trust you?" I shook my hands to the side. "Well, welcome to Trust 101. Step 1: *Honesty*. And if you don't know, trust is earned! So, just because you bought me donuts and coffee doesn't mean I'm just going to start trusting you all of a sudden," I said and walked away. What else could I do? A mix of feelings rushed through me. A dilemma between the Killian from my memory and the one standing behind me. Two sides of the same coin that I couldn't figure out.

So foolish of me to think that he and I could be at least frenemies. How could we? In my current memory, he was a liar, who hurt me and didn't even tell me or Gilbert the truth. Of course, he wouldn't say anything, as far as I knew Gilbert was his only loyal friend. The friend that actually trusted him with his life. Who would I be if I ruined their friendship? I couldn't tell Killian anything yet, not at all. And if I did, Gilbert didn't need to know. A tear dropped on my cheek, I wiped it away and half-laughed to myself, standing before my apartment door.

"What the hell?" I whispered, my apartment door slightly opened. The mat in front of the door had muddy shoe prints. I walked slowly inside my apartment, leaving my door open wide. From where I stood, I could see both the living room and kitchen. I grabbed the pepper spray inside my bag and went ahead quietly to check my room and the restroom in case someone was inside. All my things were there, nothing was misplaced. Everything valuable was there. Everything was just in place, the electronics, the TV, my jewelry, my laptop, etc. Everything... except the book. The *Illumi-*

nated wasn't there.

"Shoot, it has to be here." I went back to the living room and rechecked everything desperately, maybe I had placed it somewhere else without remembering. Ironic, right? But I couldn't find it.

I looked around slowly, noticing an antique-looking envelope on the countertop. I grabbed it quickly and started reading the front of it.

To one of the Illuminated, you might see that the book is nowhere to be found. Our apologies. The book cannot be kept and shall be passed on to other Illuminators who need the truth revealed.

I turned the envelope over and opened the black wax seal, stamped with an Eclipse symbol. A vintage ticket was placed inside. Golden letters appeared slowly in different handwriting format.

As one of the Illuminated, you are cordially invited to Kosmos. We would be truly honored by your presence.

- Anonymous

"Anonymous." At the bottom of the ticket was an address and date. The date was in about three weeks, a few days before New Year. I looked closely at the ticket frowning until I heard footsteps in the hallway and went ahead to close the door I had left open. A bag and coffee stood next to the welcome mat. I peered outside, but no one was there.

"Really Killian? I'm not even actually hungry anymore," I whispered to myself, grabbing the food and placing it on the countertop.

The next morning, I woke up starving and couldn't help but eat the donuts and coffee. I was about to take the first sip of the hot microwaved coffee when I read the sticker placed in the cup. It read *Hot Coffee with 5 pumps of Caramel Syrup.*

CHAPTER 8

LIES AND DECEPTION

"**H**OW ABOUT THIS?**"** Dani asked, holding up a pair of black glasses. I shook my head.

"He probably has a million of them," I said, imagining a whole collection of glasses on Johnny's wall.

During the week, the mall was more crowded than usual. Holidays were coming up and everybody was chaotic buying presents. I was only missing Aurora's present, which I was unable to buy in London due to the unexpected circumstances. Thankfully, earlier I found an amazing charm bracelet at a jewelry store. Dani was buying a present for Johnny, but she kept having trouble deciding what to get him. We entered store after store, but Dani couldn't find anything.

"Come on. Tell me what you bought him!" she exclaimed after we got out of another clothing store. "You are so good at gift-giving."

"I can't tell you! It's a secret and you have to figure out what your friend wants," I replied back. For days, Johnny kept telling me about a famous video game he played with Hector, so I got him a poster and figurine based on that. He sometimes posted on social media the collections he had.

"I'll just get him chocolates..." Dani pouted, giving up.

"You can't give him *chocolates*!"

"What did you get him then?" she asked.

"Not *chocolates*!" I retorted. "Fine, come on." I dragged her to a video game store. We walked around trying to find a specific video game. Dani found it and bought it. She had also bought something else but wouldn't tell me what it was. After, we headed to eat lunch. As we ate, we talked about the Daily Planner and the current wedding we had to plan. The groom expected the wedding in a forest scene, but the bride wanted it the opposite, an ocean scenery. "With a lot of shells," she had said. The ocean scenery wasn't bad, I had great ideas to go with and the forest scenery. But both of them together seemed disordered. The wedding had to be planned exactly the way they asked. Whether forest-like, ocean-like, or both. And I was running out of creativity.

"How is the wedding dress design going," I asked, taking a sip from my lemonade cup. "No, wait... she said 'with a lot of shells', didn't she?"

"She did," Dani rolled her eyes. "I mean the forest and ocean scenery are great, but not when they are combined."

"You're right. I'm having trouble with the decorations." The last idea I had was a small centerpiece of a small tree with shells

139

hanging from it. I half-laughed at the idea.

Dani let out a sigh. "The wedding is in two months, so we have about a month to plan everything while also being on a budget. I have to find a dress in the boutique or design it myself."

"You know you are an amazing designer. If someone doesn't see that, they are completely blind or just plain stupid." I smiled at her confidently. By the time we were done eating and talking, it was getting late, but we still had two more hours until the mall closed.

"By the way, I almost forgot. I have a surprise." Dani grinned. We walked out of the food court when her hands shook to the side in happiness.

"What surprise?" Good surprises were always the best.

"I got us tickets to a holiday ball. And guess what... it's in two days!" she exclaimed happily, taking two golden tickets out of her white handbag. They reminded me of the golden letters I had seen of the *Illuminated* and the Kosmos invitation.

"Wait, what? How?"

"Someone who was invited gave them to me. Here." She handed me the ticket. I grabbed it and placed it inside my black side purse.

"Someone, huh..." I mocked.

"*Don't* ask." She looked away, but I could tell that she was smiling widely. I bothered her about it. But she would keep silent at the mention of it, and I dropped the subject after five minutes. I was glad for both of my friends. At least they were having crush drama or a normal life without getting caught up in unexpected situations.

Icy fog built up in the windows again as the taxi drove us to the ball. I searched my white purse for a napkin to clean it up, but it was obviously no use since it built up again in seconds. My mind made shadows behind the window until the light reflected from it hurt my eyes. I turned away to see Dani looking out her window. It was rare to see her that way. Her eyes filled with silence, neither happy nor sad. But just there, thinking. She persuaded me to arrive together at the ball... in a taxi since she planned to leave with her 'classy' date after the party. I could have taken my car, yet I didn't want to bother with the parking anyway. It was pathetic knowing I would go home alone, but I had gotten used to it.

After driving for minutes, the driver slowly stopped. I shifted my neck to see through the windshield. Dani did the same. The line of cars moved ahead while a doorman came and let the guests go inside the huge mansion.

"May I see your tickets, ladies?" the doorman asked while Dani got out. We handed them to him, and he nodded. "You may go inside."

"Ready?" asked Dani, her face lighting up.

"Yes," I said, grabbing her arm. We walked up the steps following the instrumental music.

The ballroom was filled with so much light and ethereal decorations. I had been pulled back into another century, only with a few modern changes here and there. Aside from the painted ceiling and white lights hanging, everything else was white and gold. Women and men wore different types of clothing, from ball dresses and suits to more fashionably unique clothing. Once inside, I took off my white coat and handed it to the man standing by the wide oak doors. He went ahead to a room where all the guests' coats were stored.

"Danielle!" a voice came from one of the crowds among the people. A tall, blue-eyed, suited man seemed shuffling through the crowd towards Dani's direction.

"So, that's the guy," I whispered to her. She blushed. "You like him!"

"Shh. I'll see you later." She slowly moved towards him. As soon as he stood a few feet away from Dani, he held out his arm and gave her a purple flower. It matched her elegant lavender dress. They moved far ahead into the ballroom, disappearing among the colorful crowds.

I shivered the more that people walked inside. My off-shoulder white silk dress did not conceal the cold breeze. The long sleeves only covered my forearm and had a side slit at the bottom. I glanced into the coatroom thinking whether I should go grab my coat but decided to show off the white dress I would probably not wear again.

I started to move among the groups of people, catching small conversations. Some were about business, others about gossip, but nothing exactly interesting that made me want to stop to converse. No memories seemed to appear as I bumped into the small crowds. I pushed that specific thought away the second it came. Tonight was about having fun, not overthinking. A bar stood in the middle of the ballroom. I walked towards it, hoping for some food or dessert.

"Hi, I'm—" I was about to say to the guy passing by me holding a wine tray the second I accidentally bumped into somebody else standing next to me. "Gilbert?"

"Clara?" Gilbert furrowed his brows in surprise. *What is he doing here?*

"It was nice meeting you," he said, turning towards the two people he was talking to before I bumped into him. Then he turned away from them. He wore a gray-black suit that made him look more professional than usual and his hair was less curly and styled.

"What are you doing here?" I asked.

"We got invited?"

"We?"

He made a single nod.

"Obviously," I said, not surprised. Where Gilbert went, Killian went, and vice versa. He looked at me up and down.

"You look... great." He smiled.

I returned the expression. "So do you."

He cleared his throat. "Did you get invited as well?"

"No, my friend, who is somewhere with her date, got us tickets somehow."

"Right." He nodded. "Were you heading to the bar?"

"No," I lied. "I was just walking around..."

He rotated his brown watch in place. His smile brightened up his face, so sincere and true. The more he smiled, the more his dimples and jaw showed.

"Gram?" I heard a voice behind me say. Somewhat startled, I turned around to see a chubby man walking towards us. He looked at Gilbert with interest.

"Excuse me, I'll be right back," Gilbert said, and he walked to the man.

I nodded and decided to head towards where I had intended to go. There were a few people sitting down at the bar. Some looked lonely and others completely drunk. I didn't know which was worse.

The musical ensemble had started playing pop instrumental music, and couples proceeded to dance. People who were just talking moved to the side or went inside the other large rooms.

"What would you like, madam?" the bartender asked in an accent I couldn't recognize.

"Is it possible that you have coffee?" I said, kind of embarrassed.

"Yes, we do. In the dining room, along with the desserts and food." My mood lit up.

"Thank you." He went away to help another guest; I believe I heard him talk French to one of his coworkers. France would be a nice place to visit someday, I thought. *Maybe I should learn French.*

"Hello, Goldenrose."

And this is the moment I internally die. I sighed, turning to look at Killian with a grim smile. Unlike Gilbert, he had a full black suit. He had a smirk on his face that was unbelievably annoying. I didn't respond.

"It appears that I'm talking to a ghost." He tilted his head.

"What do you want me to say? 'Hi Killian! Great to see you! How is life going?'"

He grinned. "Yes, gorgeous. You could say that."

I rolled my eyes. *Way to go about relaxing.*

His stares were starting to increase my heart rate. I looked into the crowd avoiding his eyes, then turned suddenly at him after my palms started to sweat.

"Well, I have somewhere far more important to be."

"Which is?"

"None of your business," I replied, about to turn away from him. He squinted his eyes but didn't respond.

A beautiful woman in a red dress appeared from behind him. I shouldn't have been surprised but I was. A new feeling replaced the tightness in my chest, a feeling rarely known to me.

"Darling, I'm back. Let's go dance!" the gorgeous woman beamed. She started grabbing Killian's arm to lead him to the dance floor. He put out his hand for her to take. I watched them heading together to the dance floor. They talked and danced closely for minutes. I had accidentally made eye contact with Killian. Then looked away from them at once, avoiding his glances at all costs.

"Why do you have that look?" Gilbert asked the moment he stood next to me, making me almost jump.

"What look?" I frowned. "I don't have a look."

"Wait... are you *jealous*?" He grinned and shook his head. "I was not expecting this."

I laughed, completely confused at the remark. "I'm not *jealous,* why would I be? Seriously."

"I will say, he does have a way of being charming."

"I don't like him and I'm *certainly* not jealous. End of story."

"Or the beginning of one," Gilbert teased. He stayed silent, looking at Killian and me. "Whatever you say..." He laughed. I rolled my eyes at him, glancing at Killian. *He is charming when he wants to be.* I thought. *I may be attracted to him.* He danced gracefully. His hands were around the waist of the gorgeous woman. *No. No way I like him. I can't like him.*

"Would you like to dance?" Gilbert asked, smiling widely, and holding out his hand slowly. I hesitated, thought about it, then agreed. "Why not?"

I grabbed his hand, and we headed to the dance floor. We danced to classical music, so close to each other. I didn't falter like I thought I would have. *Not like Killian.*

"I'm sorry for leaving you earlier. I was doing bakery business for a friend," Gilbert said.

"Other than Killian... you have a *friend*?" I asked.

"Why do you say with such surprise? I have lots of friends," he replied, offended.

"I don't know. You seemed like an introverted, loner, completely serious person."

"So, you're saying I'm sad and boring," Gilbert said furrowing his brows.

I shook my head. "I mean..."

"It's okay." He laughed. "I'm not bothered."

I stayed silent for a few seconds, feeling a bit bad.

"Okay, tell me the truth. You barely know me, but am I too judgy? I'm still working on it and..." I sighed. "Just be direct."

He raised a brow and laughed. "Clara, you are an extremely, completely awful, and judgy person. *Since* I've met you, you punched me in the face and *since* then I haven't liked you at all..." he said, almost in a serious tone.

"Hey!" I laughed, lightly punching his arm. "I had to defend myself and you *were* following me!" We laughed together like two friends who had known each other for a very long time. I had judged Gilbert from the beginning when he was just nice and honest.

I hadn't realized that the song we were dancing to was over. Another similar song was being played, and the sounds of footsteps filled the air again.

"So, Killian, huh?" Gilbert said, suddenly.

"What about him?"

"You know..." He raised his brows.

"No, I don't know, and in fact don't want to speak about it."

"Frenemies then?" Gilbert added.

I shook my head. "I tried. Not in a billion years." Killian and his elegant lady were dancing not too far away. Awkward glances were shared between me and him. I had to look away again to avoid freezing on the spot. But I flustered. All of a sudden, the same brutal memories came back exactly like the first time I had remembered them. I thought I had it under control. Gilbert tilted his head by the slightest, noticing. My head was spinning again.

"I'll be back... restroom break," I explained and left the dance floor. *Why am I seeing the memories again? It isn't like I'm completely traumatized.* I was seeing and feeling the same way I had when I remembered them the first time. It wasn't like I just remembered the memories. I was there with Killian hurting me all over again. *I have to relax. Physically and mentally.* It took me five minutes to breathe calmly and head out of the restroom once it had started to become full. Instead of heading back to the dance floor, I went straight to the dining room. Piles of amazing desserts were there. I was starving, so I grabbed the few mini chocolate cupcakes my hands could take to help my hunger and nervousness. The two people that stood on the edge of the large table looked at me disgusted.

"What? Food is to eat. Is it not?" I said in my defense, walking out, and heading somewhere more silent. I walked around until I ended up in a hallway, far from the ballroom where I could barely hear the chaos.

"I have to relax," I whispered to myself, finishing the cupcake in my hand. "Everything is okay... when you are holding a bunch of sweets. Sure it is."

The great paintings and photographs inside a medium-sized room grabbed my attention. There were two entrances, so it appeared to be a living room. Both balcony windows were opened, but no one was there. So I looked around, analyzing the vintage paintings hanging on the large red walls. I stood in the middle of the room, eating the last cupcake, and looking at a canvas that seemed familiar to one I had seen at the gallery. I still wondered who the mysterious buyer was, but Max couldn't get any information.

"There you are," Killian said. He had come in from the left entrance, the one in my view. He stood next to the bookcase beside it, smiling. I shivered at the sight of him, feeling the air from the windows rush through me. "What are you doing?"

"I'm taking in fresh air. Am I not allowed to breathe now?"

He nodded at the hallway. "Can't you breathe in there?"

"You are like carbon dioxide Killian. I suffocate every time I look at you."

He smirked. "Your stares tell me otherwise." I sighed, about to head out of the room. *Thank god, there are two entryways.*

"There we go. Running off..." he began. "I don't understand why you're avoiding me."

Control, Clara. I turned back to look him straight in the eyes without responding to him. *Please, don't lose it.*

"I should at least know your reason for not trusting me at all and running away every time I'm close," he said in a more serious tone. He slowly walked closer to me. But I stepped back immediately, he noticed and stopped taking another step.

"Stay away from me, Killian," I said, my voice coming out more as a whisper than I intended.

"Why?" He stood like a beautiful statue in the middle of the room. A dark angel of death. He fitted into our surroundings like a piece of art. Like he could do nothing wrong except make you fall straight into his amber eyes. I hesitated more times than I could count. My eyes started to feel extremely heavy, and I could feel sweat coming from my palms again.

"Because I remember everything." I finally looked at him. "I don't trust you because I remember..." I tried to fight off the fear and tears, knowing that if I started crying, I would not be able to stop.

"Remember what?" His question felt like a slap on my face. How could he stand there and pretend to be confused?

In a flash, the fear turned into rage. My sweaty hands clenched. "God, Killian! I remember how you fed on me, manipulated me, made me act like a puppet, and made me believe I liked you!" I showed him the crystal necklace. It had been inside my purse all along. He looked shocked, his eyes seemed to tear up a bit, but no tears dropped. He stood there. Speechless. I threw the necklace at him. It fell to the floor with a small clunk.

"I know everything. The coffee shop, the library, the mall... You recognized me the moment we met. That's why you seemed shocked to see the necklace in the forest. *You* were the one that gave it to me." Killian's face was expressionless for some seconds.

"What?"

I turned around. Behind me, Gilbert had entered the room from the entrance feet away from me, looking confused.

"*What* did you do?" He clenched his jaw and had an angry look on his face I hadn't seen before. I hadn't regretted that I said the truth, but I didn't want to stay to hear them arguing. It was too much for me to ask for the truth from Killian. Everything would start and end with the word *blood*. I just wanted to stay as far away from him. So, I left. Away from all of the chaos. I walked out of the room, passing Gilbert's unmoving stance. A tear dropped down my cheek, I wiped it away before I passed by the large crowd. The dance floor was more crowded than it had been earlier. I walked between groups of people talking or dancing, accidentally bumping into someone who was walking opposite of me.

"Sorry," I said, but the guy in the hat I had bumped into just walked away. I shuddered, walking towards the main entrance, where the doorman stood to ask for my coat. Once he found it, I quickly put it on. Car lights flashed as some people were leaving the party. There was a taxi far away down the line of cars. A group of three people were also waiting for a ride, I didn't want to wait long. But I had no choice, there were no houses or places nearby. I regretted not bringing my car.

Gardens and forests surrounded the mansion. Only two streets ahead led to the main roads. The reminders of the Grams' house hit the walls of my mind. My own memory defied me. I could've had a heart attack right there and then. Impatiently, I thought maybe I could call Johnny, but I remembered he had an important family meeting with Hector and Dani was nowhere to be seen. I doubted she had left the party early, but I didn't want to disturb her fun either. *Winning the taxi first, it is.* I thought, looking at the almost drunken group and imagining I could just parkour inside.

"Why didn't you tell me?" Gilbert said out of nowhere. I walked away from him and the groups of people at the main entrance. He grabbed my hand, rather abruptly, and didn't let go until he led me behind the mansion where no one was able to hear us.

"Why didn't you tell me?" he repeated more calmly than the first time. "I followed Killian to the room. I heard everything." His anger and disappointed eyes made me look away from him.

"I didn't want to make it a big deal and it was a problem between me and *him,*" I said quietly. He raised his brows. "I didn't want to break your guys' friendship or hurt your feelings."

"Okay..." He nodded, trying to understand, then looked at me again. "But he hurt you, Clara. He promised me he wouldn't hurt anyone. And he hurt *you.* You should have told me." He shook his head. "Now, I understand why you didn't want to be close to him. I'm so sorry."

"I'm not scared of him, Gilbert. At least not anymore," I confirmed. "You didn't tell me either... that we saw each other for

151

the first time at the coffee shop."

"You didn't seem to remember. I didn't think it was necessary, seeing that I had only seen you once. But apparently, Killian hadn't." He shook his head, confused. "If he compelled you to forget. How do you remember everything?"

"I—" I was going to tell him the truth about my powers, there was no point in keeping it a secret from him anymore.

But suddenly he shook his head and put a finger over his mouth, signaling to stay quiet. He moved past me and looked around. There were no people, only a few trees next to us. I couldn't hear anything. Two silhouettes slowly appeared from behind the trees. Another one appeared from behind the mansion, closer to us. Their faces hid away in the darkness.

"Foolish of you to trust vampires, Illuminator," the one closer to us spoke loudly, a man's voice clear and unfeeling.

"Who are you?" Gilbert said sternly. His eyes narrowed as if he was trying to see through the dark. But it was impossible. I couldn't even guess the type of clothing the stranger had or his height.

"I don't answer to you, *Vampire*," the unanimous person said. *Vampire*. The only supernatural identity that hated vampires more than werewolves were witches. As stated in the *Illuminated*.

"Witches," I said unafraid. I thought about what the book had said about witches and Illuminators. I doubted they would hurt an Illuminator if they were trying to make an alliance with them. I couldn't say the same for vampires.

"Kill him," the so-called witch said. In less than one second the two people along with the one that was close to us disappeared.

Four people replaced them, surrounding us. Each of them had red glowing eyes. *Night* vampires. Vampires that hadn't drunk Illuminator blood or killed one. They weren't able to walk in the Sun. One of them got closer, his facial expression appearing. I knew he probably smelled the blood and craved it. No vampire could smell other people's blood unless they were under one of the four conditions: 1) the vampire was over a hundred years old (an expert), 2) the person's blood was out in the open (for example a fresh cut), 3) the vampire already had knowledge whether the person was human or another supernatural, and 4) the vampire had a deep connection to that specific person. Only one of them seemed to be true. Knowing I was an Illuminator, the vampire held desire on his face as he stared at me intensely but then turned to look at Gilbert in hatred.

Gilbert and I moved closer to the wall behind us, there was no way out. I couldn't parkour in a very long straight white wall and if I could I was kind of out of practice. Without obvious warning, two vampires quickly ran towards me, Gilbert tried to interfere in between as the other two ran to grab him. The two vampires that ran towards me, grabbed me and threw me to the floor. My body ached the moment it touched it. The two vampires laughed saying a bundle of words of "Weak" and "Be glad we can't kill you". I looked towards Gilbert; he was trying to fight off the other two vampires. But he wasn't strong enough, he didn't have the same strength as an actual vampire. Then, something clicked inside me. Adrenaline. The two vampires laughing were too distracted to see me getting up from the floor. I pepper-sprayed them on their eyes before they could even say anything else.

"I knew I should have bought two," I whispered. Thanks to my dad, I had gotten used to carrying pepper spray everywhere I went. So, I have had two in my purse since. Gilbert had punched the two vampires to the floor, they groaned. He pointed towards the back of the mansion. I nodded, and we started running that way in order to find an entrance inside. Three seconds of running until we heard footsteps behind us again. They weren't going to give up until Gilbert was dead. The four vampires stood in front of us again like statues.

"Four over two? Must be your unlucky day," the main vampire mocked, smirking.

"Make that three." Killian stood behind them. The main vampire's smirk faded away, watching Killian break the neck of one of the vampires beside him. Killian had killed an Illuminator, causing him to turn into a light vampire, from what I knew he was stronger than any of them. I shuddered at the sound of the vampire's bones breaking. He fell to the floor, certainly about to be unconscious for some minutes.

The other two pursued Gilbert. This time it was fear that clicked in. Without hesitating, I put myself in front of him.

A word passed through my mind like it had been waiting to be said. "*Memorium*," I said without thinking. Bright purple-blue light appeared from my hands, quickly creating an electric circular protective shield between me and the night vampires. They stumbled backward, afraid to hit the electric wall. I concentrated on making the shield around us. But the more I kept it standing, the more energy I lost. The vampires were not moving, they stood still, waiting. The power slowly faded away with every tiring breath

I took. *Killian, hurry.*

A few feet away, Killian fought off the main leader, finally snapping his neck.

"*Oblivio*," Killian said, snapping his fingers once. The two last vampires froze like statues as Killian walked towards them. Until they started to shift and looked around confused.

"Leave, *now*," Killian said angrily. The two vampires looked like confused little kids being grounded. They looked at each other and weirdly ran away scared. For one second, I looked at Killian, confused about what just happened. But then the purple-blue shield disappeared, and I felt myself falling. I waited to feel the physical pain, but instead, softness surrounded me.

CHAPTER 9
THE LAND OF MAGIC

E VERYTHING WAS SO TIRING. My body, my mind...
yes, especially my mind. It was burning on fire. I couldn't
help but want to stop overthinking and to want to overthink to
figure out the truth. The truth was all that mattered. I wasn't sure
why, but maybe it was a value I gained after years of watching my
dad stress over cases. Everything was always about truth. But what
do I do when that truth might hurt others? Did it still matter? Or
was there a way to figure it out and keep everyone safe at the same
time?

I woke up the day after the ball in my empty, soundless
apartment. The white silk dress was dirty with mud. The sticky
note from Gilbert read, *We brought you home. Be safe and see you
soon.* My head throbbed, thinking about everything that had
happened, about what the hell was going on that I did not know.

Killian compelled me to forget the moment after he gave me he crystal necklace because that was my last recent memory with him. I still didn't remember the one from the forest before I was found by the Grams. With the Illuminator power that I had, I thought I might've remembered by now. But I didn't and it was killing me mentally. Something else was going on. If Killian had compelled me that night in the forest, then there had to be a reason why my memory powers hadn't counteracted them. And somehow, I didn't think he had something to do with the forest incident. Or at least not on his own. Not after some witches tried to send night vampires to kill both him and Gilbert. They knew who I was and who they were. I was back at the beginning. I was missing more truth, and that is what I wanted to know.

The next few days were spent with family and friends. But no matter how much interesting chatter and funny stories were told at each gathering, I could not find myself in the moment. Only boxing at the gym and parkouring around open areas made me feel somewhat at ease. I was eager to go home, where I could be alone and practice my powers over and over again. Even at work I was rushed. I walked fast to errands, trying to finish planning for the events. Dani and Johnny must have noticed because they told me I should probably take a day off. But I shook my head and continued with the daily hurried schedule.

On the first day of power practice, I learned how to control seeing memories when touching someone. I mustered enough courage to go to public events in which I would bump into people and see their memories, no matter how bad they got. Some were so horrible that I couldn't look at the person's face due to discomfort and sadness. In the end, I burnt out. I had entered a lot of people's minds that I wondered how many memories my own brain could take in. On the third day, I realized that the purple-blue shield was made up of my happy memories. Each electric streak was filled with minimal pictures, each representing a happy memory from my life. I saw my birthdays, my childhood adventures with Aurora, funny times at college with Dani, and many more happy memories to even count. Then, I practiced until I no longer had to say the word *Memorium* and I could automatically create the colorful protection shield. On the fifth day, I figured out how to see the memories of a person I cared about by concentrating on them. Unknowingly, Johnny helped me. I concentrated on him, on his last memory or last action. The memory showed him and Hector getting out of a cafe. I called him to confirm.

"Hi, Johnny! What are you doing?" I asked, naturally.

"Just got out of the cafe. I'm going to the zoo with Hector. Would you like to join?" he said excitedly.

"No, thanks. I have lots to do, but have fun on your date!"

The more I practiced, the more I got used to feeling the power as my own. I could still sometimes feel myself without energy, but it was getting easier to maintain and uphold the magic. It was not against me but beside me whenever I needed it.

Gilbert and Killian were nowhere to be found. That was indeed expected. Gilbert was probably still mad at Killian. I wasn't sure and I didn't exactly want to know. However, something that bugged me was Killian's powers. *Oblivio.* Was the word he said to make the vampires go away. The word was the opposite of *Memorium*, therefore having the exact opposite powers. The look on those vampires' faces was of complete confusion... they must have forgotten who they were or what they were doing in the first place. The irony was what I couldn't believe. For Killian to have killed an Illuminator that had the opposite power of mine. Ironic that everything started with forgetting and remembering.

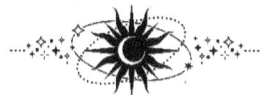

The morning I had been waiting for came faster than I could say goodbye to my family and friends. As far as they knew I was leaving for London again for a photography one-time job, where I was going to be paid a large sum of money. It was half-lying since I had already earned that amount at the gallery, and I was actually traveling. Just not to London. My parents trusted me enough to leave by myself. Aurora not so much. She had insisted on coming with me to the airport. I refused, only planning a last dinner at my apartment before leaving. My suitcase and small bag stood by the door the moment they entered. Weirdly, Dani didn't even question my trip seeing as I hadn't mentioned the "amazing job oppor-tunity" before when we were in London. Johnny, on the other hand, had requested a souvenir.

I wore my best black parkour boots, for running. Along with a comfortable black-green long-sleeved shirt that prevented the cold fresh air from making me shiver. The golden-lettered ticket laid in my hands. I walked towards the Texas City coastline. Signs in the street read 'Texas City Dike Closed'. *Closed for non-supernaturals.* I thought.

It had been a long time since I visited the east of Texas, but I remembered the funny road trip me and my family took when I was younger. Aurora and I spent the entire time at the beach competing to build the best sandcastle. Mom and Dad watched us happily helping both of us in turns. I smiled at the memory. Not long ago I was just in London looking for the best food places and worrying about Aurora's present. And now I was heading to somewhere unknown to figure out more unknown information about a hidden world with unnatural people. *Great! That made complete sense.*

Taxis and cars lined up either by the nearby park or the entrance of the dike. People held out the same type of ticket I had to the men at the red stand by the entrance. *Illuminators.* Most of them did not seem as curious or nervous as I was. Others looked around frowning and pacing slowly. I fixed my posture, walking towards the man in a suit and showing him my ticket. He revised it for a minute, making a hand gesture. The ticket flew up in flames, disappearing into the air. I could only guess that he was a witch because an Earthkalai Flamer even had its limits. The paper should've turned to ashes, not air, so the *Illuminated* explained. He wore a golden-Sun design in his red-golden coat that almost matched the black Eclipse logo, of the Sun and Moon colliding, on the cruise ship. He nodded, signaling to walk forward.

About fifty people walked farther down the dike, towards the medium-sized cruise. Other than the puzzling looks on the Illuminators' faces, I noticed there was something else in common they all had. A tattoo. I looked around at everybody, a circle-shaped colored tattoo was drawn on the right arm of each Illuminator. Each circle with a different sign, the sign of their individual power that seemed to match the Power Chart drawings from the *Illuminated*. But I didn't have one. I pulled up my long sleeve to check my wrist. Nothing. I turned around to look at the witches far behind me standing at the entrance, wondering if I had missed getting a personal tattoo. Maybe it was obligatory. Yet they just stood there receiving tickets and making them disappear. I frowned in worry and confusion, making a mental note to not show my wrist until I figured out what was going on.

I walked towards the cruise. It was a long way to walk towards it, but I enjoyed the sound of the waves hitting the shore. Two men stood at the entrance of the gangway, asking and checking each person for personal belongings.

"Excuse me, Miss, you can't bring anything. You must leave your bag," one of the men said. He pointed at the black bin next to him. I hesitated and thanked myself for only bringing my phone and pepper spray. He stared, waiting for me to follow orders. I placed the bag inside the bin. He gave me a brown card key that included a room number and gestured for me to walk forward inside the cruise. The moment I stepped inside the cruise it reminded me of the mansion during the holiday ball. Once again, I stepped into the Victorian Era.

Groups of people stood around the courtyard all around talking in small voices. I walked around for a while feeling the cruise moving slightly underneath my feet, far away from land. I stood by the olive-green wall, concentrating on seeing someone's memory and failing. There was no way I could see a random person's memory without touch or emotional connection. A silver-blonde girl, around my size, wearing a purple jacket stood by a pillar close by. A black suitcase stood close beside her. She looked anxious, so I walked towards her.

"Hey, are you okay?" I asked gently. She looked up slowly.

"You can see me?" she asked in a low voice, tilting her head to the side.

"Yes, of course... why wouldn't I?"

"Clara?" Someone shouted from behind me. I turned around, recognizing the voice quickly.

"Julien?" I asked, confused as ever. "Milana?" I stood frozen. I had never expected them to be Illuminators. "You guys are Illuminators?" They walked towards me without a hint of surprise on their faces.

"Surprise?" Milana said, shrugging. "Sorry, we didn't say sooner." I shook my head, trying to put the pieces together.

Julien pressed his lips together, starting to explain. "We knew you might've been an Illuminator. That's why your dad made us become friends with you and Aurora since we were young." Now it made sense. Julien and Milana were only children. If their parents were light-bloods, there was no doubt they would be Illuminators. No wonder my dad had pushed us to be closer to their family.

"Wow, um I have no words..." I nodded, taking in the news. "I can't believe you actually kept this from me?"

They look at each other, probably not sure what to say.

"I'm sorry Clara. Your dad told us not to until you were fully ready," Julien said. "We do live human lives. I wasn't even planning to come, but Milana convinced me."

"Do they know?" I asked with worry. "Your parents. My parents. Do they know we are here?"

"No, of course not."

"Mine either. Better to keep it from them," said Milana. "Who were you talking to by the way?" She changed the conversation. Questions raced through me. Curiosity, concern, and maybe even jealousy at the fact that I felt behind. I *was* behind. The worst part is that I understood them and their silence. Just as they hid the truth, I was doing the same.

I cleared my throat. The girl behind me stood there frozen like a statue. I shook my head. "No one." And smiled. They didn't even look at the girl once. She was practically invisible.

"Ok... well this is Nico and Ash," Julien continued, nodding at his friends. "Nico is a Joviankalai Architect and Ash is a Celestialkalai Illusionary." They both greeted me, Nico waving hello.

I looked at their colored tattoos. He had an orange circle tattoo, representing Neptune, with a black pillar in the middle. Ash had a purple circle tattoo, representing Eris, with crystals in the middle.

"I have the imagination to build stuff. Like this ship needs a ninety-nine percent of deep modern renovation." Nico waved his hands around, looking up. Ash rolled her eyes at him.

"I can make you believe you're dying in a matter of seconds," she said to Nico. He sighed and shook his head. Ash shoved his shoulder.

"Milana and I are Earthkalais. I'm a Flamer and she is Flake," Julien continued. He showed his green circle tattoo, representing Mercury, with a flame in the middle. Milana, on the other hand, had a snowflake and represented Venus.

"Whoever came up with the 'Flakes' name idea is brainless," Milana said, rolling her eyes at the sight of her tattoo. I analyzed her tattoo, while everyone nodded.

"Wait, why wasn't I able to see your tattoo before?" I asked. All those times at the gym with them, but I hadn't seen it, not even after I became an official Illuminator.

"I think it depends on how ready you are to become an Illuminator. I wasn't able to see mine or others until a few weeks of practicing my powers," Julien responded. "Take it as a sign that you are at your potential."

"Right," I sighed, avoiding the questions whether the tattoos were visible to people, other than Illuminators. If I did have a tattoo, I should've known by now. *Thank god, I have a long-sleeved shirt or they would notice I don't have one.*

The thought that I could've known much more about everything beforehand remained on my mind. All of them knew much more than I did, at least regarding their powers. I would have been more cautious. *I would have avoided falling into Killian's compulsion trap.*

"What are your powers?" Nico asked so abruptly I almost jumped.

"I'm a Celestialkalai..." I answered slowly.

"What kind?" Ash asked. I didn't have time to answer her question. *Not like I would've anyway.* Any good excuse and I would have walked away immediately. Too many *would-haves* could've been avoided if I had known the truth ages ago.

The cruise started shifting, turning everyone's attention away from me.

"We are here," someone in the crowd shouted. Everyone looked at each other. It was not possible to be wherever we were supposed to be when we had been cruising for only a few minutes. Suddenly, the cruise shook more roughly as it passed through a red barrier. A few feet further, a purple light barrier appeared between the blue ocean and sky; both barriers were shaped like large half-spheres surrounding land. People started to move towards the edge of the cruise, looking closely ahead. The walls were similar to the electric protection wall that I was able to create with my memories. The energy of the purple wall hit my body, making me shiver. And the eternal ocean that was in front of us disappeared slowly, replaced by land. *Kosmos.* The group next to me seemed to be flabbergasted. I was relieved because in this case, I wasn't alone anymore.

"You guys haven't been here before?" I asked.

"No," Milana responded. "I've heard from other Illuminators that their parents don't even know this place. But some Illuminators immigrated here with witches after the Supernatural War."

At the mention of the Supernatural War, I realized they all must have read the *Illuminated* too. Everyone here came because of the book. Witches had passed around the book to each Illuminator, maybe hoping for more allies. *But why now?*

"I guess mostly new Illuminators were invited," added Nico, side-eyeing Julien and Milana. "One of my friends didn't even want to come because he didn't want anything to do with the super-natural."

"That's *reasonable*. Since he was attacked by vampires for no reason at all," Ash continued.

"Vampires?" I asked. "Why would they attack? I mean other than the obvious reasons of course?"

Julien shrugged. "We don't know. There has been an increase in vampire attacks towards Illuminators for a while now. Those *bastards.*" His tone shifted angrily at *bastards.* Everyone else nodded, but I didn't. It felt offensive to do so. Though I disliked vampires, some of those 'bastards' were my frenemies, excluding Killian Walker. Like Gilbert, not everyone was the same.

After a few minutes, the cruise was closer to the shore of Kosmos. The sound of a whistle made everyone move in a rush towards the main exit, creating a long line of people ready to explore. Small conversations made me realize that not everyone was from Texas, some were from nearby states. Here and there, there were talks about the family they left and about their natural daily routine at home. The girl I had seen earlier stood behind me now with her jacket hanging in her suitcase. Her tattoo was purple-colored with an eye in the middle. She had the power of invisibility. *No wonder... but why am I able to see her?* I smiled at her slightly. She smiled too then looked away.

I turned around as the line ahead was moving, making sure I didn't miss anything important. Julien stood in front of me, I had to stretch a bit to look over him. Soon enough, we were getting out of the cruise and into the land.

"Everyone, please enter the passenger train in groups based on your order," a man instructed as people got out. The cold ocean breeze created goosebumps on my skin the moment I stepped out. There were large towers beside the coastline, each a few miles apart from each other.

"Those might be Illuminators and witches." Milana squinted her eyes. The Sun blocked my view, but there was movement at the top of each tower. *Maybe they are the ones creating the electric walls.* I guessed.

Another small cruise stood next to the one we had come in. More Illuminators got out as well, heading into the large train station. Guards in gray uniforms with silver-Moon and golden-Sun pins stood at the entrance. Thirteen empty railroad passenger cars stood in front of us as we walked slowly ahead. The Earthkalais entered first, then the Joviankalais, and lastly the Celestialkalais.

It was my turn to enter the 19th-century train car. Every inch of it was unbelievably luxurious, from the black seats to the brown hanging lights. The girl with her suitcase sat beside me and two other people across from us. Everyone spoke in quiet voices, some tried to show off their power, talking about hero moments.

"Hello, new passengers or should I say Illuminators! Welcome to Kosmos. Please stay seated, and I hope you enjoy the ride," the conductor said cheerfully through the speaker.

A lady and a man, with a silver-Moon drawing on their blue-silver coats, stood by the entrance and exit of the car, inspecting each of us. I looked away after making eye contact with the lady. The voices slowly decreased as the train started moving. Curious eyes looked towards the window, including mine. Taking in every detail of the unknown place. We traveled for about two hours, passing close to cold white mountains and through deep green forests, until making a stop by a city. A golden sign read *Ether: City of Aurum* in black letters.

"Conductor speaking. We are making a brief stop at the Ether Station due to some issues," the conductor said slowly. I looked out the window. A group of people stood by the train tracks blocking the way, screaming loudly. Some held posters that read *Help Arkadia! Help the City of Argentum! Equality for Arkadia!* I tried to hear what they were saying, but the thick wall of the train muffled the screams. Witches got off the train, they said something that made the people step away. The train continued passing by the people. Some wore old rags and weren't completely clean. Their sad eyes watched the grand train pass by. It made me wonder why no one helped them. I tried not to go to the conclusion, but that said much about the authority of Kosmos.

Hours later, the train drove fast through an endless forest. Some people were starting to get tired or sleepy. My eyes were failing to stay open. Until a bright light caught my eye, forcing me to wake up. The train stopped at a station almost by the edge of the forest.

"Passengers, we have arrived at Lunar Castle," the conductor informed. Everyone's shuffles, yawns, and whispers resurfaced. We stood up two by two from our seats after the man and woman gave us instructions. I was like a little kid following a teacher's orders. We stood outside the small 'Lunar Station' in groups. Julien, Milana, and their friends caught up to me. We walked together along the path.

"Don't you think it was weird at the Ether Station?" Milana asked. I nodded in agreement.

"We don't know much about this place. So, don't jump to conclusions," Julien responded.

Men in blue-silver coats led us down a forest path that ended a few feet away from us. The ones in red-golden stayed behind. As we walked closer towards the end, the bright light grew brighter. I walked faster. That's when I saw that the light came from a tall blue lighthouse. The first thing that attracted my attention once we were at the very edge of the forest was the alluring architecture of Lunar Castle.

The massive gray structure reflected off the lake in front of it. Besides it, to the left were two other gray buildings. Then, everything else was clean flat land, gardens, and statues.

"This place is a century or two behind," Nico repeated, just like he had said earlier, as we entered the castle. He wasn't wrong, but everything was still beautiful. The inside was a mixture of vintage and modern designs. Paintings I had never even seen before hung on the walls. My sister would have fainted if she had seen the castle. Guards wearing a silver-Moon pin instead of a Sun on their gray coats stood outside the castle inspecting us and their surroundings.

"They do love gold and silver, don't they," Ash stated, glancing upwards and then to the front. *Gold and Silver. Sun and Moon. Kosmos. Planets.* Everything fitted into place. I wondered if I was actually dreaming.

The men in blue-silver led all of us to a huge room, an auditorium without chairs, at the left side of the castle. On the stage stood six people: three women and three men. Three of them with Eclipse-designed colored coats: a blonde lady in a green coat, a man in a purple coat with glasses, and another lady in an orange coat with dark-colored hair. The three others only had a Moon-design in their colored coats. They waited until all of us organized ourselves inside the room to speak up.

"Hello everyone. I'm Davina and welcome to Kosmos, the land for witches and Illuminators," the blonde lady in green started. "As the new generation of the Illuminated, we are glad to meet you all, both witches and the old generations of Illuminators. The six of us are Illuminators, we are Lunar Court, your representatives," she spoke, walking around the stage.

Someone in the crowd in front of us raised their hand. I stood on my tippy toes to see the red-black sweater girl about to ask a question.

"Yes?" the blonde lady said, her brows lifting up at the sudden question.

"If you guys are Lunar Court, then what do the Eclipse and Moon designs on the coats mean?"

"Good question young lady. I was getting there..." The lady pressed her lips together. "Stellar Court, the *higher* Court, is made of three members of Solar Court and three members of Lunar Court...that would be us with the Eclipse design. Hence, there are twelve total Kosmos Court members. We will be explaining everything in detail over the next two days."

Some Illuminators nodded silently with confused expressions on their faces. The man with glasses next to her wearing a purple coat continued, "As most of us know, a certain supernatural species has threatened us over the past few years. Now, there has been an increase in this certain species, causing the population collapse of both witches and Illuminators. As your future leaders, we want to help you develop your abilities in the hope to fight against the gruesome *vampires.*" Some Illuminators cheered and whispered loudly. Most seemed to agree. I caught a glimpse of very few people shaking their heads.

They certainly didn't waste time in stating their motives. They kept mentioning witches *and* Illuminators. It was true then. Witches were really trying to ally with Illuminators against vampires. And with Lunar Court already on their side, it was working. They talked about vampires as a whole as if every one of them were monsters.

"You don't agree?" a tall guy next to me asked. His tattoo showed he was a Celestialkalai Protector, representing the dwarf planet Makemake. "I'm Ed, by the way."

I shook my head slightly. "Hi. Clara. And no, I don't," I responded. "Do you?"

"No, I'm just here to figure out how to *improve* my powers," he said. "You?"

To figure out the truth about witches' involvement with other supernaturals.

"Same reason," I half-lied. He nodded and moved towards other people, who he appeared to know.

The dark-haired woman in orange spoke next. "I know it's a life-changing decision, therefore you do have a choice. For a little less than a week, you will be training and experiencing life in Kosmos. Those who decide to leave after these days will be taken to their normal life. We will have time to talk about that later on. For right now, guards will take you to the buildings beside us, where you will be living and training. Once again *welcome* and I hope you all enjoy *our* country!" All representatives grinned widely as some

Illuminators clapped and talked. I stood there watching them closely, clapping slowly and following along.

A group of Celestialkalai Protectors walked out of the castle, as the guards led us, the *novice* Illuminators, to the hotels. They wore purple shirts and that's how I could tell what kind of Illuminators they were without having to see their right arm.

"Head to Solar Castle first, then back to Stellar, some witches will be waiting there for the night shift," the leader of the group, who wore a blue-silver coat with a Moon design, explained. The group of Celestialkalais nodded and headed out of the castle, towards the black carriages waiting outside. I saw them heading north before entering the hotel building.

In the hotels, we got separated into groups. In one hotel stayed the Earthkalais and in the second stayed the Joviankalais, while Celestialkalais got separated among them. My group stayed with the Earthkalais.

"Hello, I'm James, nice to meet you all." The man in purple who had spoken in the auditorium waved and adjusted his glasses. "On the first two days, you all are welcome to accommodate yourselves. You all were granted a random room number card key earlier. Four people in each room. Caretakers will pass by to provide food and designed apparel." Everyone nodded, heading inside the hotel. Both hotels were similar in size. They reminded me of the old elegant buildings in London. White and black walls decorated the reception area. Some people walked towards the bar on the right, gasping and reading the names of the beverages. Next to it was the cafeteria. I couldn't wait to sit down and eat.

The elevators quickly filled up; people smashed into one

another anxiously. With my room key in hand, I headed towards the stairs. Fewer people were heading that way too.

"Hey, what room do you have?" Ed asked from behind me. He moved up the stairs next to me.

"1012," I said, showing him my room key.

"Weird, I'm in 1012 as well," he revealed. "We are on the highest floor, which means we will get a great view of the outside."

I focused on my breath. *Come on, keep going.* Julien was almost right when he said I was off the charts. I had tried to be active before coming, but with everything going on, I hadn't had much time, and I hated how weak I was. I could've done better.

"I'm going to take a break." Ed panted, stopping on the fourth floor. He grabbed himself from the black stairwell.

"Ok, see you at 1012." I kept going.

Once on the tenth floor, I let myself rest for a minute. Then found room 1012. My other two roommates were there already. Funnily and strangely enough, they were Julien and Milana.

"Did you just run a marathon?" Julien asked the moment I stepped inside. The room looked like a college dorm, except wider space and more elegant. Mixed colors of green, orange, and purple decorations surrounded the room.

"I walked up the stairs," I said tiredly but collected myself. "What did you guys do to stay together?"

Julien scratched his brow. "Milana bullied a girl to exchange the room key."

"I asked *nicely...* at first," Milana said defensively, then frowned. "By the way, do you know who or where our other roommate is?"

"*He* is currently walking up the stairs too... I don't think he will make it here anytime soon," I responded. There was a moment of awkward silence, then they burst out laughing. Ed didn't come until ten minutes later, still gasping for air.

We accommodated ourselves for the next day. The caretaker had come in to give us clothes: black pants and a colored shirt based on our power classification. Either short or long sleeve. "You may have already figured it out, *but* if you have not, unlike the outside world, your tattoo is visible to every supernatural in Kosmos. Here, the clothing makes it easier to identify each of you without looking at everyone's wrist all the time. Should you choose a long-sleeved shirt, most court leaders will ask you to see your tattoo," the caretaker informed us. *So, supernaturals in Kosmos can't see our blood, but yes to our tattoo? Makes sense as to why they identified us at the dike with a golden ticket.* I frowned, grabbing a purple long sleeve shirt. *Ok, easier to conceal my tattooless right arm.* Another mystery to figure out and questions I couldn't ask. I was running out of numbers and letters to name each mystery I needed to solve.

After the caregiver left, Ed spoke up. "All the rules are so confusing..."

I agreed. "My exact thought."

"Balance," Julien added. "Everything in Kosmos is magic. Whether it is one thing or the other, everything has balance. Who can see our blood, tattoos, what supernaturals gain or lose, moon and sun, etc."

"Our 'main purpose'," Milana quoted the *Illuminated*.

Julien made a slight nod. "Who would have thought right? Us, here *maintaining* balance."

"Our first day and we already sound like true Illuminator prophets," said Ed. We all looked at each other, smiling but more likely processing the fact that we were actually supernaturals in the land of magic. At least I was.

For the next accommodating hours, Julien and Ed seemed to be getting along rather great, telling each other insults about how funny they looked on their colored shirts. Milana and I had decided to walk around the hotel during the two days. She didn't waste any time making new friends. I headed out to explore on my own while she left. She reminded me of Dani a bit. I missed her. I missed Johnny and my family. I missed everything. I couldn't believe I even missed Gilbert and Killian. I was here not only for me but for all of them. To figure out about that night, about the witches, the unexplainable vampire attacks, and why I didn't have a tattoo. Maybe, I should have become a detective like my dad. Everything that he used to tell me about being a spy just seemed so breathtaking. But like my mom, the love for peacefulness and art took over me career wise.

The first night we were all required to take a Kosmos 101 course. We headed that night to the auditorium where Lunar Court talked about how the Kosmos Courts were divided. Solar Court (the six witch leaders) and other high witch officials resided in Solar Castle. They managed most witch problems. Lunar Court, as explained earlier, was the Illuminator Court. They resided in Lunar Castle along with other high Illuminator officials and managed Illuminator problems. In between, three main members of both courts met to become Stellar Court and eventually made important decisions for all people in Kosmos. In the grand Stellar

Castle, the six leaders sometimes resided, especially during important events or meetings.

After the course, the three Illuminator orders were divided. I walked beside Ed, following the Celestialkalais to the forest behind Lunar Castle. Earthkalais and Joviankalais moved to another separate area.

"The towers at each Kosmos entry point connect to each other. Most specialized Celestialkalai Protectors help maintain a protection wall around Kosmos and witches create the red portal to let any boats or people on the outside enter the country," James explained while we walked between the trees. "The witches' portal is generally created to let anyone pass through which is why the Celestialkalai protection wall works. The walls specifically allow anyone to get out, but do not let anyone get in, especially vampires."

"Don't they all get tired?" a young man in the crowd asked.

"Yes indeed, this is what the towers are for. Every few hours both witches and Celestialkalais come together on top of each tower. The witches draw a pentagram and create a spell where witch and Illuminator magic is used for fuel to uphold both barriers for a few hours throughout the day. They all use so much magic to fuel the tower that they might feel drained for the rest of the day, hence the day and nighttime shifts."

Some Illuminators nodded in sync with others. Most of them, which must have been Celestialkalai Protectors, held their heads high as if they had just been told that their power was more important than any other.

The first night flew like the wind, the second night however was endless. Not only because Julien snored so loud in the middle of the night but because my thoughts spoke louder. Wishing and strategizing, until eventually I had arranged what I hoped to be a successful plan.

CHAPTER 10
UNDERCOVER

L UNAR COURT HAD GIVEN US a chance to leave and go back to our normal lives after two days of arriving. Some people, about less than half, had left before the actual training started. They were taken back to the cruise on the train and their close-to-home destinations like the first time we arrived. Others, like Ed, stayed to figure out more about their individual powers. I sat at the edge of the top bunk bed alone, thinking. Then quickly laid down under my covers before the knob to the room turned full circle. Milana entered the room, hands shaking side to side. I had splashed my face a few minutes earlier with hot water to make my cheeks look a bit red. That had done the trick.

"Afternoon, are you feeling better?" Milana asked, looking at me wide-eyed. "Maybe you should go eat."

"I'm not that hungry at the moment." I coughed a bit. "It will pass I hope."

"It sucks, huh. Your first day training and you get sick."

I shifted in bed. "Maybe I got too anxious. I bet Julien is jumping around, bragging."

"He may be a good fighter, but between you and me, we can both kick his ass with only words," she said.

I nodded in agreement. "You're not wrong."

She headed to the restroom and came out a few minutes later.

"I really hope you feel better soon. Have to go train with the amateur Earthkalais," she said, half-smiling. I smiled back as she turned to leave.

Everyone had woken up early in the morning by the sound of bells ringing. The caretaker walked through each floor, screaming for Illuminators to dress, eat breakfast, and go out to start the first phase of training. Kosmos seemed, including the caretaker, to be behind by decades; speakers instead of a bell would've been nice.

I didn't eat to make things more believable and wore a purple cozy sweater. My rosy skin turned pale with every tiring breath in training. The first phase was practicing actual fighting and tactics. Illuminator instructors walked around, watching how each Celestialkalai practiced. I didn't do great, but I was glad Julien wasn't around to mock me about it. The second phase was practicing our powers. There I was glad of all the drama movies I watched growing up. It was my time to act. I breathed in. *Action*. And ran to the restroom on the first floor before everyone started. An instructor came to check up on me. I explained the headaches, the upset stomach, and hollow feeling in my chest. She narrowed her eyes, pressing her lips. I kept my act going, hoping that she would believe me. Then, she nodded and told me I should get myself some tea and rest for the remainder of the day or return to training if I felt any better.

- *Stellar Court: Three witches from Solar Court and three Illuminators from Lunar Court of each order in Eclipse coats.*
- *Solar Court: Three Witches in Sun Coats.*
- *Lunar Court: Three Illuminators in Moon Coats.*
- *Solar High Officials in red-golden coats with a Sun design. Lunar High Officials in blue-silver coats with a Moon design. No Stellar High Officials.*
- *Guards in gray uniforms with a Sun, Moon, or Eclipse pin depending on their area of duty.*

I sat back up on my bunk bed, repeating everything I knew about Kosmos and their people in my head. Light and darkness seemed to be their main theme. *Light and Darkness. Killian and I.*

I sighed. "What do I do now?" I looked at my wrist. No sign of black ink over it. I tried the memory protection wall. Purple and blue colors lit up the room. I frowned. Outside the Celestialkalai Protectors worked on their full purple protection wall. I didn't understand at all.

As far as I knew everyone had a tattoo and they didn't have double powers or a protection wall that lit up in two colors. I had an eerie feeling that revealing that was a threat to me. *Everything here might be a threat to me and everyone I know.* The better plan was to figure everything out first. I started pacing around the room. There were no books I could find in the building to help me seek information, the only book that could've helped me more was the *Illuminated,* and witches seemed to have it.

The entire day was a cycle of walking down the hall, the room, and watching out the window. Finally, afternoon came along. Bringing everyone back sweaty and stressed. Loud voices of people arguing filled the hallways. I sat down waiting for the door to open. Julien and Ed entered, holding a bag of fresh clothes in their hands.

"You just won't admit it," Ed said, laughing at Julien. Their red faces filled with sweat.

"I won't because it's a lie," Julien responded.

"Admit what?" I said, slowly getting out of bed. "That he is bad at fighting?"

"Fighting and using his abilities," Ed said. Julien punched him in the shoulder and Ed winced.

"Are you feeling better?" Julien asked.

I shrugged. "A bit better I guess."

I got out of the room as Julien and Ed freshened up, avoiding making a disgusted face at the sweaty odor as I walked by them. It was announced yesterday that there would be piles of clothing at the reception for people to get and change each day. I headed there to get a fresh pair of clothing. The crowded elevator called me as I passed it by. But I ignored it and walked down the almost empty stairs towards the reception to waste time and avoid the tiring people. Some, however, walked up the stairs, wincing in absolute pain.

When I got the fresh pair of clothes, I headed to the red-walled cafeteria and followed the fresh delicious smell of food. The introverted girl from the cruise sat at the far edge table eating a piece of some strawberry pie in a plastic tupper that reminded me of Killian and the London coffee shop. I headed her way and stood across from her.

"Hi," I half-smiled. "I don't mean to disturb you. I just had a quick question."

"It's okay," she said in a soft and eerie voice, shaking her blonde curly hair out of her face.

"By any chance did you see a Celestialkalai Eidetic during training? I got sick and couldn't be there this morning."

She sat there thinking for a few seconds, her vivid blue eyes looking around the room. "Now that I think about it, I didn't," she said, staring back and forth at the strawberry pie and me. "*Actually,* I don't think there was anyone there with memory powers?" She shook her head.

"That doesn't make sense," I added out loud.

The girl made a slight nod, then suddenly looked at me strangely. "You have them, don't you?"

I frowned, a slight panic going through my brain.

"You are the only one that has become aware of my presence even after I have tried to use my full powers on you..."

I shook my head. "That doesn't mean I have memory powers... *maybe* you need more practice."

She narrowed her eyes and spoke in a low soothing voice. "I don't know why you can see me. But if you do have memory powers, you should be careful. I've heard dangerous stories from a family member who used to work at the Archives department in Stellar Castle. Finding an Illuminator with memory powers is rare. Sometimes none exist for decades. If anyone finds out they might use you to their advantage."

I stayed silent. If she was right, then I saved myself earlier by acting sick, without being aware of the rarity of my powers. That meant I had to keep it a secret for the time being.

"Your secret is safe with me," she whispered, going back to eating her strawberry pie. *Do I trust her? Should I ask her, or should I leave?*

"A piece of enlightenment Clara..." The girl curled her lips before I turned my back to her. "The universe works in mysterious ways, it's up to you to figure it out." She went back to eat her pie quietly.

"Thanks." I walked away to get myself a large cup of coffee from the coffee maker at the counter. Something told me I would definitely need more than one.

Soon the night came when I headed back to the room, holding the second cup of coffee and thinking about my next steps. Everyone was there telling stories about their day. Milana talked about how she was a better fighter than her opponent while Julien and Ed argued with each other. They chattered about other people's powers and the coolness of it all. I listened and laughed. That's until they started practicing on their own.

"You are going to set things on fire, Julien," I warned when he started playing around, holding a lighter in his hand, and making flickers of fire.

"That's what I'm here for," Milana responded, glancing at the glass of water nearby. Ed shook his head. I stood up from my crouched position and headed to the restroom to change into a black long-sleeved shirt I had gotten and black pants.

"By the way," Julien started to say while I fixed my space after coming back, "Clara, you never showed us your tattoo or told us the power you had? I'm starting to think you are not one of us." He joked.

I turned and everybody was facing me. Milana lightly punched him.

"Celestialkalai Protector," I responded without hesitating.

"Wow," Ed blurted, shocked. "Now, I'm curious."

"Show us!" Milana said. I shook my head.

"Not today. I'll show y'all at practice tomorrow."

"She's tired and fragile, let her be," mocked Julien.

"I'm not. I'm just not in the mood," I replied. "Goodnight." I got into bed and closed my eyes. I hadn't done anything, but my eyes stung. Two large cups of coffee no longer helped me get energy. After years of drinking so much of it, I needed more than that to stay fully energized and awake. Everybody else started shuffling too, getting ready to sleep. I waited patiently until the room was silent enough. Until everybody was paralyzed, and Julien's snores concealed the sound of my steps in the dark.

The lighthouse shone brighter than the Moon itself, guarding the forest for strangers. I opened the door to the soundless hallway, looking forward and backward while I headed for the stairwell. My feet throbbed as I met the steps, walking slowly to not make any sound and making sure to quietly close the creaking doors. I looked up and down, hoping no one was awake or in sight. Just like in the castle, candle lights and lightbulbs hung at every corner, only most of the time were the candle flames awake.

At the faintly lit reception area, two guards stood outside behind the clear glass. They wore a silver-Moon pin, like the guards outside Lunar Castle. I had noticed that that's how everyone could tell who they were or what position they were in. High officials and Court members had a unique drawing on their coats, either Sun, Moon, or Eclipse, while guards had a pin. One guard shook himself awake, while the other one fell asleep against the glass. I couldn't reach their memories, not unless I made contact with them. The invisibility power of a Celestialkalai would have been handy. I moved to the left, passing the bar and towards the cafeteria. *There must be an emergency exit somewhere.* I thought as I looked around. But there wasn't. My only last hope was an open window. I hid between the tables, checking each window I could and glancing back and forth at the guards.

I sighed slightly. None of them were open.

"Okay then, I hope plan *Z* will work." I ran quickly towards the elevator and pulled down the fire alarm next to it. Both of the guards shook awake at once. I hid behind the bar, wincing from the loud noise. I let out a breath, feeling bad for scaring everyone awake, but the damage was necessary, and it was done. For five seconds, I waited behind the bar. I couldn't hear or see the guards at all, but I had to get out before more people appeared. Quickly, I peeked from the huge countertop. Nobody was in sight. I ran out of the hotel and towards Lunar Castle.

Without the Sun, the night was slightly colder, it made me shiver as I ran. The dim lights made it easy to hide in the dark. I ran behind the hotel, and towards the back of the castle, concealing myself behind the pine trees. I waited for the beam of light from the lighthouse to pass by before I kept moving. Other guards or witches from the castle ran to the hotel as the room lights shone and the alarm sounded endlessly. Behind the castle was pure silence and darkness. A filled trash bag sat beside one of the back doors. I guessed workers were getting ready to rest. To my luck, I was right. The door opened right on time and a kind-looking man with a beanie came out with more trash bags.

"Do you need assistance?" I asked, appearing from the darkness and trying out a British accent. The old man made a small jump, a scared look on his face.

"My apologies for frightening you." I drew back and spoke in a well-mannered tone, like some people in Kosmos did, trying not to burst out smiling.

"No need, Miss," he said, looking curious.

"Alright, I must hurry to clean, or I won't hear the last of it," I quickly said, entering inside before he asked questions.

"Thanks, Killian," I whispered to myself once I was far enough from the man for him not to hear.

I walked down a darkened hallway until I reached the kitchen. I had expected it to be somewhat filthy, but it was the exact opposite. If I had the same elegant kitchen, I would probably have baking problems and never want to stop cooking. Every inch of the largely onyx kitchen was crystal clean. No smell of food was detected. The counters were left empty with only pans hanging from the pan holder on one of the walls.

"Oh girl, what are you wearing?!" a lady with short red hair said, coming out of a supply room holding a blue bucket of water. I stumbled back. She wore a sky-blue apron with a white shirt and a long black skirt.

"Hello. Um... I'm a new worker." She glanced at me strangely, up and down.

"New worker? Ah, I see!" She moved her head sideways, inspecting my clothing. I looked at myself, wondering if I had dirt or a stain. "I thought the Court was joking when they said they wanted more modern workers in the castles. Your parents must be modern lunatics, dressing you up like this. Certainly nothing like the good sturdy fabric, you need to do proper work," she rasped, shaking her head.

I held my offensive look back, only nodded, and stood silently.

She continued as she walked past me into the kitchen. "I'm Lia, the current housekeeping manager in the castle."

"Clara."

"You must be a light-blood, almost every employee here is either a light-blood, a poor witch, or an Illuminator family member from Arkadia."

"Yes. I'm a light-blood," I responded. "I traveled a long way from... Arkadia. I even had the chance to pass by Ether."

"Did you attend the protests earlier at Ether or Ark Station?" she asked, placing the bucket inside one of the lower drawers from the island countertop.

"Protests? Not exactly. I was too busy trying to get here on time to notice or do much." I wondered why protests were happening in the cities of Kosmos.

"You are in luck... to have been hired here I mean. My sullen heart really goes out for the poor people of Arkadia." She shook her head and approached me. "Come girl, I'll show you to your room."

I didn't move. "Before the grand tour, may I know where the washroom is?" I asked, embarrassingly.

She sighed. "Sure but run along. I'm rather tired. Out the door, down the hall to the left." She pointed towards a white door behind me. I nodded once and headed out of the kitchen through the glass door. Stairs stood in the middle of the hallway. I looked behind me, the lady was gone. It was my chance. I walked up the stairs until I could find the exit to an actual castle hallway that was not flooded with workers.

Soon enough, after the twisted stairs, I was out of the workers' area on the third floor of Lunar Castle. The castle's elegant hallways gave it away. Tapestries and paintings hung on the dark brown walls. Long black, silver, and blue designed rugs decorated each hallway and stairs. I looked around before stepping into other hallways, hiding the shadows of the dimmed vintage lights.

"It was a false alarm," a man said, walking in sync down the hallway to my right.

"We should come back to promote some better fire alarms from France." The other man beside him laughed. "If the Court decides to actually meet us." They wore black plain suits, so they weren't guards, witches, or workers. Maybe light-bloods, but it was impossible to tell the difference between a human and a light-blood without seeing their blood. I sighed. *Here it goes, focus.*

I walked down the hallway, bumping into one of the men, and hitting his shoulders. *Library. Focus on a library.*

For a second, the memory came to me. The path to information.

"My apologies," I said, stumbling back. "I'm so clumsy." The man nodded confused. *Clumsy, really?*

I made a small smile and walked away. The library was upstairs on the fifth floor. My path towards it was easy, the castle was oddly empty with only some workers walking around finishing their cleaning duties. Their slight stares followed me as I passed.

CHAPTER II
KING OF WRATH

LOOKING AT A LARGE NUMBER of books in the library made my eyes watery. Both for happiness and stress. It was going to be hard to find clues in the three-floor library. For minutes, I had lost myself within the shelves, searching silently one book after another. Until I heard footsteps and voices not far from where I stood. I froze, quickly shoving the piece of paper into my pocket. Light gleamed between books. Without looking, I almost stumbled back. A stack of books on the floor fell, making a loud thud. I grabbed hold of one of the shelves to prevent myself from falling and moved down to another shelf, but it was too late. A guard stood about five feet away from me shining a flashlight right on my face. For a second, the light blinded my eyes. I turned around to run and hide, but another guard was already behind me. He grabbed me by the arm with a firm grip. I shook trying to release it, but he was too strong. *Shoot.*

"Walk, criminal," the guard holding me said, pushing me forward. I rolled my eyes at him.

"I'm not a criminal. Let go of me. I'm a new employee that just came from Arkadia," I explained.

"You don't have to explain to me. Let's see what Sir Kaan from Stellar Court has to say," he responded aggressively. I looked at him angrily. His grip hurt my arm. We walked downstairs and passed some hallways. I recognized the hallways from the first day we came to Kosmos, we were on the first floor.

We walked by the auditorium, made some turns in a long hall and onto a small hallway that led to a silver door with a Moon sign in the middle, the symbol of Lunar Court. The other guard with the flashlight knocked on the door, then waited a few seconds to enter. Behind the silver door was a dark room with silver chandeliers hanging from the roof. Bookshelves in the walls surrounded the entire room, making it look like a large study room. Only a large brown table sat in the middle. And at the end of it sat a man with dark short hair looking down at what seemed to be a large map and files. Behind him stood two other people in orange clothing I hadn't seen before, also looking down at the large map, pointing here and there.

"Sir, we found this girl roaming around the library," the guard said, releasing me from his grip. I glared at him. He went to stand by the silver door.

The seated man looked almost disinterested at first, he stood up and looked at me. He looked young, handsome even, but maybe a bit older than me. He wore a large black coat with gray stitching designs and feathers at the collar. I suspected he was 'Kaan from Stellar Court' as the guard had said earlier. A serious but curious look came upon his face as he looked at me straight in the eyes. His dull gaze was cold. I could've sworn he could see through my soul. I looked away for a few seconds, clearing my mind. Thinking that at that point anything was literally possible.

"What is a *girl* doing in the castle at this hour?" he said coldly, looking at me and then at the guards behind me. His voice was firm, strong, and filled with certainty. Goosebumps traveled across my body before I spoke.

"I'm a light-blood," I responded steadily. "A new employee from Arkadia." *Self-control Clara. Pretend you are acting. Don't lose it.* He narrowed his dark eyes.

"You say 'Sir'," he shot. "If you were from Kosmos you would say, *Sir.*" I tried my best to stay calm. The better I behaved, the faster I could get out. Yet, a tinge of fear and anger crossed my mind. His gaze made me feel intimidated and I wished it didn't. *Worse than Killian.*

The silence was interrupted by the opening of the silver door behind me. A guy entered, walking towards Kaan, and standing next to him. He seemed to freeze for a second, staring at me. The design of the gray pants and dark-blue hooded sweater gave me a hint that he wasn't from Kosmos. And if he was, he chose to be modern. His hair was dark with a blue streak of hair dye, reminding me of something that I couldn't exactly place. He whispered something to Kaan that I couldn't hear. Then, Kaan looked at me coldly, smirking.

"*Apparently* you are a liar as well, Miss De Rose."

My breathing stopped.

"Now, would you like to tell me the truth or should my assistant here, Axel, make a truth spell?" he said, his words filled with power. "I sense your silence means yes? What is your power, Illuminator?" He sneered like a sociopath.

I didn't speak, or worse, I couldn't speak. Of fear, anger, and most importantly concern for my safety. The less I said, the more of an advantage I had. Even so, I needed a good enough reason as an explanation. Axel took a step forward. I was about to step back but had forgotten there were guards behind me. I quickly thought of what to say.

"I'm a Celestialkalai Protector," I said, looking at him. "Protection powers... Sir," I added.

"Let us see then." Kaan grinned. I stood there without words. If I showed him he would know that not only am I lying, but I have different powers, and I couldn't let that happen.

He sighed, annoyed. "Lying again, are we?"

Axel moved forward, he was so close to grabbing my arm.

"Memory powers," I spoke at once. "I'm a Celestialkalai Eidetic."

"Show me your tattoo," Kaan demanded.

"I don't *have* a tattoo." I lifted up my sleeve, turning my arm to show that I wasn't lying.

Kaan stood quietly and expressionless. I couldn't tell what he was thinking, and that made me anxious.

"Bring Mister Montova," he said towards Axel. He nodded once and got out of the room without glancing back.

"Shouldn't you be resting from today's training, Miss De

Rose? Why were you at the library?" Kaan asked, seconds later. *To find out the truth about what witches are planning to do with Illuminators and vampires.* I thought, but I didn't say. Of course, I wouldn't say. He walked towards me slowly, making him more visible. Up closer he looked younger, maybe my sister's age.

"To find out why I didn't have a tattoo like the others," I responded. He watched every move I made, making sure I wasn't lying. My dad had told me that most people didn't look straight in the eyes when lying or they moved their hands. I tried not to do either. The door opened once again, and Axel came in. He walked towards Kaan, but this time another young man, wearing a large black coat like an old-fashioned businessman, was behind him. He stood a few feet away from me. Looking back and forth from me to Kaan. I looked at him. His hazel-gray eyes shone under the light like the light-brown highlights in his dark hair. The three silver rings on his fingers shined brighter with designs I couldn't make out. He didn't display any type of emotion, holding only a straight face.

"Shall I send word to Stellar Court about this incident, Sir," Axel said, his voice almost a whisper.

"No, it is not necessary. Not a word to anyone," he said loudly. Everyone, except the hazel-grayish-eyed young man, nodded.

"Adrik, escort Miss De Rose to one of the main suites... on the fourth floor," Kaan said to the hazel-eyed man 'Adrik'.

"Why am I being held hostage?!" I said. Other than entering without permission, I hadn't stolen something or hurt someone to be held.

"Take it as a small vacation, Miss De Rose," Kaan added, smirking. "Anyone in your place would have been extremely excited."

"My friends will be looking for me," I said defensively. Kaan looked at me.

"They will understand." He waved a hand of dismissal and sat back in his chair to look back at the large map.

Adrik grabbed me by the arm. The same arm that the guard had grabbed earlier. I glared at him as he walked me out of the silver door room towards the stairs and the fourth floor. After walking up the first-floor steps, I winced from the pain in my arm. Adrik looked at me, just as expressionless as Kaan. He released the pressure from his hand to my arm, it still hurt but not the same as before. I noticed a scar under his left eye, it was only distinguishable when standing close enough. We continued silently until we were on the fourth floor. Walking down an empty hallway with only a million rooms.

"Don't try to escape. You'll waste your time... and mine," he said roughly. We stopped at the door and Adrik opened it. He released me, nodding for me to go inside. I looked at him blankly as I went. The moment I stepped in he closed the door. Keys shuffled and the lock turned. There was no point in checking. I was a prisoner.

The main suite was on the west side of the castle. It was bigger than the rooms at the hotels. Same vintage and mixed modern vibes. A fireplace stood across from me, beside it a bookshelf without books, and the door to what I guessed was the restroom. I inspected around, shuffling through shelves but couldn't find anything useful and sat on the annoyingly comfy bed. I felt something in my back pocket as I sat down. I took the hidden piece of paper I had in my pants. A map. I had forgotten I grabbed it before I was caught.

The unfolded map sat before me. It was neatly drawn, showing me the whole country of Kosmos surrounded by cold mountains and gloomy forests. There were three entrances to Kosmos: West Entry (the main entry everyone uses), then North and South Entry (only used for officials, leaders, train cargo, etc.). I remembered how we kept heading north during the train ride, passing Ether. In that case, we had entered by the West entrance of Kosmos. The country was mainly divided by Ring Forest and Ingla River with Star Lake in the middle. Lunar Castle at southeast, with Stellar and Solar Castle up north. The cities Ether and Arkadia were on the west side of the country.

I sighed, my eyes getting heavier by the second. I was unbelievably tired. I laid down, but I didn't want to sleep. A teardrop fell on the light-beige pillow from my cheek, making a dark brown stain. *Don't cry, not now.* I thought of my family and friends, wondering what they were doing right this second. The thoughts of them held me together. Mom and Dad must have been at home, probably baking. Aurora stressed about her job. Dani and Johnny working on the wedding. They all thought I was in London, living my life as a photographer. I looked at the white roof, letting myself enter my peaceful mind and dream of being with those whom I cared about.

I was awake before the Sun lit up the room. Someone knocked on the door, and I sat up quickly. A lady had come in, placing dark clothing at the foot of the bed. Then leaving without saying a word. Before she closed it, I saw Adrik standing by the doorway. He wore similar black clothing he had worn yesterday. It reminded me of Gilbert's fashion style, just the opposite colors.

"I will return in five minutes. Kaan requires your presence," he informed, looking at his silver pocket watch.

I proceeded to change after he left. I put on the Celestialkalai long-sleeved shirt that was neatly placed on the bed. This one was different from the shirt they had given us yesterday at the hotel. The shirt was made with better quality fabric and had the Eclipse design like the one I had seen on the cruise ship. I was also given a black coat with long-cut sleeves and pockets on the inside. Both items of clothing made me feel smaller in size, but I guessed I had to manage.

"Oof, I look like a pirate," I said to myself, looking in the mirror.

Adrik waited for me just outside the room. He walked ahead of me and led me towards the staircase, this time without forcibly grabbing my arm. Like last night, the castle was soundless and unmoving, it gave an eerie aura. We walked downstairs back to the first floor. Adrik's silhouette was much taller than mine. Once on the first floor, we walked towards a wide room that was almost visible from the castle's entrance. It had a large dark dining table in the middle filled with nothing but a few plates on the two opposite ends. The two-doorway entrance room and hanging pictures on the brown walls reminded me of the gallery room from the holiday ball mansion.

"Enter," Kaan said the second we stood by the doorway. "Please, sit." He sat at the end of the black table, eating silently. I could easily tell now based on his casual clothing that he was only a few years older than me; it made him look skinnier. Instead of the large coat he wore last night, this time he wore black pants and a black knitted sweater. A black-threaded necklace stood around his neck showing a white crystal that looked similar in shape to the purple one I had found in the forest. I walked and sat at the head of the table, facing Kaan while Adrik stood motionless by the doorway.

Even sitting feet away, his stare made me shiver. He nodded at Adrik, to which he took as a sign to wait further away from the dining room. Adrik glanced at me for a second and walked away to stand by a room door that was visible from the corner of my eye.

"My apologies for my unmannerly behavior last night. Country policy changes have been taking up most of my time. I'm Kaan, a member of Solar and Stellar Court. Nice to meet you, Clara De Rose." I stayed silent. "Everyone else is at Stellar Castle, therefore it's just us this morning," Kaan informed.

I wondered what important meeting required all high officials and Court members to attend Stellar Castle. But I decided not to ask and continued staying in silence.

"Suit yourself," he said, nodding towards the plates. I had not eaten for a long while and the food at the table smelled amazing. *Except* for the pancakes. After eating breakfast in London with Dani, pancakes and juice had started to make me nauseous. The biscuits and coffee, however, had made my mouth watery but eating would have made me seem like I was okay with being a prisoner and I absolutely wasn't.

"Or not," he continued, eating peacefully.

"Why am I here?" I asked.

"You willingly entered the castle."

"Why am I held *hostage*?"

He smirked at me, chewing up some food. "People would die just to enter the castle, and you want to leave so soon?" He shook his head, clearing his throat. "I never said you were hostage, Miss De Rose. You are a guest."

"The lock on my door says otherwise."

I stared at him, waiting for an actual answer.

He shifted in his chair. "We haven't seen an Illuminator with memory powers for years." Exactly what the girl had said earlier. But even though that answered a million questions, I couldn't understand how that could be possible or why it would matter.

"How do you know that?"

"Witches have records for every supernatural species," he said. "For safety..."

"Or for power." I frowned at him. "It isn't a secret that witches have been trying to ally with Illuminators."

"That is indeed true," he replied. "Witches have been trying to *maintain* peace with other species for years, allying with Illuminators will be best for everyone. Don't you think so?" He talked in the most uncaring way, like allying with Illuminators was nothing or like he didn't care at all about the situation.

"I'm supposed to believe *you* want the best for your long-lasting vampire enemies?" I shook my head in disbelief. Other than power, what else did they want? What else did Kaan himself want?

"I'm not the enemy here, Miss De Rose."

"You are not the ally either," I responded.

"But I could be."

"I don't think so." I crossed my arms. Kaan stared at me unemotionally.

"Very well then, I don't think you have much of a choice."

I glared at him without speaking. Now, I was at a complete disadvantage. With Kaan now on the enemy side and Adrik spying on me, I would be unable to leave the castle. Yet I couldn't help but stay quiet and act like I cared much for witches. Kaan stood up suddenly.

Adrik seemed to hear the noise of the creaking chair sliding through the floorboard and came to stand by the doorway.

"Excuse me, Sir." A guard appeared next to him in the doorway. Adrik moved away from the doorway before the guard could accidentally touch his shoulder.

The guard continued speaking to Kaan. "We have found the um..." He looked at me. "The person you sent us to..."

"Finally," Kaan responded, a boast in his face. The guard nodded and left the doorway to walk back outside the castle. As soon as Kaan walked out of the other doorway, I stood up to walk out from the other.

He glanced at me once and looked at Adrik.

"Tell Axel to meet us in the library and to bring the house-keeper," Kaan ordered. Adrik nodded once, watching Kaan walking out of the castle's main doors.

"Come with me," Adrik said. He was about to turn around

when he noticed I wasn't following him to the stairwell. "What are you doing?"

I didn't respond.

"You can't go outside." He warned and walked quickly beside me before I took another step.

"Don't worry. I'm not planning to run away... yet."

He made a very slight frown. It was the closest facial expression he could make that was not close to nothing. "You are more than a bodyguard, right? Based on your choice of clothing and not-so-respectful manners to *Sir* Kaan, it appears you were hired for something else. Aren't you *a bit* curious as to what Kaan is up to?"

"No. And I can't let you figure it out either."

"So, you like being treated like a puppet then? Are you that loyal to him? Is money that important to you?"

"The only person I am loyal to is myself. And it's none of your concern." He grabbed me by the arm again. I hated that.
"I'll go. On my own." He let go of me and nodded for me to go in front of him. I rolled my eyes at him, walking forward.

In a matter of seconds, I was back inside my jail room, left alone with no hope in sight. I paced back and forth. Then I walked to the balcony, feeling the warm breeze entering the room through the white curtains. From afar I could see Illuminators walking out onto the training grounds, walking in sync like soldiers in a war.

CHAPTER 12
ROCK-CLIMBING

"TIME TO MEMORY TRAIN, Miss De Rose," Kaan taunted, an expression of gloating. If I knew he wasn't an enemy maybe that expression would have made me think the opposite of what I thought. That smile was nowhere near a genuine smile, and I didn't think it would ever be. I walked up to a smaller library on the third floor. Adrik walked behind me, watching me like a hawk. He stayed in the hallway watching at every corner of the room.

Axel was already in the library when I entered. The woman, Lia, who I had seen the night I broke in, stood next to him motionless. She looked at me curiously but didn't speak. Two chairs sat, about three feet away from each other, in the middle of the small library.

"Sit," Kaan demanded. I sat down before he sat in front of me, lights cast shadows underneath his eyes. "Now, show me what you can do."

"I can see other people's memories, only with physical contact," I said, hoping to sound genuine enough. Axel nodded at Lia to move forward. I looked at the sudden fear in her eyes. She had seemed so brave when I met her and now, she walked slowly towards me, maybe in panic of standing close to Kaan or fear of me and my power.

"Show me." Kaan's cold voice echoed through the room.

I looked at Lia. She gave me her hand and I nodded to let her know it was ok. I grabbed her hand and tried to focus on a specific memory, one that would prove I actually saw it and was telling the truth.

Kaan looked angry, he sat in the dining room. The table was filled with different meals and desserts.

"What is this?" He spoke so loudly.

The woman stood frozen. "It is a chocolate dessert, Sir. Came from a great baker in Ether," Lia replied.

I didn't need to finish the memory. I released the woman's hand, and she stepped back quickly.

"Why don't you like chocolate?" I asked out of curiosity, half-smiling. From the corner of my eye, Lia's lips seemed to twitch. "You should try it, but I doubt that it can take your sour mood away." I sat up straight in my chair and crossed my arms.

Kaan stared angrily at me from the mockery, then held an unsettling smile. He eyed me closely without even flinching.

"You're lying. There is much more you can do that you are not showing." He sat up in his chair, making me feel small and weak. But I tried not to look away from his stare and stayed unmoved, glowering at him.

"The more you stay silent, the longer you'll stay here, Miss De Rose," he acknowledged. "Let's see how much you can take." At once, he broke the stare and stood up, looking at Adrik. "Escort her back to the room."

I hadn't seen Adrik come in; he now waited by the door inside the library. Kaan walked out without looking back. Axel left the room after him, weirdly smiling at me and Lia rushed behind him to go back to her duties.

I stood up at last. Adrik walked in front of me this time, sometimes glancing towards me as if I could disappear into thin air. His mysterious glare looked around. I recognized that look so well because of how much I used it. He was analyzing every inch of his surroundings. He always was, and I didn't know why.

"Why *do* you work here?" I asked him as we walked upstairs. He didn't respond. I knew he wouldn't, but it was worth a try.

"I assure you that is not to make new friends," he said as we stood outside the main suite, sounding serious. I frowned at him, entering the room. He looked at me dead in the eyes like something had sparked anger in him. Whatever it was, I would never know.

The hours passed by while I was kept locked in the main suite. It made me anxious thinking about what was going on that I didn't know. I sat down concentrating on Lia, trying to see her memories. Information that would help me get out of the castle, but it didn't work without any actual connection.

After a few minutes, Lia came to leave lunch. She passed into the room slowly. I looked behind her, but Adrik was nowhere to be seen. I got up, accidentally bumping into her, dropping the food tray and glass cup on the floor. Water spilled on the red-blue carpet.

"I'm sorry, Miss," she blurted. I frowned at her formalities.

"No, it's completely okay. I'll help you clean and take everything back."

"But you can't," she said, shaking her head.

"Yes, I can," I said firmly.

We both grabbed the messy utensils on the floor and walked down to the third floor. I looked around me, but Adrik was nowhere in sight. Lia walked in front of me, looking around every ten seconds. I placed the utensils quietly in the tray she held.

"Go ahead. You won't get in trouble," I whispered, trying to reassure her. She nodded and walked towards the third floor and to the twisted stairs I had taken that headed to the workers' area and kitchen. Once she was out of sight, I walked around the hallway and passed by the small library from where I could hear shouting. The door was a few centimeters open, but I couldn't see anyone inside.

"Figure out more. Do it soon." It was Kaan's voice.

"Yes, Sir," a lower voice said, Axel's.

"If Clara has memory powers, then there has to be someone that has the opposite powers. Her balance. Find that person and bring them to me," Kaan exclaimed. "We will need both to move forward with the plan."

"Yes, Sir."

"Also, start with the *other* plan. Everything has to be ready for when we have both holders of the Eidetic powers."

"Yes, Sir," Axel repeated.

"Miss?" Lia spoke next to me in a whisper, she stood a few feet away from me and held another food tray with a cup in one hand and cleaning supplies in the other. I came back to my senses and moved away from the room, towards Lia. She raised an eyebrow at me. I grabbed the cleaning supplies from her hand. Then she just shook her head. I walked behind her, back to the suite. We were about to step onto the fourth-floor stairs when we were stopped.

"What are you doing?" I turned around. Adrik stood behind me, glaring suspiciously from me to Lia.

"I accidentally dropped Miss De Rose's meal tray—" Lia started to say. She was taking the blame for me.

"I was helping her," I interrupted. "Am I going to be scowled at for being nice?"

"Come on. Let's go," he said, looking at me and then turned to look at Lia. "You can go later to clean."

"Food fell, Adrik... to the floor," I grimaced. "It's not *my* room, but it shouldn't stay unclean for so long."

"She will go later," he repeated, turning to Lia. "You will certainly need more than a bucket of a few supplies."

"Yes, I'm aware. I was going to return after... for more," Lia muttered. She gave me the tray as I gave her the supplies. I looked at her, mouthing "Thank You" before Adrik walked ahead of me.

I was back in the room in less than thirty seconds with Adrik looking at me annoyed. I sat down with the tray on the small table. A ham sandwich, apple slices, peas, and mashed potatoes stared back at me. Even the glass of water seemed bland. I was hungry for not eating in the morning, but the feeling had gone away. The conversation I overheard earlier struck me. I couldn't help but think about what Kaan meant about moving forward with his plans. And that the other person who had the forgetfulness and opposite powers of mine was Killian.

I was kept in my room the rest of the day, waiting anxiously. Lia had come about an hour ago taking away the untouched food tray. I sat in the bed, analyzing the room second after second and trying not to fall asleep.

"Hello, Miss, it is about to be midnight," she said after closing the door slightly behind her, the cleaning supplies in her hands. "Was your lunch satisfying?"

"Drop the formalities, Lia. I think we both know you hate them." I looked up at her.

"Well... you are not wrong," she responded with a grin, her shoulders slightly relaxing.

"What's so funny?" I asked.

She shook her head. "You broke into the castle only to be caught. That's rather foolish, don't you think, child?"

I frowned. "You are mocking me?"

"In fact, I am."

"Well, there is something I need to figure out, being caught actually helped me more than I expected."

Lia frowned, but she stayed silent.

"By the way, thank you for helping me and taking the blame. But I don't understand why you did it," I whispered in case Adrik was close by.

"I dislike the bodyguard, seeing him annoyed brings me joy

for some reason," she confided. I did too, if he even got annoyed anyway.

"Are you sure it's only that?" I questioned. "You fear him, don't you? Kaan?"

She started cleaning the floor. "Everybody does. Even members of Stellar Court are bloody scared of him. He is one of the leaders that has been around since Kosmos' rise. His magic helps him stay young."

"He was around during the Supernatural War?"

"I believe so? Along with two others from Solar Court. Everyone else was new and chosen to become leaders of Kosmos by the people after the war; most of which migrated here like me. As far as I know, Sir Kaan was already automatically in Solar Court, then rose to Stellar Court a few years ago."

"How did you come to be here? You are not supernatural... are you?"

"My husband was a witch. He died in Arkadia, fighting two vampires that had entered Kosmos after the war. Afterward, I filled out paperwork and got a job here as the first housekeeper..."

"Wow, I'm sorry." I shook my head. "I doubt any vampires can get in now with the barriers around Kosmos."

"No place involved with magic is safe right now, especially not Kosmos."

I nodded, and she sighed.

"I haven't seen anyone talk down to him in my many years here... Sir Kaan I mean." She half-laughed. "That's why I helped you. You are courageous." She finished cleaning and left silently out of the room.

Sometimes being alone and overthinking wasn't such a bad idea. About two hours after midnight, I took the linen sheets off the bed and tied them together to make a rope. It was late and I didn't expect anyone to come in the middle of the night.

There were four sheets in the bed, the rope would be long enough to drop me on the balcony of the third floor. I frowned, looking around the room. *The bathroom.* I took off the shower curtain first and then one of the curtains from the window and tied them together along with the first strand of sheet rope. I could drop to the second-floor balcony by jumping. It was a tricky and physically dangerous plan, but I hadn't practiced parkour and running all those years for nothing. I turned off the lights from the room and headed to the balcony. Most of the guards guarded the front of the castle, so I hoped to not be seen through the moonlight or the lighthouse.

I tied the sheet rope to one of the pillars, making sure it was secure. I turned one last time towards the room, then back towards the outside. The light from the lighthouse moved at a steady pace.

"Ok, here it goes," I whispered. "The only option is surviving." I stepped off the balcony grabbing the rope. My hands were a bit sweaty and shook with nervousness. *You have to make it.* Slowly, I slid down the rope, trying to reach the third-floor balcony, making sure to take a steady step on the rocky wall. I took a breath as I grabbed myself from the balcony poles. The lights in the room in front of me were out. *Good.* I flew a few more feet down to get to the second floor, but this time I had to jump. I grabbed myself from the last part of the rope and jumped onto the second balcony. The door to this balcony was open and the lights were on. I tried to reach the rope from where I stood to hide it from the window view. Then I moved to the side, where I wouldn't be seen from the window. *Parkour time.* I stepped to the balcony, looking for places I could hold myself to. The blue rope nearly disguised itself with the gray bricks, making my run away easier. Like rock climbing but without the secure ropes. *Breathe.* I shook my burning hands. Then held myself tight with every move I made. Just needed a few more feet to reach the small window on the first floor. I was extremely relieved once I reached it, and I jumped to the ground. I hit the hard floor, realizing I missed the humid smell of grass.

From the top, I saw the dark-blue sheet rope dangling from the balcony. I hid in the shadows. Running straight to the Ring Forest wasn't an option, I wouldn't make it far with my aching muscles. I walked to the front of the castle where about ten guards stood, deciding to run around behind the castle to the other side, hide in the trees, and run to the stable instead.

My feet slightly hurt, hitting the Earth's surface. I watched the guards and made sure not to be seen. With the protection shields around Kosmos, I guessed leaders were not used to having someone from their country breaking in or breaking out. The guarding system was not as great.

Horses stood peacefully inside the stables. Only in the moonlight was I able to see the horses, their breaths sounding almost in sync with the low chirps of the crickets. I chose the wide-awake black horse, it was easy to camouflage in the darkness. I beamed at him and petted him slowly. He seemed comfortable or so I hoped. I put on the saddlery and the reins rather poorly.

"I think this will do. Hopefully?" I said to the horse. "Okay, come on." I opened the door and took the horse out.

"Do you need help?" I half-jumped at the voice that spoke in the dark. I turned around to see the blonde Celestialkalai girl standing behind me, looking like an angel.

"Shoot... you scared me!" I said, frowning. "How are you here?"

"Perks of invisibility. I have been here for about two hours, just inside this stall," she said, pointing at one of the opened stalls a few feet away, her blue eyes sparkling in the small light. "Do you want some?" She held a clear plastic tupper with grapes inside it. "I brought my own food from home. A few meals..." That explained why I saw her carrying around the suitcase when we came to Kosmos. "I told them I was allergic to a lot of foods..." she said after seeing my frown. I grabbed some of the purple grapes, feeling my empty stomach agreeing with me.

"I hadn't seen you?" she continued curiously.

"I broke into the castle," I said. She stayed silent for a few seconds. "And you were right. About the danger."

"And now you are running away?"

"Yes..."

"Okay... I'll help you." She nodded slowly and started towards the black horse in front of me. "I love horses and have ridden a few times. This is how you do it."

She showed me how to put the saddlery correctly and gave me a few tips on how to control the horse. I looked at her somewhat confused while she explained some details about the horse riding, not because I didn't understand what she was talking about but because I didn't know why she was helping me.

"You are wondering why I'm helping you," she spoke softly, stroking the horse. "I like your aura and bravery... and there's a feeling that I *should* help you."

"Thank you." I smiled at her. "I don't even know your name."

"Irene Grace. And you are Clara De Rose."

"Very nice to meet you, Irene." I shook her hand.

"Okay, Midnight is ready." She smiled at the horse, who stood calmly. "Wait here." Irene walked back inside the stable in which Midnight had been seconds earlier. She came back out holding a brown backpack and taking out a white shirt. "Purple will attract more attention. Hope it fits."

I grabbed the shirt and went into the stable to change. The white button-up shirt fitted in nicely. I folded the purple shirt.

"I can take it," Irene suggested once I was next to Midnight. She was a Celestialkalai after all. I nodded, handed it to her and she placed it inside her bag.

I shook my hands ready to leave. "This is my first time riding a horse, so please be nice, Mister Midnight," I said, getting on the horse. "There is a first time for everything right?" I looked at Irene. She nodded in assurance.

"Oh here!" She rummaged in her bag again, getting out two medium sandwich bags with three chocolate chip cookies each. "For the trip."

"Thank you, again." I beamed, taking the bags and placing them inside one of the pockets of my coat. "Will you do okay here?"

She tilted her head. "I will. No worries. You are valiant, Clara De Rose. I wish you the best on your journey."

"Thank you," I repeated, even though I had said it more than a thousand times.

Before I turned around, she stared at me and said, "By the way, I did say the universe works in mysterious ways... but it is usually always on your side." I glanced back at her, regretting not spending more time getting to know her and leaving her on her own in Kosmos. Yet as I turned back around towards the moonlight, a feeling of certainty ignited inside of me, telling me that I was ready to do what I had been meant to do from the beginning.

Irene waved goodbye. I led the horse out of the stable, it was time to take action. I shook in sync with the horse till it started to run at a normal rate, leading him straight towards the Ring Forest. I took one last glance at Lunar Castle.

From far away, I could tell guards were starting to take notice of us. They moved forward, arranging themselves into a mob. A sudden white, almost clear wall appeared around them. For a second I thought someone was using their magic to stop me. But I turned around again and couldn't believe my eyes when the guards seemed to move *very* slowly, close to a halt. I took one last glance at the stables for Irene. She was nowhere to be seen, probably hidden out of sight again. I turned back to the dark as Midnight ran faster into the forest, heading into the shadows.

I had never thought I would have to ride towards a forest in these conditions. Running away from a country that was home to some Illuminators, light-bloods, and witches. But that wasn't my home and never would be as long as lies surrounded it. Because I knew something the people of Kosmos didn't know. Leaders are not leaders if they only care about themselves. I didn't know what

Kaan or Stellar Court planned for Kosmos, but people I cared about were involved, and I wasn't going to let them get hurt. Not in this supernatural story.

CHAPTER 13
SILVER RINGS

L IGHT FROM THE LIGHTHOUSE vanished as I rode deep into the Ring Forest. I didn't know for how long I had been riding, but my back killed me. I stopped and walked for a few minutes. Midnight walked next to me, breathing tirelessly. I could only hear my footsteps, owls hooting in the trees, and the chirps of crickets on the ground. I wasn't sure how many exact hours it took to get to Ether, but I had to get there fast before Kaan sent every guard to look for me. Besides that, it had started to drizzle. The light of the Moon slightly shone through the leaves, but it was already too dark to see more than a few feet ahead, and the rain wasn't helping. I tied the horse reins to a small branch so that I could see the Kosmos map again. It had only been a few seconds until Midnight made a slight movement next to me.

But it wasn't the only sound I could hear. I turned around as quickly as I heard the leaves rustling. Adrik was already behind me. He grabbed both of my arms, preventing me from using a memory shield. Midnight moved away from us, scared.

"I don't want to hurt you," I said, distracting him.

"That implies I'm capable of being hurt," he responded uncaringly.

"You should rethink that."

I moved my leg against him, making him lose balance and causing him to release one of my arms. But he balanced himself quickly and tried the same trick on me. I fell to the floor and grunted. Adrik stood beside me like a statue.

"To your *functional* power, it was demanded that I take you back to Lunar Castle *unharmed*." He lowered his hand in front of me to help me stand. The three silver rings on his left hand glowed in the dull light, over the black gloves he had on.

"You don't seem like the type to hurt me, even if you had the chance to do so," I said, grabbing his hand and focusing on his mind.

Smoke and Fire. Burning hot and excruciating fire. Three silver rings on the floor. Sparks of flames and a house burning down slowly.

I stood up with Adrik's help. The shocking memory passed my mind another time. Adrik stood about two feet away in front of me holding a serious face. I would not go back to Kaan, not without warning Killian about what was going on or finding out more. Without hesitating, I tried to punch Adrik in the face. He tried to grab my wrist but missed when I pushed it away with my other hand abruptly. My heart beat faster. With not enough energy in my body, I forced my legs to take one last stand. Only my mind could help me fight.

I created a memory shield between us, making him stumble back giving me time to walk away from him and towards Midnight. When there was a large amount of space between us, I took the shield down.

"You should be afraid you won't get far," Adrik said, looking straight into my eyes. I ignored his words and showed him the silver ring that I held in my hand.

"This is important to you, isn't it?" I flashed the ring back and forth, inspecting it. The small symbols were almost impossible to see in the dark, but the silver ring seemed to have a vine design around it.

His eyes turned hard and stone-cold rather fast. "I'll hunt you down until you wish you had gone to Kaan instead if you don't give me back that ring." I flinched at his abrupt anger.

"I'm sorry, but you can either find the ring before it gets lost in mud or let me go." I threw the ring in the air as far as I could, Adrik watched it fly far away from him. He looked at me for a second. I thought my trick hadn't worked, but he turned around and walked in the direction of the ring. I sprinted towards Midnight, untied the reins, and headed to the golden city. This time without trying to stop.

From afar, I could see the city lights of Ether. I pulled my hair up into a ponytail to seem less recognizable and because I was sweating. I watched around, then proceeded straight into the City of Aurum. Ether was the City of *literal* Gold. It made complete sense after I crossed a golden bridge over a stream towards the entrance. Not larger than Star Lake I assumed. The bridge at Ingla River was certainly larger to cross.

Languages I hadn't heard of before passed through my ear and out the other, hearing people switch from their unfamiliar small talk to English accents in public. Women wore lavish dresses while men wore vintage wear. But here and there were people with modern-looking clothing yet with no phone in hand. Like in the castles, only electricity for light was available here and there. Still no modern machinery was insight, no technology, and no way to contact anyone outside Kosmos. However, organized neighborhoods and old-time business buildings stood all around, it all seemed isolated but exceptional. Some people walked down the main street, staring at me. I got off the horse, trying to fit into the busy street.

"Excuse me, sorry to disturb you. May I know where I can find a library?" I asked the man selling gorgeous handmade ceramic plates on the sidewalk.

He grinned. "Yes, Miss, down the street, inside Ether Station."

"Thank you."

I could tell some people were Illuminators based on their tattoos or their colored clothing. Others were either rich witches or light-bloods. If this was Ether, I wondered what Arkadia looked like, being the City of Silver. The number of people awake in the streets was surprising. They looked so comfortable with each other like there was no worry in the world. Maybe Kosmos was all they knew, maybe the outside meant nothing to them. I saw the sign of the library after I walked inside Ether Station. I tied Midnight's reins to a pole close to the entrance of the library.

"Stay here, okay?" I whispered to Midnight, hoping he could understand. "Don't let anybody steal you."

Small whispers echoed from inside the library. I walked in silently, thinking about ways I could ask questions without being too obvious. Some people buried their heads into books, while others stared at them amused. All of a sudden, a young guy in a red coat bumped into me, getting scared and accidentally dropping his book. He picked it up, rubbing the cover with his hand.

"Why were you standing there? Almost gave me a *heart attack*," the guy complained dramatically, his messy black hair falling over his eye. He stood with the book in one of his hands and the other on his hip. The weird stance almost made me laugh.

"I'm sorry... I didn't realize this was the 'walk and read' part of the library," I responded. He narrowed his eyes, then made a small sigh.

"Is that a book about how to make bombs?" I glanced at the book in his tanned hand.

"What? Of course not," he half-laughed. "What do I look like to you, a *bomb* maker?" He hid the book behind his back. "Don't answer that." And walked slowly towards the exit, leaving quicker than I came in. His red coat swinging behind. *A reader... I should've asked him!*

I walked out of the library a second later, looking around for the red coat and tan-skinned guy. A lot of people lined up to take the train. He stood in line to buy a ticket. I grabbed the horse reins and led Midnight with me towards the guy.

"Wait, I need your help!" I screamed loud enough for the red-coat guy to hear. He turned around surprised.

"Making bombs?"

"No..." I looked at him confused.

"Why would I—" He stopped, looking shocked. "Is that your horse? It's so lovely."

I nodded, surprised at his amusement, and whispered. "I'll give you this horse. If you help me find a way to get out of Kosmos."

"Well, unless you are acquainted with a Stellar Court witch or high official, who can create a portal. The only way to get out of Kosmos is by crossing the divided line and passing the red portal in the ocean."

Of course. I sighed, but I needed to get out of Kosmos one way or the other. "I'll give you *lovely* Midnight... if you help me buy a ticket then to the West Entry."

He sighed, seeming to hesitate as he looked at Midnight.

"I'm doing this for Midnight," he said, taking the reins. I smiled at him.

We stepped forward to buy the tickets. "Sir, two tickets to ship this gorgeous horse and myself to Arkadia and another to Zephyr Port."

"Yes, that will be a hundred seventy-five *Kosniz*," the ticket collector said. The guy got out the *Kosniz*, each blue and red bill with an Eclipse sign, and paid for the tickets.

The conductor informed us that the train would pass by the West Entry before going to Arkadia. All passengers were supposed to be on board in ten minutes. More witches and Celestialkalai Protectors were going to start their shift before sunrise. The guy, whose name I didn't know yet, had gone to the back of the train to put Midnight inside a train car. I sat down next to the window. After a few minutes, the guy entered the train and sat next to me. The conductor announced the departure.

"Clara." I half-smiled. "By the way."

"Franko..." he informed. "With the K, not the C."

"Clara...with the C, not the K."

"Nobody writes 'Clara' with the K."

"Yes, they do," I said as a matter of fact.

"Where?"

"Somewhere that I can't remember..." I answered. "It doesn't matter." I was interrupted by the conductor's announcement; we were leaving Ether Station. The train car was half-filled. People talked in whispers. I avoided looking out the window. Watching the city and trees fly by made my eyes feel more tired than they already were. Franko proceeded to read his book quietly. The ride was going to take a few hours, and I didn't know what to do with myself, other than eat the chocolate cookies Irene had given me.

"Do you want some?" I asked him, holding out the second bag to him. He frowned at first but looked at the bag and grabbed it.

"Thank you," he said, leaving his book down and starting to eat after seeing me eating in silence.

After ten minutes Franko was back to reading his book and I was starting to slowly doze off.

"Why would you want to get out of Kosmos?" Franko asked suddenly, closing his book and looking at me. His question shook me awake.

"Why do you want to make bombs?"

He nodded. "Right... no questions then."

I nodded back.

"I know it isn't my business, but you can't possibly get out of Kosmos at night. Cruises leave daily," Franko informed. "Each morning."

I shrugged. "I'll find a boat."

"A boat? What if there are no boats?"

"I'll swim then."

"You will *die*. And no one wants to die in ice-cold water, take it from that human sinking ship film." He lifted his eyebrows.

"I will at some point die if I stay here anyway, so running away is a better option," I answered. He shook his head in disapproval and went back to read his book. I could tell he had more questions, but he didn't ask.

The air had become colder as we reached the West Entry station, we were closer to the ice mountains. I still had the black coat I was given the day before at Lunar Castle, but it wasn't enough to conceal it. The conductor announced our arrival.

"Hope you don't die and if you do... *I* told you so," Franko said. He grabbed something from inside his coat. "Sandwich for the trip?"

I was about to ask him why he had a soggy sandwich in his pocket but decided not to. I responded "Sure" instead. The train stopped. I got up and headed towards the exit.

"Actually, don't eat the sandwich. It might be disgusting!" Franko screamed. I wasn't planning on eating it anyway. I made a single nod and got out, throwing the sandwich in the trash can by the door.

Most Illuminators rushed around the station, following high official orders or just looking for a place to rest until morning's sea trip. I wasn't sure where to go from there. I hadn't seen any boats when we arrived at Kosmos. A lady, not too far ahead, was giving directions to Celestialkalais about when to start the guarding shift. I headed in her direction. She wore a red-golden coat with a Sun design, a high official witch.

"Hello, may I ask where I can find the boats?" I said after the Celestialkalais left.

"Boats? The *cruise* leaves in the morning," she replied.

"I'm aware, but it is an urgent matter, and I must leave right now." I grabbed her arms pleadingly, and she bounced back immediately.

"Do you have verified permission from Stellar Court to get out of Kosmos *by* boat?"

"No, I do not."

"Therefore, I cannot help you."

I gave her a bitter smile and walked away, knowing well where the boats were located by the touch of her arm. There was a warehouse, not far away from the station and guarded by Illuminators.

The ocean waves hit the shore gently as I headed in the direction of the storeroom. Moonlight barely lit the place, but the front entrance was visible thanks to the four torches that stood close to it. Two Illuminators, a Joviankalai and Earthkalai, stood by the entrance. One of them stood close to the tall, medium black table that held two clipboards.

"Hi, I came to get a boat," I informed.

"Your verified permission?" the Earthkalai asked, getting one of the clipboards and a pen from the table.

"I already showed it to an official. She approved."

"Are you an Illuminator or witch?" He stared at me up and down.

"Why does it matter?"

The Earthkalai crossed his arms. "You should have more respect, woman."

"You should mind your own business," I shot, creating the memory shield. Both Illuminators bounced back from purple-blue streaks.

"Blue? How?"

I walked closer to them. Their backs hit the wall of the gray warehouse. The Earthkalai tried to stop the electric wall by hitting it with ocean water but failed. The wall was able to protect me from his power and most likely others to some extent, as long as I could sustain the magic and concentrate enough. Something touched my leg, plant roots were grabbing me from the ankle. I looked at the Joviankalai, he had biological powers. He could control plants. I moved closer to them until the electric wall was one inch away from touching them.

"I don't want trouble, so let me pass," I demanded. They both nodded and raised their hands. I decreased the shield when they both started to run towards the West Entry train station. I quickly moved inside the warehouse. The medium-sized boats stood on the right. I grabbed the white one with the paddle already in it and pulled it outside. I hurried, seeing a group of people running in my direction, pushed the boat towards the water, got on, and started paddling as fast as I could. The hands that helped me with opening a cryptic book, boxing, parkour, and leading a horse were starting to hurt. I should have been concerned but I paddled. There was no time to rest.

A person was already swimming my way in a matter of seconds. Another Illuminator, possibly Earthkalai Liquis, tried to bring the boat back by changing the current of the ocean. An electric shield helped me counteract the action and slow down the power. But I couldn't stop the Illuminator and paddle at the same time. I still had a long way to go to hit the purple protection wall and red portal. The person still swam towards me. I breathed deeply before launching myself under the ice-cold water.

The current pushed against me, making it harder to swim fast up north. I kept my eyes closed as I swam under. It was dark, so I couldn't see anything either way. Unable to hold my breath for more than ten seconds, I swam up to get air. The Illuminator, who was following me, was no longer swimming. He had grabbed the boat to reach me faster, he was only a few feet away.

"You're not going to make it. *Give* up." He screamed under the frosty air and sound of the waves. I ignored him, looking intently at the water. Something was moving under me. Sharks. When I looked back at the Illuminator, he smirked. From the purple shirt, I guessed he was a Celestialkalai Illusionary. He could create illusions.

They aren't real. I repeated it in my head, even though they seemed completely authentic.

In the distance, people stood on the shore just watching. I closed my eyes, swam faster but this time I stayed above. The 'non-real' sharks swam fast towards me. I breathed and just swam. *They aren't real.* I collided with nothing, the sharks evaporated like smoke.

In a matter of three feet, I passed the protection wall. Then swam a few more feet to the red portal wall. I didn't have the luxury to turn around and witness the look of the Illuminators as I went through. I closed my eyes, quickly focusing on where I wanted to go. I was weightless.

Magic had always amazed me. It was impossible to just disappear and get somewhere else completely far away in less than a second, except of course maybe in space. Just like that, before knowing the actual truth, *magic* had been completely out of the world... literally. But I stood inside a restroom of Zatara Sunset, and there was no doubt.

I stood in the orange restroom stall, shivering down to my bones. My clothes were heavy and soaking wet. I sighed, getting out of the stall and heading to the vanity. Thankfully, there was only one person inside a stall, taking their time in the restroom. I took off the black coat I had. I should've taken it off seconds before I swam in the ocean, but I was too concentrated to get to the portal to even think about it. So, I took it off now, held it above the sink, and squeezed it to release the water. Then, I put it back on the moment the cool AC air hit my skin and fixed my hair. I breathed steadily, opening the door to get out of the restroom and hoping to not embarrass myself among the people.

The restaurant was not as filled as usual. But that didn't stop me from accidentally making eye contact with someone moments after walking out of the restroom hallway and into the open space. My face was cold under the bright lights and my fingers were like frozen ice pops. I tried to avoid eye contact, looking down at the ground and walking towards the exit.

"Excuse me, ma'am," the man standing by the entrance asked. "Are you alright?" I ignored him, walking out of the restaurant. Once outside, I stood by the balcony, looking up and inside the restaurant in case Gilbert and Killian were around. But I didn't think they were, especially since they usually sat by the balcony on the second floor. The duo's table stood empty and lonely, waiting for its daily new visitors.

The only way to figure out where they were was by looking at their current memories. But I doubted I had a close connection to either of them to locate them. It was worth a try. I closed my eyes and concentrated on Gilbert first. *Where are you?* I thought. But my mind stayed blank as the night sky. I tried Killian next. *I truly doubt it.* I visualized him and repeated his name in my mind, cringing at the sound of it.

A 4-star hotel. Standing by a bar, drinking whiskey, talking to a person next to him.

"That actually worked?" I said out loud, seeing the clear memory. I opened my eyes, shaking my arms awake. The hotel I saw was nearby. I believed I had seen it before, just a few buildings away from Zatara Sunset. *Why was I able to see his memories but not Gilbert's?* I shook the thought out of my head, concentrating on my surroundings. I walked through the Riverwalk as the sky turned slowly to twilight, anxious to get to the hotel and inform them of everything that had happened.

With the pace I was walking in, it took about three minutes to ultimately enter the hotel. I could see the bar at the far left and I walked towards it. Not surprisingly, Killian stood by the counter. From the side view, he looked unbelievably serene and daunting. As if he had heard my thoughts he turned, making eye contact with me.

"*Goldenrose*," he uttered, walking towards me and crossing his arms. "What a surprise." He looked unbothered at the fact of my disappearance. I tried to speak, but before being able to ask where Gilbert was, my body shifted sideways, and my vision started to become blurry.

"Clara?" I turned around. Gilbert stood by the entrance of the hotel. I leaned on the closest white wall next to me. Shivers went through my body. I wanted to walk towards Gilbert. To stay balanced. But my feet failed at their main job. So I let the darkness drag me deep into a safe place until I felt nothing at all.

CHAPTER 14
EIDETIC POWERS

T HE SOUND OF GLASS AND METAL crashing into each other was what woke me up. Or maybe my body reminded me how hungry I was in my sleep. The soft blanket protected my body from the cold air. I still wore the soaked clothing from last night. I shook a bit as I put the blanket aside and slowly got up.

Clearly, I was in Gilbert and Killian's hotel suite. Two suitcases stood inside the closet in front of me, one black and the other white. Clothes of opposite colors hung from the racket. On one side were the white, beige sunlight colors, and on the other the black, blue night colors. There were only a few color mismatches here and there.

I sat up on one of the twin beds. On the other beside it was a neat pile of clothing. I suspected that was for me. Once again the blue jeans, brown long-sleeved shirt, and brown coat fitted me nicely. Even if it was during bad circumstances, at least now I knew why they did.

I agonizingly made my way into the kitchen, where the sound was coming from. The hotel suite gave gray, white, and rustic color combinations. Sunlight spread from the two windows throughout the living room and kitchen. I squinted. From the counter to the fridge and stove, Gilbert walked quickly around the gray kitchen. Cooking. And a sweet mouth-watering smell filled the entire space.

"Good morning," Gilbert smiled, looking up while holding a cooking pot filled with what seemed to be hot chocolate. I half-smiled back, feeling a bit uncomfortable all of a sudden.

I heard a shift in the living room. Killian sat on the gray couch, reading a book from the tiny shelf beside it. He smirked, looking at me. I rolled my eyes.

"Morning to you too, cupcake," Killian said. "How is it going?"

"Pretty amazing, *considering* you're here." I crossed my arms. He sighed and went back to 'read' the book.

"I'm sorry that he is here. He has more strength," Gilbert explained, his face somewhat sympathetic.

"I know," I replied. Gilbert got more ingredients out of the refrigerator. "Thank you for the clothing, by the way."

"Killian already knew your size..." He looked at me, furrowing his brows. Killian had told him everything that happened between us those few days in London.

"Right. I happen to clearly remember," I said. Killian closed his book abruptly. Gilbert and I wavered a smile at each other. He concentrated deeply on cooking and baking, while still looking from Killian to me. Killian turned to look at me, waiting for me to speak, but I had no idea where to even start.

"You didn't manage your *death wish*," Killian sneered, breaking the silence.

"That's because I don't have one," I responded.

"Sure, you don't, darling."

"We were trying to contact you for the past few days," Gilbert added.

"By *We*, he means himself," Killian corrected.

I sat down on the couch, in front of Killian, my legs weakening. I hadn't eaten in days and running away had made me physically fragile. "About that... *we* have a huge problem," I began, staring at Killian. He frowned in curiosity.

Gilbert offered me a plate of delicious-looking breakfast that thankfully didn't include pancakes. I could've devoured the omelet if I wasn't talking at the same time. *Start at the beginning.* I told them everything from when I received the ticket to Kosmos, when I met Kaan, what I overheard, my powers, our powers, to when I ran away and found them (well... except the part about how exactly I found them). Killian looked expressionless, and Gilbert nodded, eating chocolate cookies at the same time.

"So, this Kaan... is the king of Kosmos," Killian questioned. I slowly opened the soggy folded Kosmos map I had in the pocket last night and showed it to them, the ink still intact.

"Not exactly, he is part of both Solar and Stellar Court. He and other court members in Stellar Court make the overall decisions."

"Kaan didn't want anyone to know about you or your powers?" asked Gilbert. I nodded. After a few seconds, he said, "Why did you break in?"

Curiosity. I thought. But was it only curiosity? Did I go there to just find out the truth and not do anything? *No. I did not.*

"Illuminators are supposed to *maintain* balance. As far as we know witches are trying to ally with new Illuminators to get rid of vampires and I think that's not fair. And I wanted to figure out more about... everything," I admitted. I had been waiting my entire life to do something more than just go to work and live normally. Of course, my life before knowing I was an Illuminator was still great, but I remembered the way I would read fiction books. How I had a spark of hope that magic was real, how as I grew older I had forgotten that spark. But I felt it again. An actual power that was mine, a power I could use for good.

"Sounds pretty cultivating *considering* you wanted nothing to do with the supernatural," Killian teased.

"Shut up, Killian."

He sat up on the sofa, clearing his throat. "Fine. *In other words*, it was all mere curiosity."

I gave a slight nod. "Yes, but after the ball... I thought something more was going on."

"Not surprising that witches would do anything to make vampires disappear," Killian continued. I silently agreed with him.

"So, Stellar Court could be planning to fight vampires with the help of Illuminators. And Kaan is after you and Killian for another reason," said Gilbert, sitting back on the sofa next to me. *Maybe a selfish one.* I thought.

"That's a theory. He is either with Stellar Court, planning something on his own, or both."

"Now, what is the long-term plan?" Killian asked, looking at me for an answer. I shook my head.

"That's the problem... I don't know. But I *do* know that we need to find a way to stop the anti-vampire groups or Stellar Court without getting caught by Kaan first."

Gilbert and I sat next to the kitchen countertop while we ate more delicious food and chocolate pastries he had made in silence. Killian had to leave for a while. "Life or death situation," he said. The clock kept ticking, mocking my thinking for a plan. Nothing would come up. Without having other people who could give us information, we were helpless. I couldn't call my friends, who were still in Kosmos, and they probably hadn't received their phones yet. I tried to call Milana with Gilbert's cell phone just in case but no response. Same thing with my memory power. For the first time, I couldn't move forward.

It was around two hours after waking up when Gilbert and I sat in the living room once again. The opened windows brought downtown noise inside, making the day feel more normal.

"Clara, thank you for trying to get more information... for helping us." Gilbert stood by the window, his eyes staring into space.

"I'm sorry that I couldn't even figure out anything about your parents' death."

He shook his head, starting to sit next to me. "I understand. With everything going on, you could've died multiple times."

"If things go sideways, I could always turn into a vampire," I mumbled.

"You don't mean that, do you?"

"I don't know," I spoke. "I had considered it when I was young, but now that everything is *so* real. I don't think I would like to be a vampire. Besides, can you even be an Illuminator and a vampire at the same time?" There were pros to being a vampire. But being lonely and watching everyone you love grow old was the worst con. I didn't think I could ever handle so much pain and I didn't want to.

"Haven't heard that story before, so maybe not..." he said, shaking his head. "I don't recommend it... becoming a vampire I mean."

"To be like Killian. Absolutely not." I couldn't even imagine knowing and being bothered by Killian for a lifetime. Actually dying seemed to be the normal and best option.

"Then that makes my gift much more meaningful." He got up from the couch and went towards a drawer in the kitchen. After getting something from the shelf, he walked back to the couch, sitting next to me. In his hands, he held a small black box with a white bow in it.

"A small late birthday present." He opened the box and held a small clear test tube with a red liquid. I couldn't tell what it was until he shook it a bit.

"Your blood?"

"Light blood and Illuminator blood to kill vampires, right?" He held out the small box to me. I took it carefully. "Just in case you ever need it," he added.

"Can I use it on Killian?" I half-smiled, unsure if I was trying to be sarcastic or not. His face turned somber.

"He told me everything, Clara," he clarified. "Trust me when I say that neither of us were in the forest that night. And as far as I can tell, in this case, he is telling the truth. You should talk to him."

I sat up. "I don't blame you, Gilbert. You have been an amazing friend since the beginning, and Killian is your friend, so I understand..."

"*But?*" he said, waiting for my second response.

I shook my head. "*But* to be honest, I can't even look at him. Every time I do, I feel so angry that I want to slap him or something."

But not kill him. I had been waiting for Killian to mess up on something else, something where I could hurt him. If he ever did, would I want to kill him too? Maybe I wouldn't because he was still Gilbert's friend. I couldn't kill his closest friend. That would be as if someone killed Dani.

"Still, I'm sorry, Clara. I would've tried to stop him if I had known everything else," Gilbert said, looking at me, his head lowering.

"I know," I said in the silence. "But... if you still feel sorry. You *can* give me the recipes for the amazing pastries you made."

He shook his head. "Nice try. Those recipes will go with me to my grave."

"Really?! Pinky swears I won't tell anyone," I half-laughed. "Not even a small, *tiny* hint?"

He shook his head again and got up from the couch. I got up as well, looking at the clock that stood next to the entrance door.

The small box was in my hands as I walked back to the kitchen.

"I have to go finish some bakery business errands," Gilbert said, grabbing his bag and computer from the table. "You can stay if you like to wait for your clothes to dry. The door automatically closes anyway."

"Thank you." I nodded and slightly waved the box. "And Gilbert, I do trust you." The solemn look on his face disappeared, replaced by a slight smile I watched before he turned around.

The second he closed the door, I checked on the bed sheets and clothes I had thrown into the washer and dryer earlier. They were dry already. I fixed the bed, folded my clothes into a plastic bag, and headed out of the suite. I walked downstairs to the first floor, eager to get home. Killian stood at the bar talking quietly with Gilbert. I walked faster the second we made eye contact. I guessed Gilbert noticed and turned around to look at me. Then, he approached me.

"Is something wrong?" I asked him, stopping. His face was with slight concern and confusion as always.

"No, it's not a big deal. Are you okay?" he asked. I crossed my arms and yawned.

"Yes. I'm just really tired and have a lot of errands to do, so I'm heading home. If anything..."

"I'll let you know Clara." Gilbert smiled, his brown bag over his shoulder. "You can always come either way."

"Well, I'll see you later."

"Yes."

"And don't let Killian follow please."

He turned around to look at Killian drinking from a glass cup at the bar. "I don't think I'll need to stop him. But just so you know, between the past situations and now, you would be safer with him."

I shook my head, not sure what to say to him. Not even sure what I felt about Killian. "Bye." I waved, walking towards the exit of the beige building.

Five knocks on the door and I already knew who it was. I had planned to go to the mobile shop to get a new phone. Yet I had woken up an hour earlier with my head spinning in circles and gurgling in my stomach, making me feel sick about every ten minutes. I got up from the couch, the empty medicine bottle falling to the floor. I managed enough strength to head to the door and open it. Johnny stood across from me, his smile disappeared from his face at the sight of me.

"Clara, are you okay?" I nodded, closing the door behind him. He grabbed my shoulders. "You look sick. Have you ever eaten anything?"

"A sandwich."

"Since when?" Johnny frowned.

"Yesterday... I'm not that hungry really. Everything seems disgusting to me." He touched my forehead with the front of his hand. "Oh god, you are burning up."

"I drank medicine," I mumbled. "Don't worry it won't take long to work its magic."

"Magic? You and your old imagination." He raised his eyebrows at me. "*Magic* doesn't exist, Clara. And you are truly ill. Now, come on, sit down." He walked me back to the couch. "I'll make you something to eat and go to the store afterward."

I flopped back into comfort, pulling up the flowery quilt back over my body. I missed the warmth of the Sun, but opening the balcony curtains over two inches made my head hurt even more. As if he had read my mind, Johnny walked to the balcony, opening the doors slightly enough to hear noise from outside. "The noise will make you feel better."

"I need silence," I said. "And peace... no offense. Of course I like having you here Johnny." I closed my eyes, hearing him move things around in the kitchen. From metal pans and the fridge door. I had no idea what he was making until he came to sit next to me probably ten minutes later.

"Oatmeal and orange juice." Johnny beamed at me. I slowly got up, wrinkling my nose at the sight of the food.

"I am not eating that. I think I'm going to be more sick if I do," I said, shaking my head.

"But you love breakfast, including oatmeal and orange juice," Johnny frowned.

"I don't know, it doesn't seem as appetizing to me as it used to."

"In that case." He got up, took the plates to the kitchen island, and came back with another white plate. "A sandwich then again. Just eat and maybe I can bring you lunch later." I grabbed the plate. Even though I had eaten one the day before, a sandwich definitely smelled better than anything else for breakfast.

"Thank you, Johnny. You are truly like a brother to me," I said, taking a bite out of the sandwich.

He smiled back. "I had called you to check out how it was going since you said you would only take a few days in London. But you didn't answer, and I got worried, so I came. I was actually about to leave thinking you were still gone."

I swallowed the piece of sandwich, feeling my throat burn a bit. "I lost my phone on the way here. Long story," I said when he looked at me, eyes wide in curiosity. "And *mentally* gone, but I'm still physically here. Thanks to you I will survive. I have no idea what I would do without you, truly."

He tilted his head, watching me eat. I knew he probably wouldn't leave until I was done. I was already halfway through the sandwich when Johnny returned from cleaning the plates and kitchen. "You did have time to clean though, of course."

"It didn't look perfect," I responded. I had started to have a runny nose and shivers, but I didn't think I would get sick. I rarely did.

"I will call Dani, tell her you are sick, and I will come late to work," Johnny said, coming back to sit down.

"No!" I looked up at him, swallowing the last piece of sandwich. "You can't be late, and you can't let anyone know. Please, Johnny, don't say anything to anyone. *Especially* Dani, we're already slow in progress at the Daily Planner. I'm taking a small break and I'm sure she needs your help. The Daily Planner needs you. Dani needs you. And I will be fine."

"You know I didn't need the entire speech." He shrugged. "It will do."

I raised a brow at him. "Besides, if you told Dani, *she* would tell Aurora, and you know how that will go..."

"Your parents would drop everything and come at once."

"Exactly." I nodded. "And thanks to you, I'll be great now. Go to work, okay?"

Johnny raised a brow. "Ok, but with one condition."

"Ok." I was fully aware of what he was planning to say.

"I'll come back with a whole meal and a movie marathon of vampire movies."

"The whole series?"

"The whole movie series and seasons for all these days you have a break."

"Fine."

"Great." He smiled, grabbing his bag and sweater from the sofa and heading out. Leaving behind the silence once again.

Time had passed by slowly and fast at the same time. Steady when I was alone but quick-paced when Johnny would come by. I had been asleep with fever and flu nonstop for a few days, falling asleep now and then. Sometimes cleaning and making myself some food. For a while, I was alone at peace. No noise. No sound. Not even my voice. I had barely woken up from a dream when I heard the five knocks at the door once again. *Gray walls slowly moved in, surrounding and suffocating me.* I had woken up, feeling out of breath and relieved that Johnny was finally here. Shivers passed through my body from the cold dream. I remembered the gray somber walls. The uncanny loneliness.

I shook the eerie thoughts out of my head the moment I met Johnny's chipper eyes. He held a bag of fast-food burgers and a box of chocolates in the other hand. I frowned at him.

"Chocolates?"

"Hector gave them to me at work... as a 'pre-date' gift." He shook the box. "Nice right?"

I nodded at him. "I guess chocolates are better than nothing I guess?" He nodded at me, entering the apartment. I closed the door and went back to the couch.

"Oh, by the way," he started, putting the bag and chocolates on the center table. "Are you still helping out that London couple?"

"What couple?"

"The one that dresses opposite of each other."

"Oh, right," I recalled, remembering the whole couple scenario of Gilbert and Killian. "Yes. Giving them a few ideas."

"Are you sure they are a couple?"

I furrowed my eyebrows at his question. "Yes. Why?"

"I bumped into one of them, the sunshine one, on my way upstairs, and he asked me if you were okay..."

"Gilbert came?"

"If that's his name... yes," Johnny said, organizing the food on the table. "I told him you were ill, and he wished you the best in your recovery. He also said he had important news. And when you could, meet him and his *friend* at their place." I sat back on the couch, turning on the TV while Johnny connected my laptop again with the HDMI cable. Whatever Gilbert had to say must have been important for him to come visit.

"So, what do you think? Couple or not?"

"Maybe they broke up with each other, Johnny," I said, looking at the screen for the last movie we wanted to watch. "Maybe that's why he wanted to meet up. But we aren't here to talk about anyone except—"

"The fact that you have been on the *wrong* team this entire series," Johnny interrupted. "I don't know what you see in vampires."

I grabbed one of the pillows behind me, hitting him in the face with it. "Haven't we rewatched the movies like a *thousand* times? Some of them aren't evil."

"But some are." Johnny moved the pillow from his face. "Don't ever turn into one, please, you'll be horrible at it."

"Not even thinking about it, John."

"Don't call me that... *Valerie*." He teased, holding out to me the wrapped burger after he sat back on the couch. The corners of my lips turned upward automatically. Looking at Johnny I really wouldn't have known what to do without his presence. I missed Dani too. But I had spent more time at the library with him than with Dani out at parties that I didn't always fit in to.

We stayed up late debating the best main characters and watching the movie bloopers. Only if Dani had been here, it would've been more chaotic. Yet she hadn't answered Johnny's five calls after work. "She had left early to run some errands anyway," he informed. I hoped she was doing well.

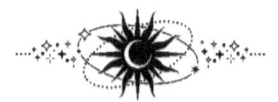

Black coats were my favorite when the Sun shone bright during cold weather. Even then, entering Gilbert and Killian's hotel building, I could feel the warmness of the heater in my face and through my skin. Gilbert sat on one of the brown lobby sofas, this time reading a book, while Killian sat on a stool at the bar. He turned to look at me as if he had sensed my presence from afar, but I approached Gilbert first. At the sound of my boots coming closer, he looked up. "Clara."

"Gilbert." I smiled. "Good morning."

"Good morning." He closed his book, putting it on the side table next to the sofa. "How are you? I met with one of your friends..."

"Johnny."

"Yes." Gilbert stood up. "He told me you got sick."

"I'm better now, thank you," I said, still feeling Killian's stare from behind Gilbert's silhouette. "Johnny said there was something important you needed to talk about..." I continued, moving to the right to hide away from Killian's stare.

"It isn't a considerable method, but Killian has a plan that can help us stop the witches."

"What is it?"

"He called some of his vampire friends. They informed him that they are coming together at a bar with a group of supernaturals, including witches, that are against the Court's beliefs. Maybe they can help with a plan to stop the hate between supernaturals. They could also help with keeping you and Killian safe, with a counter-tracking spell or something similar." We did need to be safe, at least until we figured out what to do.

"With my powers, they might be able to help me locate the *Illuminated* too."

Gilbert nodded, his eyebrows drawing together again. "But I won't be able to go with you."

I sighed and looked over his shoulder where Killian walked towards us. His white teeth in sight, arms crossed. "I'll try not to kill him," I said, quickly showing him the box he had given me from the pocket of my coat. Gilbert shook his head.

"You still need a wooden stake. Besides, he won't hurt you again and if he does, it won't be you hurting him," he joked. I shook my head at him, turning around and walking out of the hotel. He waved goodbye and turned back to his friend.

Fresh air blew over my face the moment I stepped outside the hotel. The Riverwalk was lonely in the morning, especially during the week. Only a few restaurants were open, and people sat where the sunlight could hit their skin. I didn't walk in the shadow either, the nice warmth hit my back.

"Hungry, Goldenrose?" My back froze. *Well, that didn't take long.* Killian started walking next to me, smiling. I ignored him and kept walking.

"You're still avoiding me," he said, still staying nearby until I got to the end of the Riverwalk, and I could see taxis just ahead.

"Leave me alone Killian. Just because we have a common friend *and* enemy doesn't mean I have to talk to you," I said, turning to him at once annoyed. His dark hair shined in the Sun as he moved closer to me. I stepped back at the same time, and he stopped.

"Will you come with me?" he asked. I shook my head. "We can go in my car."

"Done that," I said, walking away from him.

"It wasn't me, Clara. In the forest, I wasn't there," he admitted. "Don't be afraid of me."

After everything and Gilbert's statement, I somewhat believed him. I didn't exactly trust him, but I trusted my memory. With my powers, I would've remembered. But I didn't, which meant something else had happened. Someone else had to be involved.

"I'm not going with you, Killian." I stopped to look at him again, reminding me of the brutal memories of him in which I clearly remembered.

He fixed his posture. "Very well then, we just won't go. I'm the one that has the address, and taxis are so slow these days, don't you think?"

"Are you serious?"

He made a single nod and walked towards a black car that was parked in the same spot the black truck was parked last time. I rolled my eyes but followed him anyway.

"You don't have to come." I walked out of the office of my apartment complex, with a new key in hand. If I had known I was going on a road trip I would have probably gotten more physically and mentally ready. I insisted we should make a stop at my place so that I could get the third set of keys for my apartment, take another quick warm shower to ease my sickness, and drink more medicine. The manager, Ms. Robins, was kind enough to save my actual key in the office till I got back from *London*. She had advised me to get another set in case I lost my other keys.

"You don't keep a spare," Killian asked, following up the steps beside me.

"My parents have them. And I can't leave it under the mat or tell my parents why I need my key back. I suspected they wouldn't let me bring items to Kosmos, so I brought the simple stuff just in case, such as my phone."

"Well thought of, Goldenrose. You are a genius." He smirked.

I shook off his compliment as we approached my apartment door. "Wait here. I won't take more than fifteen minutes."

"I'll wait, love." He winked before I headed inside. As expected, I was done and out of the apartment in less than fourteen minutes.

"Your neighbor is *interesting*," Killian started as I locked my door.

"Interesting?" I asked. Jake, my neighbor, had never spoken a word to me. The only way I learned his name was when there was a pizza delivered to my door that was meant for him. Other than stumbling by him on some mornings, the cargo pants man had never even smiled. Another Adrik Montova for the matter.

"He greeted me most amusingly."

"What did he say?"

"He *asked* me if I was your boyfriend." Killian grinned. "Then I said yes..."

I turned to him and frowned. "You said *yes*?"

"The conversation was entertaining. Don't look at me with those judgy eyes," Killian waved his arms in the air. I darted a gaze at him. He continued, "When I said yes, he said 'Interesting' and left. By experience, I'm sure he is your stalker."

"Why does that concern you?" I said, now walking towards the front passenger seat of Killian's rental car.

"It doesn't. I'm letting you know what happened outside your apartment door while you were gone."

"I'm sure you made that up out of boredom."

He unlocked the car, keys dangling in his hand. "All you have to do is ask him."

"As if I would ever date you."

He grinned before getting inside the car. "As if you could ever resist me."

After the awkward conversation with Killian, we drove in peaceful silence for ten minutes along the long road. Too silent that it was starting to worry me.

"How long until we get there?" I asked, turning away from the window.

"To the bar?" Killian shook his head. "I have no idea. That's not where we are going... at least not yet."

"What? Then where are we going?!"

He didn't answer.

We drove for another five minutes, in silence again. I didn't have my actual old phone with me so I couldn't call my family or my friends to tell them I had been doing fine. The thought of them alone without me to protect them bothered me, they could be in danger for all I know. Yet, I was going away with a vampire and without a cell phone.

"Lunch," he suddenly said. Some stores appeared down the next visible street.

"I already ate, and we don't have time. We should be hiding, not be in plain sight."

"No one comes to this restaurant during the day," he informed. I glared at him. "Don't worry. I don't plan to *eat* you."

I rolled my eyes at him. "That's comforting."

Killian made a turn into the plaza and parked in the only small restaurant around. The business sign read 'Break the Fast', and transparent pictures of nice-looking dishes and pastries hung in some of the windows. Killian got out of the truck. So did I after making sure the small, gifted box stood safely inside my coat pocket. I followed Killian towards the entrance. He opened the red door for me before I could protest.

I hated admitting that Killian was right. *But* he was right, only four people were sitting down. Two women sat quietly eating and two men talked in low voices. Killian walked in front of me and sat at a table by the window. I sat in front of him, looking around and avoiding his annoying stare. In less than a second, the waiter came to get our order.

"What can I get for you." The red-headed girl twinkled, holding in her hands a small notebook. She stood closer to Killian and eyed him closely.

"Hi! I will have a chocolate muffin and a hot coffee with five pumps of caramel syrup," I demanded.

The girl nodded silently, continuing to look at Killian.

"I will have a strawberry pie and a plain hot coffee," Killian said, staring at her and back at me. The girl flashed her lashes at him. "Of course."

"You know her?" I asked after she was out of sight.

"I've seen her before."

"That's not surprising."

He didn't say anything but just kept staring at me. I looked out the window instead, crossing my arms and scratching my nose. But it was starting to get annoying and awkward after two minutes. I was out of breath, feeling my heart beating faster with every second that passed. "I'll be right back."

I walked off from the intimidating situation, trying to slow down my pace. Once in the restroom, I could breathe again. *Why am I sweating?* I paced for a few seconds, trying to calm down. Then, washed my face with cold water, fixed the strand of hair sticking out my half-ponytail, and headed back to the table. The girl who had taken our order was sitting on my seat, saying something to Killian. The wooden tray with our food stood on the table. She stood up and looked at me up and down. I approached them, faking a smile.

"Hi again! *We* are in a hurry. So, would you be *so* kind as to put this in a bag to go," I grabbed the tray and slightly shoved it towards her. "Thanks!"

She vaguely smiled and left with the tray. I rolled my eyes at Killian and walked outside to wait for him.

After about two minutes, he came out of the restaurant holding the bag and smiling.

"Really, Killian?! We don't have time for this."

"Is that what you are mad for?" He smirked mischievously.

"Or is something else bothering you, Goldenrose?"

I shook my head, unable to keep my annoyance under control. "You know what? What's bothering me is that you seem to *forget* I'm not your puppet anymore, Killian! And honestly, I can't even tell what's more pathetic. The fact that you were bored with your life to compel someone to hang out with you or that you're a coward about it," I ranted. He stood there with no response. And I felt a small dust of regret, even though I meant every word. With nothing else to say, I got into the car, holding tightly the small box that Gilbert had given me. My head pounded but I wasn't sure if it was because I was angry, actually hungry, or both.

I checked my watch for what felt like the twentieth time. It only had been three minutes after we got out of the restaurant when Killian broke the silence and said, "Someone is following us."

"What?" I turned around to look out the window. A black car followed behind us, two men sat in the front, the same men that had been in the restaurant.

"We have to lose them," I said. "Fast."

"Don't you think I know that, love?" Killian drove faster and turned onto a lonely and less busy street. "Come on," he said, honking the horn. The two cars in front of us moved out of the way, but others kept driving slowly. Suddenly, a black truck appeared from another street, almost stopping our tracks. Killian drove quickly past it, passing the red light and turning into a deserted road. They still followed.

Out of nowhere, a fire started to ignite from the trees. That would mean that it was either Illuminators or witches that were following us.

"It might be an illusion," I said. The trees fired up one by one next to us.

"Is this an illusion too?" Ahead of us, stood a dark tunnel. I looked around for my phone until realizing I didn't have one.

"What is your password?" I asked, grabbing Killian's phone.

"143GR," he said. I opened it. A notification of a message showed up on the screen. *Your Appointment with Zhaak has been accepted for tonight at 9 pm.* I didn't pay much attention to it, proceeding to search for our location on the map.

"No, it isn't. The tunnel isn't an illusion." The map showed the long dark tunnel, it had been there for a few years. Entering the tunnel felt like entering a portal. Dark, quiet, lonely until you could see the light. Except this wasn't the case. The tunnel was a few miles long with no visible light and no cars but ours to light up the road ahead. I couldn't tell if we were still being followed until more flames appeared behind us.

"Any bright ideas, Ms. Illuminator?" Killian said.

I frowned at him at the sudden change of nickname. "I'm working on that, Mr. Vampire." I closed my eyes and tried to concentrate under the stress. The purple-blue light shined between my hands. It expanded slowly around me, then around the entire car like the purple barrier that protected Kosmos. Killian drove faster. We were able to see a bit of the road ahead of us with the purple-blue light. The fire behind us stopped the moment it hit the barrier. But it didn't stop the people from following us. The other end of the tunnel was just ahead along with an intersection that could take us back home.

"Can't you use your powers? Make them forget?" I asked, filled with adrenaline.

"Yes, I can. Downside: It only works on two people at a time. But I can't do that if I'm concentrating on not crashing," he responded, out of breath.

I hesitated. "We have to switch, quickly."

"I won't let you die, Goldenrose," he reassured. He swiftly jumped to the backseat with his vampire speed. I grabbed the steering wheel. The car went slightly sideways as I moved to the driver's seat. I balanced the car back to the road before we went straight to the wall.

"Are you ok?" Killian asked.

"Yes." He turned around watching the drivers of the cars behind us.

"*Oblivio*," he murmured.

From the rear mirror, I could see the driver of the black car panicking. The truck behind them stopped as well. It almost worked. But another car behind them still followed us quickly.

"I can't use my powers until the five minutes of their forgetfulness is up," Killian said. "We have to keep driving."

"I think I know where to go," I urged, remembering the way close to town.

CHAPTER 15
FOR GILBERT

I T WAS THE CLOSEST IDEA I had in mind to lose them. I wasn't sure how many people were in the car, but they still followed behind us. Killian's power could've been more helpful if there were fewer restrictions. Even after five minutes, each team followed one at a time. I had been to this mall only once. Today it was crowded like it was the weekend.

"If you wanted to go shopping, you know you could've just told me, Goldenrose," Killian said. I rolled my eyes at him.

"Hiding in between people, they won't find us," I explained. I quickly drove around the parking building to find a hidden parking spot and got out of the car to get inside the mall. Before entering the entrance that was a few feet away from us, a black truck and car stopped abruptly, closing in on us. Two people got out of each car and walked towards us. I quickly created a memory shield around me and Killian, glad that humans couldn't see the magic unless it was intended.

"Who are you?" I asked, turning to each person, inspecting their moves, and trying to look at their wrist. Two of them were Illuminators: one Earthkalai Aires and one Celestialkalai Illusionary.

"Your friends are so easy to bribe," the man I had seen in the restaurant said. He looked at Killian. "You saved us a lot of time by stopping in the restaurant."

"Who sent you?" I asked this time. The man's eyes fixated on me.

"You must be Clara. The entire Kosmos is looking for you. I'm going to receive a hell of a lot of money when I send the holders of the Eidetic powers to Kaan from Stellar Court."

"You are wasting *your* time if you think that's going to happen, mate," Killian said, looking back and forth between me and the man. He slightly nodded at me, and I released the protection wall. We started running towards the entrance. With a lot of people in the mall, none of us were able to use magic inside. Even if they couldn't see it, our hand movements and actions would attract a lot of eyes. Almost every store with a sales sign was crowded. The most famous stores even had waiting lines outside to stop the huge crowds. Killian could've run faster than me, but he moved at my pace in between the people. The witches and Illuminators still followed behind trying to walk at a normal fast pace to avoid stares. I turned around, and the man who had spoken earlier was only a few feet away.

"Over here, love." Killian and I blended into the crowd ahead of us. There was a band in the middle of the mall, people surrounded them, cheered, and sang along.

"Clara, come on we need to run more ahead," Killian said. I walked next to him into a less crowded store. We entered the large store, hiding in between the women's clothing.

"We should go to the first floor. There must be an exit down below," I said. Killian walked in front of me, getting his phone out of his pocket. He grabbed a lonely man who was inspecting cologne by a fragrance counter.

"Hello there, mate, you will do me a huge favor," Killian said, grabbing the man by his white shirt. The man nodded obediently. "Take a good look." He showed him a picture on his phone.

"You will go outside, to the parking lot on this floor, second row to the left, and as quickly as possible find this car. Then drive it to the entrance of this store. Understood?"

"Understood." The man nodded, looking into Killian's eyes and his phone back and forth. I handed the man the keys to the car, he hurried off running. Killian looked at me.

"Let's go." I broke the stare.

A laughing couple went ahead of us on the escalator. Killian stood beside me. He was so close to me that our shoulders almost touched. I stepped a bit back so that my back touched the handrail. I inspected him as he looked around us. He looked so serious and faintly narrowed his eyes at every person he would see.

"You still have it?" I frowned, looking at the crystal necklace around his neck. Killian looked at me without responding, his eyes relaxing. Then, I looked away as we got off on the first floor from the stairs.

"Wait," I said before he took another step ahead. "I don't care why you still have it. I'm more concerned about the fact that it's glowing." He stopped and looked at the necklace. I stood in front of him, touching the crystal around his neck. A sudden memory came to me.

A small lake. Crystals underneath. Star Lake from Kosmos. Witches making a spell. Kaan's white crystal. The strange words of a spell being made.

I stood silent for a while, confused about what I saw. Killian frowned. "Well, Goldenrose I would like to know what you saw..."

"You got this from Bellives Pendants? Right?"

"Yes. What's wrong?"

I shook my head. "I think they are tracking us with this," I said, letting go of the crystal. "We need to crush it."

"Once again..." Killian smiled, raising his brows. "You are a genius."

"I'll explain more later, just take it off." He took off the necklace right away and threw it to the floor. He looked at me in assurance before stepping over it, crushing the necklace into small purple and bluish pieces.

"Hopefully, that worked," I said, walking towards the exit of the store. Killian walked behind me. His car was perfectly parked just outside. The man he had compelled got off and gave Killian the keys. "Now, forget this ever happened or that you ever saw us." Killian looked into the man's eyes. The man nodded and walked back inside the store. I saw his eyes adjusting to reality. Not long ago that was me. A confused person with unreadable memories.

"I don't understand," I said out loud, taking another sip from the hot coffee we had ordered earlier. Killian drove us back into the city, looking behind us through the rear view mirror every thirty seconds or so.

"Which part out of everything," Killian responded, his eyes now on the road.

"The crystal vision," I said, taking a look at the cars around us as well. "I saw crystals at the bottom of Star Lake, the lake from Kosmos. How could a crystal from Kosmos end up randomly at a London jewelry store?"

Killian shook his head. "It could be a coincidence. But yet again, at this point nothing is."

"Why did you give it to me? The necklace, why that one?"

"You were looking at the store..."

"Or... you were trying to show off."

"I happened to choose that one. Not sure why but I did," Killian looked at me for a second then looked back at the road. "Every person would have loved a luxurious necklace. As you remember, that includes you."

He turned to look at me again, I rolled my eyes at him remembering my reaction when I first saw the necklace. "It was a pretty necklace. I'll give you that. But that doesn't explain why I now had a vision of Star Lake when touching it, why Kaan has a similar one, or how the witches were even able to track us with it."

Killian turned to me. "Mystery after mystery, Goldenrose. Here I thought you would've loved the ride."

"If only the *ride* stopped once in a while to catch my breath or think," I responded, looking away from Killian. With everything that was going on, my mind was a non-stop loop and wondered if at some point it would explode. I stayed silent for the rest of the drive, overthinking about how the necklace was connected to Star Lake. Yet my thoughts kept being interrupted by one bothersome thing: the true reason Killian got the necklace from Bellives Pendants.

I paced back and forth in my apartment, closing my eyes and trying to remember any clue that I could have forgotten from my time in Kosmos. Everything had happened so quickly that I probably missed many things. But I couldn't think of anything important that could've helped us.

"Darling, you are making me dizzy." Killian sat on the couch watching me pace around and finishing the chocolate muffin. I glared at him for one second, annoyed at his gaze.

"They might know where you live, Clara," Gilbert said worriedly through the phone. He was on his way to my apartment. I called him to inform him about what had happened as soon as we were back in the depths of the city.

There were three quick knocks on the door. I went ahead and opened it, not before checking who it was. Gilbert entered, half-smiling, holding his phone in his hand and ending the call.

"I know, but running away is not an option," I said, watching Gilbert walking in to sit on the couch next to Killian. "We have no idea what Kaan is up to, except that he needs us for some crazy, unknown reason."

"Don't you think it's odd? He has people following us but hasn't come to the place he knows we could be," Killian said, moving his hands in the air.

"Maybe he was just trying to scare you off?" Gilbert suggested.

"Or maybe it was a distraction," I thought out loud.

"A distraction for what?"

I sat down, shaking my head, and wishing that reading minds was an Illuminator power. "I have no idea."

Maybe I ran away from Kosmos too soon. Maybe if I had stayed longer, I could've gotten more information. But I didn't, and now we were sitting ducks waiting for Kaan or anybody from Kosmos to strike. How was I going to live with that? How was anybody around me able to survive that?

"You should head to sleep, Clara," Gilbert said. "It's been a rough day. We can stay here if you'd like, just in case."

"No, it's okay. I don't think I'll sleep, anyway. But thank you." I got up from the couch. Gilbert got up after, followed by Killian.

"Right... see you tomorrow then?"

"Yes, as always," I replied. Gilbert walked to the door.

"Goodnight," he said, opening the door and walking out. Killian followed behind him, his black jacket sparkling under the kitchen lights.

"Killian... wait," I quickly said without thinking, catching me off guard. He turned around. His eyes brought shivers through me.

But not the type of shivers I expected. "Thank you."

His lips curled up, making a slight nod. "Careful, Goldenrose. You're starting to sound like you care." He winked, walking into the hallway and closing the door quietly. I went ahead and locked it, cursing *What the hell did I say?* under my breath.

I turned back to get the brown coat I had left on the couch earlier and got the blood tube out of it to put inside my purse. A phone ring suddenly sounded. I looked at the table where the sound came from. A cell phone stood on the edge of the wooden center table. I grabbed it, realizing it was Killian's phone. He knew I didn't have one at the moment and had left his on purpose. The notification on the screen caught my eye. It read *Gilbert's birthday in a few weeks. Meet the warlock for Gil's information at 9 pm.*

I frowned upon it, wondering why I didn't know Gilbert's birthday was coming up and why Killian was meeting a warlock for information. What information did Killian need about Gilbert? The realization hit me. I quickly grabbed my brown coat and purse, leaving my apartment at once.

I hoped Killian hadn't left yet. It was getting colder by the hour and the breeze made my hair flow in the air as I walked to the parking lot. Killian's rental car was still parked in the same spot, but no one was inside. I looked around. Killian was nowhere in sight either. I walked towards the car and checked if the back seat doors were open. They were, which meant that Killian was somewhere around. I got inside, placed my brown coat on the seat, and hid in the shadow of the passenger seat. It wasn't until a few seconds later when from afar, I saw Killian get out of the apartment community office holding a closed glass bottle and a rectangular snack in his hands. He had probably gone inside to get food from the snack machines by the public gym. I hid quickly back into place. He opened the door to the black car, placing both the bottle and snack in the cupholder. The second he closed the door, I sat in the middle of the backseat. He turned around at once when he sensed me.

"Clara, what are you doing?" He half-shouted, frowning but not exactly frightened. I showed him the phone.

"You never told me Gilbert's birthday was coming up?" I lifted my eyebrows, showing him the notification. He grabbed the phone from my hand.

"Get out, lovely Clara," he sighed, shaking his head.

I shook my head. "I won't. Aren't you going to meet a warlock to figure out what happened with Gilbert's parents?"

"Not surprised you figured that out. But I'm going alone. So, Goldenrose... get out," he demanded with a grin.

I shook my head again. "I won't because I'm going with you." I stood up and jumped into the passenger's seat. Killian just stared at me as I put my belt on.

"Well then." I sat back, nodding my head at the wheel. "Go on."

He sighed. "You are unbelievable." He shook his head.

"I was a *genius* earlier." I gloated at him, finding his annoyance funny. I saw him smirk in the shadows, driving out of the parking lot.

We drove for about thirty minutes to the outskirts of San Antonio as stars in the sky started showing up.

"Where exactly is this place anyway?" I asked.

"A house," Killian responded, making twisted turns around a deserted forest.

"In the middle of nowhere?"

"They like isolation. Zhaak and his wife." He made another right turn into a more lighted-up but deserted street. Only from afar, I was able to see two houses. The radio faltered with every second we drove into the street and slowly stopped when at the same time a sudden crashing sound was heard from the front of the car. Killian frowned as the car slowed down the rocky road.

"What just happened?" I said, watching the car completely stop.

Killian shook his head. "I knew I should have kept the truck... wait here."

He got out of the car, opened the hood, and checked around. The bottle of mocha iced coffee and a strawberry fruit grain bar sat in the cupholder. *Of course, strawberries.* I sat inside the car for only one minute, then sighed, and got out with Killian's phone in my hand. He stood in front of the hood, moving things around.

I checked his phone. "There is no service."

"What in the hell is this?" he whispered angrily, walking back inside the car, trying to turn it on and failing. He came back to the front of the hood, his hands dirty from grease and oil.

I shook my head at him. "Do you think you can fix it?"

"You should've asked this before getting into the car," he half-laughed.

"Wow, something that Killian cannot fix. Finally, I know you are not invincible Mr. Killian Walker," I taunted. "How many years have you been alive again?"

He smirked. "And you know how to fix it, smart pants?"

I shook my head. "My dad was a detective. He took his cars to the auto shop... and the times he fixed them I was working. But I can try to see his memory and find a clue about the problem."

He shook his head, brooding.

"So, you think you can fix it or not?" I asked.

He nodded. "Of course. Now, it's a matter of honor," he whispered, frustrated. I walked back towards the car to get my brown coat. Once I put it on, I came back to light the built-in flashlight on the phone towards the engine where Killian couldn't see.

"This is beyond me." He said after three minutes. "We have to walk towards Zhaak's house."

"Okay then," I teased. He made a slight glare at me to which I raised my brows by the sudden act. "I didn't say anything." He walked towards the back of the car to get a clean black shirt. I turned around when I saw he was going to put it on.

"Goldenrose, if you want to look at me all you have to do is ask." He mocked. I sighed, my cheeks starting to get warm in the dark.

"Just hurry, Killian." I heard the trunk close, a car door closed, and doors being locked a few seconds later.

"Come on, De Rose," Killian said, appearing beside me and walking past me. I followed next to him, the smell of wintergreen circling in the air.

I crossed my arms tightly, hearing the cracking of branches moving around us. Killian held out the bottle of coffee.

"Thanks," I said. He smirked, opening the strawberry grain bar wrapper.

"Want some?" he said, biting into the bar.

"No, thanks. You?" I asked, showing him the bottle. He shook his head.

I took a sip of the delicious coffee. We walked in silence until the second I heard something moving in the forest. I moved closer to Killian.

"I thought you said you weren't scared." Killian raised a brow.

"I'm not." I shook my head. "I'm an Illuminator and you are a vampire. I have nothing to be scared of." He smirked. "Get over yourself, Killian. I can kill you."

"Likewise," he said. I frowned at him. "But I won't."

I rolled my eyes, watching him glance at the time on his phone before putting it in his pocket. "I thought you weren't a planner?"

Killian tilted his head. "Are we asking each other normal questions now?"

"*Trust 101*, remember?"

"Zhaak sends the notifications automatically and..."

"And it saved on your calendar," I finished his sentence. "Got it."

He nodded, taking another bite from the grain bar. I stared intently at the forest surrounding us. No matter how much greenery I saw, the hidden forest night memory never re-surfaced. At this point, it was not worth spending a second overthinking about it.

I turned to Killian, finding another question hovering in my head. "What you are doing for Gilbert, why now? Hasn't it been five years?"

"Five years without knowing the exact truth." He shook his head. "I never brought it up. He wanted to figure it out on his own. He went to the crime scenes and questioned the police department. And nothing. Then I found a warlock, made a deal, and here we are."

I nodded and stayed silent. At least there was something both Killian and I agreed on. Gilbert was a good person, and he deserved to know the truth about his parents' unknown death.

We walked silently when Killian started smiling.

"What are you smiling about?" I asked.

He shook his head. "Nothing."

"Now, you have to tell me because—"

"You are curious." He finished my sentence, shaking his head.

"Are you not saying?" I glared at him. "Ok then... but I do have another question."

"Ask me."

"How do you manage to stay calm all the time? You are a vampire, but all of this seems normal to you."

"Well, Clara De Rose. Welcome to *Vampirism 101*," he lectured. "Getting used to immortality for years. Just enjoy life."

"Enjoy life? Right? Because you don't have to worry about dying..." I replied, half-smiling.

"Are you scared of dying?" he asked, looking at me seriously.

"Some part of me. Yes," I said. "But I'm more scared of dying and not being remembered."

He half-smiled again. "Dear Clara, *I*, as one the Eidetic holders of forgetfulness, would never forget you." I was unsure of what to say. But my head surrounded itself with the word. *You.* Irene had said that magic was unpredictable. As the Eidetic holder of forgetfulness, only Killian could fully forget me, if his power counteracted. *You can forget me, Killian. And I would be the one to remember it all.*

"I have another question," Killian continued. "When you portaled from Kosmos, how did you know where we were?"

I looked away from his eyes, hoping the dark could consume me because I couldn't fully lie. "I saw your memories..."

"You wouldn't be able to see them unless you had a connection to me?" He stopped in his tracks, staring at me.

I let out a sigh. "There's only one thing connecting us," I looked at him, "and that's our friendship with Gilbert. Nothing more."

"Sure, love," Killian responded. "But not believable." I ignored his reply, only to walk forward. He glanced at me every few seconds without saying anything, and I was glad it was dark; that the breeze freshened up my face.

We took a turn, walking past the two houses we had seen. A large house stood at the end of the street. As we walked closer, I could see the bright red color of the house. A porch light lit the entrance and only a downstairs window showed signs of life inside. Once on the doorstep, Killian pressed the doorbell. I heard shuffling behind the door.

"Hello. Please state your names," the voice of a woman spoke through the speaker next to the door ring.

"Killian Walker and Clara De Rose. *We* had an appointment

with Zhaak," Killian informed.

"Come on in." There was a sound of a lock turning, and a woman in a flowy pastel green dress opened the door and greeted us.

"Zhaak, darling. It's Killian Walker," she said gently behind her. A man in a black robe appeared from the vine-filled stairs behind her.

"Killian Walker! Come on in." He walked downstairs, opening his arms to hug Killian.

We walked inside the earthy house. A blend of brown and green filled the entire structure. The walls shone in a glossy brown rustic color and plants hung from every space they could be hung from. Killian smiled as he hugged Zhaak.

"And this is?" frowned Zhaak, fixing a strand of sky blue over his black hair.

"I'm Clara De Rose. Nice to meet you, sir," I said, extending my arm.

"Don't call me '*sir*'. I'm Zhaak." He hugged me quickly, smelling like soil and salt. "And this is my wife, Ava."

"Nice to meet you," Ava said, smiling at me and Killian. I smiled back.

"Ava, can you help me set up the floor, please? No time to waste," Zhaak said, walking to the living room. Ava followed behind, her dress flowing in the air.

"They seem friendly," I whispered to Killian.

"Beyond friendly," Killian responded as we walked to the living room. Different aromas and scents surrounded the entire home. I had just entered a candle store.

"Please, sit." Zhaak nodded at the orange pillows on the wooden floor. "Do you have the picture?"

Killian searched inside his jacket pocket. He got out a picture of Gilbert and his parents when he was younger and handed it to Zhaak. Ava placed four white candles around the four orange pillows and with a flick of the wrist Zhaak lit them up.

The four of us sat in a circle. I sat in between Killian and Ava. In the middle lay Gilbert's photo, a green candle, and a salt-made circle.

"Everyone hold hands," Zhaak said. "We will start the spell."

"Is that necessary?" I asked. Zhaak nodded, closing his eyes, and opening his arms. Ava did the same, grabbing Zhaak's hand and mine. Her hand was soft and warm. I looked at Killian, he beamed, holding out his hand. I rolled my eyes at him, grabbing his hand and expecting it to be cold. Except, it was the exact opposite. His warm hand counteracted my cold one. I closed my eyes at once.

"Breathe in and breathe out. I will start the spell that will help us see the specific memory we are looking for. With the photo, we will all search, see, and hear the same thing," Zhaak informed. He started chanting a spell in Latin and my mind shifted to another place immediately.

"Albert," a woman in a green jacket asked tiredly. "Do you remember our first hike with him?" Albert shook his head, smiling in the air.

"Of course, I do, Gillie. It was hardly a tiny mountain. I had to carry him for half of the entire hike," the man named Albert behind her smiled. Gilbert's parents. They laughed at the thought.

"Are we almost there?" Gillie wondered after a minute.

"Not yet. The cabin is on the other side. Down a deserted mud road," Albert responded. He wore a green vest and carried a black backpack.

"I understand they chose a far cabin for their safety, but this place is still dangerous." Gillie sighed as she climbed up the lifeless mountain.

"I know, but you know why we need to meet the light-bloods. They are the only ones we have met in England, and they know much more," Albert responded. "We need to do this no matter what... for Gilbert."

Gillie nodded. "For Gilbert." She whispered.

They climbed for a few minutes, without speaking. Saving their breaths for each step. Everything was serene. The warm breeze moved Gillie's long curly hair, making her ponytail messy. Albert mumbled under his breath, frustrated at the sight of flies over his brown eyes.

"What was that?" Gillie asked the second the ground moved in the slightest.

"Hold yourself. I think it's an earthquake," Albert screamed. The mountain shook more abruptly with every passing second. Rocks at the top fell at once down the mountain.

"Albert, we are not going to make it," Gillie said. "Just in case, I love you!"

"No, we have to!" Albert shot back, a worried look on his face. He pointed at the tree a few feet away. Gillie nodded, trying to walk towards it and failing to move upward. She looked up at the mountain and then at Albert. Her face was filled with both sweat and tears. Instead of trying to walk towards the tree, she walked

down to Albert, grabbing his hand.

"I love you," Albert whispered to Gillie once they were close. The earthquake wouldn't stop, and even if it had slowed down only for a second, it didn't stop the rockfall. Gillie and Albert fell, following the pace of the large falling rocks. The earthquake stopped in twenty seconds, but it was too late to save their lives.

A knock was heard at the door of Mr. William Gram's house. His face was so similar to Albert's, almost like he was his twin. He walked towards the door, passing the kitchen where Mary Gram baked pastries. He opened the door.

"Hello, are you a relative of Mr. Albert Gram?" the officer asked.

"Yes, I am his brother," William frowned. Mary stood next to William at once.

"Sir, I regret to inform you that Albert Gram and his wife had a terrible accident. They have passed away," the officer said. "These are the hospital and case details." He held out a yellow envelope which the brother took in disbelief. William shook his head and Mary started crying.

"Sorry for your loss," the officer said, turning around to leave.

"What?" a soft mumbling voice said behind them. They both turned behind them to see the silhouette of a fifteen-year-old Gilbert. He stood shocked and ran to his room.

"Gilbert, you have to eat, honey," Mary said. It was late at night, and he wore a black suit, matching Mary's dress and William's suit.

"Come on, son. You didn't eat the entire day," William pleaded.

"I'm not hungry. If you'll excuse me," Gilbert whispered, standing up from his chair and walking out of the house. He walked down the forest path, crying until he got to the daisy landscape and sat down to stare at the picture where his parents and him stood happily.

"Clara. Clara..." The voice of Killian brought back. Everyone had their eyes opened. Zhaak and Ava frowned at me. Ava's hand was no longer in mine. But I had been holding Killian's hand too tightly. A tear dropped down my cheek.

"I'm sorry," I said, wiping the tears away and standing up at once. "Excuse me. I need some air." I walked towards the entrance door, got out of the warm house, and walked in the direction of the car.

"Clara." Killian followed behind me, grabbing my arm gently. I turned around to look at him, wiping away the tears in my eyes. He stood silently, frowning.

"I'm okay." I looked at him, moving my arm away from him.

"So, where is the broken-down car we need to fix?!" Zhaak appeared from behind, saving me from the edge of crying more. "There is no car here."

"You guys should go fix the car," I suggested, not fully meeting Killian's eyes yet.

Killian nodded. "This way." And walked away towards the street, looking back at me for a second. Zhaak followed behind him, glancing at me as he did.

"Would you like some tea?" Ava asked gently from the doorway.

"Yes... that would be nice." I walked back into the house and let the fresh air dry my face from the fallen tears.

The scent of vanilla passed through me from the oil diffuser standing a few feet away, bringing me sudden peace. I sat on the chair, my hands on top of the countertop. Ava's footsteps were soundless as she walked around the kitchen, placing two white cups the middle of the counter, inches away from my hand. She sat next to me with ease.

"You and Mr. Walker seem to care so much about your friend," she said softly as I took a sip from one of the white cups. *Green tea*.

"We do." I nodded. "Gilbert has been a great friend. Since I've met him, we have gotten along very easily."

"What about Mr. Walker?" She frowned, starting to drink from her cup. I shook my head without responding.

"I'm not sure we are at the *friends* part."

"You can't both care about the same person without caring for one another," Ava acknowledged, placing her cup back on the countertop. I stayed silent, wondering whether she was right. The only connection Killian and I would ever have was Gilbert. The only reason we were even talking was for Gilbert. We both cared for him, but did we care for each other? Did I care for Killian? Did he care for me?

I took a sip of tea, trying to erase my thoughts.

"You should get ahead. They must be done," Ava said suddenly, getting out of her chair. "Zhaak may be a warlock, but he does know a lot about cars."

"Thank you." I smiled at her, getting out of my chair. She grabbed the cups, turning the counter corner back to the kitchen sink.

Killian and Zhaak stood next to the black rental car, now parked by the driveway, talking quietly. Once Killian saw me, he nodded. Zhaak turned around and waved at me.

"Thank you for everything," Killian said to Zhaak.

"No worries. You guys aren't the only ones that have lost themselves on this path," Zhaak smiled. He patted Killian on the back, watching him walk away from the car. His brown eyes followed him and then at me.

"Thank you," I said, walking past Zhaak. "It was nice meeting you."

"Ms. De Rose, wait," Zhaak said. I turned around to look him in the eye. "Your power is a gift, Clara. Not a curse," he smiled. "You are valiant by blood. You'll do well in remembering that."

I smiled at him, not knowing exactly what to say, and kept walking to the car where Killian already waited for me inside. Zhaak waved at us as we drove backward and out of the lonely street.

I stayed silent the entire way through the main road. I kept seeing Gilbert's memories again as I had been there, and I could feel the feelings that the memories gave. They were full of sadness and grief, a feeling I rarely felt and a feeling I wished would never feel. A feeling of utter death.

"What did you see?" Killian asked, in the silence. He didn't look at me and I didn't either, but I could tell by his voice that he was curious and sensitive about it.

"I saw Gilbert and his parents... I saw them dying." I tried to keep my voice steady.

"I saw it. It was the only thing we all saw," he informed, his eyes still on the road and his voice full of emptiness. He was a vampire, it would be easy to guess he was used to death. But I wasn't and I didn't think anyone could be used to death. Not even Killian.

"And I saw when the Grams received the notice. Gilbert's face was full of shock, he cried endlessly," I continued. Killian nodded, looking at his planet bracelet without saying anything. In my mind, each bead seemed to light up. I stared at him before looking out the window. He glanced back only for a few seconds. His eyes glimmered in the moonlight, telling me what his voice couldn't express. And for the first time ever, I could see through his soul like an endless black hole of sadness.

I was thinking so much about Gilbert, but I never truly thought about how Killian must have felt. I never thought how much he missed his family or how much guilt and regret he carried around for all these years. I knew him without knowing him at all. And even though I had never lost family, at that moment a part of me felt like I had, like in another world I had been alone.

The night went by slowly. *Time* came by slowly. Even though I wanted to ask about the car malfunction, Killian and I hadn't spoken after the entire ride. We glanced at each other, knowing that there was nothing to say after the visit to Zhaak's house. Now, I lay awake in my bed for an hour, the classical music slowly playing.

The songs got deeper and sadder. But not even the greatest lullaby could help me sleep. I sighed, getting up from the bed and heading to the kitchen instead, deciding to clean. From the kitchen to the bathroom, my room, and the living room, I cleaned until it looked spotless. Time had now decided to go a bit faster than usual. It was 2 am when I finished and sat down on the couch facing the large bookshelf.

What did Kaan want? What can I do instead of sitting around?

My eyes slowly got tired and my headache increased from overthinking. I caught myself lingering deeply into my bookshelf as if I was hypnotized. Flashes of pictures quickly came into my mind. The book itself connected with me.

An Illuminator reading the book. The Illuminated. The book sat in the hands of other Illuminators. A white house. Axel and some witches asking around or making spells to look for it. The papers sitting on the table in the silver door room at Lunar Castle. The paper Kaan was reading.

Then it struck me. Kaan was not reading a map. He was examining copied pages from the *Illuminated*. That is why he had two Joviankalais, most likely Archs, with him that night in the silver door room. They were able to see the symbols or words and tell him everything they saw or even trace it by hand.

I didn't know how the book had lost itself between the hands of different people in a matter of hours. I wouldn't be surprised. A black book with a weird title would have caught every person's attention. Only to some people's surprise was the emptiness inside and to others a whole new world they needed to learn about. But that meant, the witches had lost track of it after trying to pass it on to a potential new generation of Illuminators. That's what Kaan was looking for. The actual book. And from what I could remember it was close by inside a small white house.

"Hey, it's Clara," I spoke to Gilbert on the phone. "Sorry to have woken you up."

He took a second to speak. "It's alright. I was already awake. How do you—"

"Killian let me borrow it," I explained. "Long story." I couldn't see Gilbert's expression, but the slight silence helped me guess he was frowning out of curiosity.

"Is something wrong?" he asked.

"No, the opposite actually," I replied. "I think I know what to do. I just need time."

The next morning turned out to be the most productive time. Even though I didn't have much sleep, I had something to look forward to, a plan that I was ready to initiate. I had woken up with a start, getting ready for the rest of the day. I grabbed my black coat and purse to head out. Gilbert and Killian were running last-minute errands. Or that's what I thought before opening the door.

"Killian? What are you doing?" I said, confused. He sat down on the floor with his back against my apartment door. I moved back, opening it. Killian shook awake. His back almost hit the floor.

"Good morning, gorgeous. I am bodyguarding," he said, standing up at once and moving aside. He wore a gray shirt and black pants. I smelled his cologne all around me. *Smells nice.*

"What?" I asked. Getting out of the apartment and locking it. "I don't need a *bodyguard*."

"Gilbert said otherwise," Killian replied. "Besides, I have nothing to do today. I'm all yours, Goldenrose."

I sighed and started walking downstairs. I needed to run some errands before sunset. "Where are you going?" he asked, following behind me along with his wintergreen smell.

"Going to buy a new phone, to keep in touch... with Gilbert and visit my parents."

"I'm going with you."

"No, thanks. I'm very great on my own. Thank you anyway." I handed him his phone. He took it slowly, smirking at me. Not wanting to ruin the semi-happy mood, I ignored him and unlocked my car. I walked towards it, but he still followed me.

"Says the girl that came running to me two days ago and got into my car yesterday." He mocked. I rolled my eyes, trying not to smack him in the head. I didn't want to give him the satisfaction, so I kept walking. "Kaan is looking for both of us. Don't we have to team up together," he added, still behind me.

"Sorry, not sorry. I have to go..." I made a lopsided smile and opened the door to my car. Killian stood in my way, closing the door before I could get in. Then took my car keys faster than I could react.

"Killian! Give them back! I'm in a hurry... Killian." I tried to get the keys from his hands. He kept walking backward away from me and grinned.

"Seriously Killian, it's *not* funny." I sighed. "You do realize that I can kill you right?"

"I'm completely aware." Killian smiled. *But I won't. I won't kill him for Gilbert.*

I rolled my eyes at him, still following him. "Give me the keys, *Killian.*"

"I'm driving," he said, ignoring me. "And we are going in my truck." He winked at me mischievously and walked towards the rental black truck that was parked across from my white car. I followed Killian once again, walking behind him, annoyed that it was always him who got to drive.

"One day, Killian Walker. I will manage to bother you as much as you have annoyed me," I added.

"It isn't bothering, if you enjoy it, is it?" he smirked, opening the passenger's door for me.

CHAPTER 16
HAPPY NEW YEAR

"I COULD'VE JUST COMPELLED them to give you a *better* deal," Killian said, standing outside the cell phone store. An hour ago, he had told me he wanted to come inside to 'help me out'. I shook my head and went in by myself.

"I can get a deal on my own." I showed him the new phone I got by swinging it close to his face. I was surprised that the store was open since it was New Year's Eve. However, they would close earlier, which is one of the reasons I was in a hurry.

"Right, because you are so persuasive," Killian responded. But I wasn't looking at him, instead, I was looking inside a gift store that was only two stores away from the cell phone shop.

"Come on," I said, walking towards the store.

"And stubborn." Killian walked behind me. "What exactly are you looking for?" he asked, but I didn't respond.

"Clara, wait." His voice changed to seriousness, grabbing my arm to get my attention.

"What is it?" I tilted my head, ready to listen.

"I want to say I'm sorry," he apologized. Killian was actually apologizing. "I'm sorry for hurting you and lying. For everything."

I narrowed my eyes. "Is that the reason why you've been following me everywhere?"

"There are a thousand reasons why. Being sorry is one of them." He ran a hand through his jet-black hair.

I wasn't sure what to say. When people change their habit, it usually takes a while. Not long ago Killian had hurt and compelled me. I remembered and I probably always will. He continued, "I don't know what happened that made me lose control."

"You are a vampire in nature, Killian," I said as a matter of fact. "I can't forgive you now. But I am here standing in front of you *because* of you. You lost control but didn't kill me therefore I am here. And that's saying a lot." He nodded in understanding. The least I could say was that I didn't feel threatened by him anymore not only because I had power but because he never hurt me to the point of actual death when he had the chance to. Besides the blood lie, Gilbert trusted him. *I* was beginning to learn some good parts about him. Since the crystal necklace's memory, he hadn't lost control. He kept us alive. He was a few days late, but he apologized and seemed to want to change.

"Trust 101." I put my hand out, a sign of starting over again.

"Trust 101," he repeated, shaking my hand with a smile.

The store was small but abundant with merchandise. I looked

around until I found the hats and a pair of glasses. There weren't a lot of cute pairs, but I found some that would work great. Aurora and I used to play spies often when we were younger. Dressing up in disguises and using walkie-talkies, we liked imitating our dad's detective voice.

"Here." I turned to look at Killian and showed him the glasses. "Undercover glasses." When he didn't take them, I put them on. Catching him by surprise. He smirked as he looked in the mirror. *Show off.* I glanced at him, realizing that this was the first time I had genuinely seen him smile. A smile that didn't include him teasing me.

"How about a hat? Black hat? This one!" I gave it to him. It read *You Only Live Once.*

"That's ironic." Killian brooded. He put a cap on my head too. I took it off to read what it said. *Partners in Murder.*

"Really?" I glared at him. "You're making me regret what I said seconds ago."

He waved his hands in the air. "It's a joke, Clara." I shook my head and started walking towards the cashier to pay for the glasses. The man smiled at us and then furrowed his brows.

"Good afternoon, Mr. Brian," I said, looking at his name tag.

"Hello," he answered. "Two pairs of glasses and a hat?"

"Yes," I said. "Do you accept card?" I searched through my purse for both my card and cash.

"That will be twenty dollars," Mr. Brian said. "And no, we don't, ma'am, the card machine is not working properly at the moment."

I sighed. "Can I pay you half the price? I just came from

buying a cell phone because I was robbed, so I don't have any cash. My frenemy here doesn't have a job, and I only have ten dollars in cash with me," I briefly explained. "I *promise* to come back to pay the rest."

Brian hesitated, glaring at me and Killian. Back and forth. "Are you two together?"

I laughed. "Me? With him? Of course not! Not even in my dreams."

"Get a man who can find a job at least," Brian said, shaking his head.

Killian grimaced at us, offended. "I do have a job, Clara dear... in London."

"Sure you do," I teased.

"Fine, ten dollars it is," Brian responded. I looked at him kindly, paid him, and left the store. I couldn't help but feel delight as I walked out.

"And that is how you get a deal," I told Killian. I had proved him wrong.

"So lying is better than compelling someone. Noted, Golden-rose."

"Half-lying."

"About the 'not having money' part or the 'not together' part?" he smirked, walking to the truck.

"Both," I said without looking at him.

The next stop was meeting my family. There was no need to tell Killian where the location was, it appeared he remembered from last time. He didn't ask and just drove through the peaceful street. Too peaceful and so quiet, who could ever imagine ruining such a beautiful street?

He nodded when I said, "It will only take a few minutes," and got off the truck, walking through the trees and towards the house. I took my glasses off and knocked at the door multiple times, eager to finally see my family. Aurora opened the door.

"Clara! We were worried! You didn't answer your phone," she exclaimed, giving me a hug. "Mom! Dad! Clara's here!"

I smiled at her as my parents came. "I'm sorry. My phone got lost. I just came from buying a new one." My parents hugged me, they smelled like chocolate.

"We were upset you would miss New Year," my mom said, while my dad went to the living room.

I shook my head. "I said I was only leaving for about a week or so, Mom."

"I love it, sister," Aurora glowed, showing me the charm bracelet I had gifted her. My dad came back from the living room with a golden wrapped-up present, handing it to Aurora, who then held it out to me. My sister had not given me a present during the holidays, she said it would take a while, but that it would be worth it. "Come on, take it. It is from me, but we all choose it," Aurora smiled, swinging the small box in front of me.

"You didn't have to! It was my birthday just a few days ago," I reminded them. I took the gift and opened it to reveal a box with a lovely Sun and Moon ring. It almost reminded me of the silver rings that Adrik wore over his black gloves.

"Thank you!" I beamed at them. "It's so *beautiful*."

"I never get to see you much anymore, and I want you to think of me every time you wear it."

"With or without a ring, I could never forget you. I could never forget any of you," I responded, hugging Aurora again. Her warmth made me feel comfortable and at ease. My mom's eyes became teary.

"Oh no, you cry I cry." My dad hugged her. "So don't cry."

"No, don't cry please," I said, looking at Aurora and my parents, trying not to sound emotional. Aurora pushed her hair behind her ear sheepishly and disappeared into one of the halls, while my parents went back to the kitchen. I closed the door behind me and followed them to figure out what they were baking. The oven was closed, but I could easily recognize the smell. I bent down to look inside. *Cupcakes.* My stomach made a slight grumble. I sighed sadly at the cupcakes. They looked too delicious even without the frosting on top.

"I can't stay." I frowned. "There is something extremely important that I need to do... for the photography job." I didn't like lying to my parents, but I couldn't just tell them that a powerful witch was hunting me and that I was hanging out with a vampire.

"You've been busy lately... with *photography* jobs," my dad muttered, looking directly into my eyes, knowing very well what he was trying to do.

"It has nothing to do with..." my mom added.

I looked at my dad, making sure to not flinch or move a lot. "No, I'm ok. With all of it. Nothing *weird* at all. Don't worry about it."

"You better not be lying... I can't tell anymore," my dad joked, checking the timer on the oven. *Learned from the best.* I let out a breath, glad that they trusted me enough to not ask a lot of questions about my personal life.

"Hey, Clara!" I turned around at the sound of a voice I recognized.

"Dani? What are you doing here?"

"She was helping me with fashion advice," Aurora said, appearing from behind. "New job and everything." I raised my brows in surprise.

"You definitely got the best!" I smiled at Dani. She wore a black feathery jacket that made her stand out and a bright gold watch I hadn't seen her wear before.

"You like it?" she asked, noticing my gaze and moving her arm slightly.

"Really nice," I responded, reminding myself to look at the time on my phone. Time was moving fast.

"*Well*, it was nice seeing you all. I really missed you. I'm sorry I can't stay for the New Year's party."

"Other work stuff *in* New Year?" Dani asked, curious. I nodded and went ahead to give a goodbye hug to my parents and Aurora. I told them I would be back soon as I walked to the entrance door. Dani followed behind.

"Your car is not here," Dani noticed, the moment I opened the door.

"A friend drove me here."

She furrowed her brows and looked around. "A friend?"

"Don't look at me like that. It's a friend, who I met a few days ago that's helping me with the job…"

"You are the one always judging, not me," she added. "But then again I get more into trouble."

"You usually do a lot, which is kind of unnecessary..." I stopped realizing what I said. "Okay, I'm sorry." Dani shook her head but smiled unbothered.

"Be safe, Clara," she added in the silence, her voice with worry.

"I should be the one saying that," I joked and hugged her again. "Be safe too. I care about you, that's all I'm trying to say." The strong cherry smell of her perfume encircled me. "And I always am," I assured, releasing from the hug, turning to leave, and giving her one last smile before she closed the door.

"Did something happen?" Killian asked after I sat down inside the truck. Nothing happened. I should be glad that nothing happened to them. I should be beyond glad, but instead, heartache and a feeling of loss rose in my soul. I was leaving my family to walk towards danger *again*, a place I might not come back from this time.

It's the right thing to do, Clara. I thought. *It's the right thing to do*. Because if I let the witches and Kaan go through with whatever plan they had then not only my family will be hurt but others as well.

"Nothing happened," I responded, shaking my head. He nodded and started the truck. I glanced back to the house, feeling homesick already, hoping to actually come back again soon.

We were driving downtown to meet Gilbert at Zatara Sunset and arrive together at the white house, where I believed the book was held. That was the plan. The streets of San Antonio

Downtown were extremely busy. I didn't even want to imagine how crowded the Riverwalk was. Killian parked his truck on the edge of a street, close to where we could walk quickly onto Zatara Sunset.

"Where are you going?" I asked him when instead of walking straight into the paths of the Riverwalk, he took a turn down a small alley. The golden buttons of his black coat gleamed in the dull lights.

"There's another entrance this way, love," he responded, walking in front of me.

"So now you are the expert in *my* city?" I marveled. "Great... and not surprising."

He smirked, walking down the alley and taking a turn to the right. We went up the stairs from the building in front of us, where there was an entrance to the restaurant.

"After you, Goldenrose," he said, opening the door for me and nodding for me to go ahead.

"How did you even know of this entrance?" I walked into a large kitchen room. Cooks and employees walked around the kitchen, cleaning, making some dishes, taking out orders, and talking about rumors.

"Mr. Walker, nice to see you again," a lady holding two plates in her hands said.

"Mr. Walker, hello," another man, who was fixing a plate exclaimed.

"Did we just enter a world where you're famous?" I joked, walking in front of Killian. "Of course, you compelled them."

"It might be a shocking surprise to you, but I didn't," he

responded. I raised my eyebrows at him.

"*Only* to not say we meet here," he added. "That's all." I greeted everyone I passed and walked out of the kitchen. Soft and chill music played all around the restaurant. The same man with the mustache I had seen twice before, stood behind the counter. I never knew his name and never had closely inspected his face. Zatara Sunset had given me warmth and tranquility all around to the point that my awareness had lowered.

"Hello, Mr. Walker and Ms. De Rose. Mr. Gram has been waiting for you on the floor above," he informed. I looked at his name tag. It read *Mr. Leonard Miller, Owner of Zatara Sunset.*

"No news today, Mr. Walker," he added, looking at Killian.

"Thank you, Leonard." Killian nodded. We proceeded to walk up the stairs.

No doubt, Gilbert stood next to the same regular table on the edge of the lonely balcony. He examined some papers. The sleeves of his white shirt rolled up in his arms. He looked up at the sound of the balcony door opening.

"Hey," I said. Killian and I approached him.

"Hey," he answered, putting his arms beside his hips. Killian frowned at him.

"Business Papers: One. Mr. Businessman: Zero. You need a drink, mate. I'll be right back," Killian said, winking at me, and walking out the balcony without another word.

Gilbert blurted, "You know I don't even drink..." But Killian was long gone to hear him.

I frowned, staring at Gilbert. "It does seem you need a drink.

What are you doing?" I asked, looking at the papers all over the table. The writing and numbers made my head spin. It had been a while since I had seen any mathematical calculations.

Gilbert sighed. "Bakery business. Uncle William and I decided we want to open a bakery right here."

"You mean here in San Antonio?"

"There's an open space across the street."

"Really?" I said, not expecting the news. I walked towards the balcony. "I hope everything goes as planned." The hanging lights shined brightly above me, illuminating the balcony just like down below, where people walked in and out of the restaurant.

"Just a few minor complications. Nothing really serious," he continued, starting to pick up the papers into piles. "How did it go with Killian?"

"He was beyond annoying," I replied, explaining what had happened for a few seconds. Gilbert's brows moved up and down through the small anecdote.

"That is what I call a normal day with Killian." He sat down in front of me.

The balcony door opened a few seconds later. I turned around to see Killian holding a bottle of whiskey and a man behind him holding a tray with three tiny glass cups. The waiter placed the cups on the table and turned to leave. Killian opened the bottle and poured whiskey into each glass. He passed the first glass to Gilbert. Then passed another to me.

"Come on, princess. It is New Year's Eve," Killian said. I rolled my eyes at him, grabbing the glass.

"He is not wrong. But I don't drink," Gilbert added, putting all his materials in his brown backpack that sat in the empty chair.

"Only one Gil... to us."

Gilbert hesitated. "Alright, *only* one." I turned to him, surprised that he agreed with Killian, who now sat next to him. The sunglasses I had chosen for him earlier were hanging from his coat.

"To friendship." Gilbert held his glass in the air, only taking two sips from his cup.

Killian smirked. "I doubt Ms. Judgy here agrees to that." He raised his cup, drinking all of its contents.

"That would be reasonable because you and I are far friends," I said. He only kept smiling, sitting back in his chair.

"You guys could try to be friends. It would make everything much better," Gilbert suggested, his voice sounding more relaxed.

"Yeah, well. If your little sidekick here was less infuriating." I glared at Killian.

"*Infuriating*? Yes, that makes sense..." Gilbert said to Killian, to which he rolled his eyes.

"If you could be more fun." Killian shook his hands to the side, mocking me.

Gilbert raised his brows at me. "He just said you *aren't* fun..."

"Shut up, Killian," I said. "And whose side are you on Gilbert?"

He lifted his arms, drawing back. "I'm just here." Gilbert smiled back and forth when neither Killian nor I spoke.

"Ok... to acquaintances." I hit their glasses only slightly and drank one tiny sip to taste it, regretting the decision the moment the disgusting flavor touched my tongue. Gilbert shook his head in surprise while Killian sat back in his chair.

I had set my glass on the table when Gilbert and Killian's eyes moved towards the balcony door. The second I heard it open, I turned around to see a young man with a Polaroid camera hanging around his neck walking towards me. He wore jeans with a brown sweatshirt that matched his eyes.

"Excuse me. I'm sorry to disturb you," he started, standing next to me. "You are Clara De Rose, right? I come here sometimes to take Polaroid pictures. But I've seen you in the art gallery before, where Max works. I have some pictures hung in there too." I looked at him again, trying to remember if I had seen him before. But I didn't recognize him at all.

"I'm sorry I've never seen you before," I smiled, apologetically.

He continued. "I just want to say that you have been such a *flourishing* inspiration, and if you could please sign my camera." He made a lopsided smile. Killian raised his brows and stared at us.

"Of course," I responded. It was the first time someone actually recognized me outside the gallery and even made a pun at my flowery photographs. He passed me his camera and a permanent marker to sign it. In print, I wrote my signature, *Clara Valerie De Rose*. Making each *A* look similar to a star.

"Here you go," I smiled at him as he took back the camera. Killian sat up in his chair, grabbed the bottle of whiskey from the table and started to pour on his and Gilbert's glass cups again.

"*Another* one for Clara?" Gilbert proposed.

I shook my head at Killian and raised my eyebrows at Gilbert. "I don't drink *either*."

"*Neither* do I," Gilbert realized. "You're a bad influence,

Killian. Thanks, Clara."

"Very well then," Killian said, raising his glass. "For you, darling." And drank until his glass was empty.

"Would you guys want a free picture?" the young man still standing next to me said.

Gilbert nodded. "Yes, please."

I frowned at him but didn't object. The man moved a few feet steps back so that everything was in the frame. I moved my chair close to Gilbert and Killian did the same.

"Smile," the young man said. The flash lit the entire balcony for two seconds. We all smiled like little kids taking a picture with a celebrity. Like we had been friends forever. The young man grabbed the Polaroid and handed it to Gilbert, who had stretched his arm. "Thank you."

"It was nice meeting you," the guy grinned, walking towards the balcony door.

"Likewise," I replied.

"I'll keep it." Gilbert looked at the picture. Neither Killian nor I bothered to see it while he placed it inside the pocket of his white shirt.

At that exact moment, Gilbert's phone started ringing. He frowned at it and stood up to answer it, walking a few feet away to the edge of the balcony.

"Hello, Uncle William?" Gilbert said. I glanced at Killian wondering what was wrong. Killian looked at Gilbert, staying silent. I couldn't hear anything of what Mr. Gram was saying, but I hoped the silence didn't mean anything bad. After a few seconds, Gilbert hung up the phone, turning around to look at us.

"What happened?" I asked at once, frowning at Gilbert's worried face.

"It's Mary. She fell from some stairs." He shook his head in disbelief.

"What?" I said. We weren't close enough, but she had been so nice to me. Even the first time I spoke with her, I felt a motherly connection.

"Uncle William said she would be alright, that it was a minor incident, and she just hit her head. But I have to go back to London."

"I'll go with you." Killian stood up.

"No, it's alright. Stay with Clara. You guys have to figure out about Kaan. I'll be alright." Gilbert picked up the piles of paper from the table and placed his brown bag over his shoulder. He was right to go back to London with his family, instead of staying here. It would be safer for him to leave for now anyway. For Gilbert and William, I hoped that Mary would be okay.

I stood up and hugged him. "She will be okay."

"I know." He nodded.

"Mary is strong, mate," Killian said, giving him a quick hug.

"Be safe. Whatever happens please call me," Gilbert said, looking at me and Killian.

"You too," I responded. He turned away, walking fast out of the balcony door and out to the Riverwalk. Killian and I moved to the balcony to see Gilbert one last time, but he didn't turn around or waved goodbye. His silhouette slowly faded in the shadows of the colorful buildings and crowds until he was unable to be seen.

Killian turned to me.

"Once again it's just us, Goldenrose." He acknowledged without smiling or teasing. I nodded, looking at him and deciding that the universe had once again managed to keep us together... and that to some extent it wasn't that bad.

Based on the memory, the white house was located in the rural areas of San Antonio. I concentrated on seeing small memory flashes of where the book was. I couldn't tell whose exact memory I was seeing, but I had a feeling it was the book that helped me see them somehow. The book itself was magic after all.

"Turn right in the next street," I instructed, pointing to the right. The map on my phone showed that a small town was close by, about ten minutes away. We rode away from the sunset. Houses and ranches came into view as we entered the small but largely populated town. People walked outside comfortably. A group of friends got out of a bar, laughing about something. I wondered about the social events I had missed after knowing I was an Illuminator. But I wasn't regretful of knowing the truth. Without it, I would have probably been lost more mentally than physically.

"It's that one." I pointed at the only white, cottage-looking house that looked exactly like the one in the memory. A feeling of déjà vu went through me like I had been there before. I was kind of used to it by now, being at a place in my mind without actually being there at all. Killian parked a few blocks away from the house.

"Ready?" I asked, turning to look at him.

"Since always, De Rose," he answered. I half-smiled at him. Who would have thought I would be going on road trips with a vampire? *Exactly, me neither.* Much less as a supernatural.

Killian followed behind me. I concentrated on seeing the memories and the path in front of me. People were talking and having fun in their backyards, families celebrating New Year's Eve. The further I walked the less sound I would hear. The small house stood apart from other houses, making it seem haunted.

"It's this one," I said, stopping in front of the white and red brick pathway.

"Stay behind me." Killian started walking in front of me, but I followed next to him till another memory emerged, giving me a warning look. "Clara."

"Wait, something is wrong," I realized. "The book, I don't see it there anymore." I tried to concentrate on the book again, but everything was completely blank.

"I don't hear anyone's heartbeat inside," Killian informed. We looked at each other in confusion until my phone started ringing. *Unknown.*

I looked at Killian. He nodded at me to answer it and I did.

"Well, hello, Miss De Rose. Let's pick up where we left off, shall we?" a cold voice said. One that I had rarely heard but could completely recognize.

"Kaan," I whispered and proceeded to put the phone on speaker.

"After running away, I thought you had lost your memory." He laughed. Chills ran through my back at the sound of it, his cold voice and mocking laugh. "Get it? Because obviously, you *can't.*"

Killian and I stayed silent, looking at each other.

"But Mr. Killian Octavious Walker surprisingly can make you

forget. Temporarily, of course." He laughed again. *He knows.* Killian tensed up next to me, his eyes sharp as he observed around. I couldn't tell whether he was confused, shocked, or suddenly angry as I was.

"What do you want?" I asked harshly, making sure to keep my voice as steady as possible.

"Better question. What do *you* want? Have you checked in on your little half-vampire friend? Do you want to say hi?"

"Clara, whatever you do, don't fall for it!" Gilbert screamed through the phone, going into complete silence right after.

I froze in place. "Gilbert?"

Killian's jaw hardened. "I suggest you think twice before hurting him, you bastard," he threatened.

"*No*, then?" Kaan said. "Maybe your dear sister wants to greet you."

In the background, I could hear crying and muffled sounds. I closed my eyes at once, concentrating on Aurora and her mind. *Where were you? Where are you?* I saw flashes of Aurora's current memory. She sat inside a gray room, tied in a chair. The reflection of the glass wall in front of her showed her mouth was tied up with a cloth.

"This time I'm telling the truth, Ms. De Rose," Kaan spoke. I opened my eyes, feeling them getting heavy. "Follow my orders, if you want to save your friend and your sister," he continued. "Can't wait to see you." He hung up.

The front door of the house opened the second everything had gone silent. Axel appeared holding the *Illuminated* in his hand, smiling mischievously.

"Still looking for this?" He shook the book. Killian proceeded towards him.

"Killian…" I warned, trying to stop him, but it was no use. He proceeded towards Axel quickly. With a flick from his hands, Axel stopped him. I couldn't hear or feel anything, but I guessed what he was doing. Killian slowly fell to the floor, touching his head and grunting from pain.

"I wouldn't do anything stupid, *Vampire*. We are not the only ones here," Axel said, withdrawing his hand. Others appeared from the dark. Witches *and* Illuminators. Among them were Milana and Ed. I looked at them, trying to find a hint of empathy in their eyes, but there was none. They looked at me like I was a complete stranger. Killian stood up slowly.

"I'll give you two choices: one, go with me willingly to Kaan, or two, kidnap you and take you by force. Your choice." Axel smiled, his voice was no longer a whisper.

A black van drove down the street and stopped in front of the house. Killian looked at me, there was no hesitation between us. We both knew what was necessary to do. I walked towards the van.

"Good choice," Axel said, behind us. Two Illuminators came to my side the second I walked ahead.

"Don't touch me," I said when I saw they were about to grab my arm. Killian shuffled behind me, avoiding the Illuminators from grabbing him as well. They nudged us into the van.

The black-tinted windows made it harder to see outside. It was the two witches that sat in the back that I noticed second, due to the dark-colored coats that seemed to glow slightly in the dark, then a Celestialkalai in the driver's seat. Killian sat to my left, still a bit shocked but trying to inspect the doors. As soon as the door closed behind him, his arm slowly moved towards the lock, maybe in hopes that he could try to get out. I reached out for his arm and shook my head at him quickly, feeling the slight force of Illuminator magic. The Celestialkalai had quickly created a purple electric shield, surrounding the van's walls. In the slight purple light, Killian looked like he wanted to kill everyone. And he probably would have if it wasn't Gilbert's life at stake.

Ed entered the van sitting in the passenger's seat without looking back. I remembered how he said he disagreed with the witches' ideas. *Maybe he could help.*

"Ed, you need to help us," I pleaded.

"Be quiet," one of the two witches behind me said.

I ignored him and continued. "Ed, please... you said it yourself. You don't agree with any of this."

"I changed my mind now," he responded with no emotion in his voice. "You can't see where we are going, so a little sedative won't hurt."

There was a sharp sting in my neck, then coldness running through it. I turned to look at Killian, the purple shield light decreasing in my eyes. The witch behind him put a needle in his neck, the syringe filled with a yellowish liquid. Killian gritted through his teeth. Whatever they injected him was not the same as what they injected me with because instead of feeling pain, I felt weak. I slowly dozed off watching out the window, seeing the colorful light and hearing the sound of fireworks exploding far away in the dark sky. *Happy New Year to me.*

CHAPTER 17
SECRETS OF SOCIOPATHS

I F I WAS GIVEN A CHOCOLATE BROWNIE for every time I had an uncalled sleep and awful awakenings, I would have probably owned a chocolate brownie bakery by now. Instead, I sat tied up in a chair with ropes inside a large room of an abandoned factory. I winced, putting my head up. My neck hurt from having my head sideways.

Across from me sat Killian, who was starting to get awake too, looking somewhat frail. Gilbert sat in between us, his face red with blood dripping a bit from a small cut on his cheek.

"Gilbert!" I shot, trying to sit up in my chair and ignoring the pain in my wrists from the ropes.

"Hey," he responded weakly, making a tight-lipped smile.

"Are you okay?" I asked quickly.

"Are *you* guys ok?" He looked at me and Killian worriedly.

I wasn't, but I nodded anyway while Killian tried to untie his hands. Instead of having his face a bit rosy, it was completely pale, like he was actually and definitely dead.

"It's no use, Killian. They used that garlic, salt, and sunflower petal mixture," Gilbert said.

"*Allium*," I corrected. I remembered the mixture I had read from the book. The one that was created by Illuminators with the help of witches years ago. Its purpose was to make vampires feel boiling pain and weakness. Now, I knew it worked, but I kind of wished it wasn't Killian I had to see to know so.

"I'm going to murder everyone." Killian gritted through his teeth. "Once I get out of these ropes."

"You are *not* killing anyone, Killian," I responded, shaking my head at the thought of death. I tried moving my tied-up hands, but like Gilbert said it was no use. Red marks and pain appeared with every hand movement I made and decided to sit still. I took a quick look around. There were no windows and only yellow lights lit up the large, tall gray room. We sat in the middle of what seemed to be an abandoned manufacturing area. There was no way to tell our actual location or how long we had been unconscious. Except that it was cold and smelled moist. I was about to ask Gilbert what he knew about Aurora when some noise was heard outside close by.

The black double doors on the left of the large room opened, creaking with every movement. Axel walked into the room along with Ed, Julien, and two witches. All their faces were vacant and somber as if they had just left a funeral. Ed and Julien closed the black doors behind them in a guard-like manner. They walked like robots, standing around the room and inspecting. Axel walked to the middle of the room, wearing a dark blue suit. His curly blue-black hair was messy and shiny over the light. It fell over his face, he ran his hand through it to push it back.

"Finally, the trio is awake." He mocked, smiling towards Killian and Gilbert. But not looking at me.

"*Where's* Aurora?" I asked the second he finished speaking.

"Kaan has her," he said without looking at me. I closed my eyes, trying to concentrate on her recent memories. All I saw were dirty gray walls, similar to the walls that currently surrounded us. Knowing she was somewhere close by made me feel somewhat relieved.

"Let us go," Gilbert demanded at once, taking me out of my mind. His worried look reminded me that he was in a hurry to London. Mr. Gram waited for him to support Mary.

"Do you have somewhere to be, Gram?" Axel tilted his head. "Oh, wait. You do? How is it going with you Aunt?" I looked at Gilbert, panicked.

"You had something to do—" Gilbert snapped. Axel shook his head, clicking his tongue and shaking his head.

"We didn't. Her fall was just perfect timing," he continued, cutting Gilbert off, who looked more furious than ever. By his mockery, I could tell he was lying. I had barely known Mary and just hearing Axel making fun of her fall made me angry. Gilbert didn't have to be here; they had used him for leverage to get Killian and me.

"What do you have against us?" I asked Axel, wanting to know his reason for helping Kaan. "Let him go. Kaan only wants me and Killian."

Axel smiled mischievously, walking to me. I smelled smoke and fire the closer he got. "You look so much like someone I used to know?" He lightly touched my cheek. The coldness of his touch made me shiver. I moved my head to the side, away from his hand.

"Celeste..." he whispered, sounding like a complete maniac. "She was a photographer too, you know. I always bought her photographs from the gallery."

Always bought her photographs? I kept my breath steady. *He was the unknown buyer. The one Max couldn't figure out!*

"Used to know? Wouldn't be surprised if *Celeste* or whoever she was left you, *Witch*," Killian said coldly, moving in his chair.

Axel moved his hand from my cheek but stood inches away from me. He looked at Killian and Gilbert then at me, furrowing his brows.

"I don't understand. Why are you still friends with these... *vampires?*" I didn't respond. "I mean being bitten by one must have been really rough for you. But not for the vampire who did it, right?" He turned to look at Killian and smirked.

"Shut up," Killian demanded.

"How do you know about that?" I asked, shocked. Nobody knew about what had happened between me and Killian except Gilbert.

Axel laughed, mocking at our confused and alert faces. "You can remember now," he said, snapping his fingers.

The coffee shop Killian and I met in. The times he had bitten me and made me his puppet. When he gave me the crystal necklace. The night of the ball. All the lost memories, including the only night

*I couldn't remember. The night before I woke up at the Grams' house.
It all came back.*

In less than a second, everything came to light. I was no longer
in the room as flashes of memories came to my mind. I remembered
the day at the cafe when Killian and I met for the first time. What
we were eating and the worker with a blue hat who served us. The
day at the library when I bumped into the guy with a black hat and
found the *Illuminated* in the cart. And then at the holiday ball
when I bumped into a random guy as I left after arguing with
Killian about what I remembered. The way I felt when I
remembered everything again. Anger and disgust rose the same way
they had when my powers slowly appeared and knew Killian had
hurt me.

My heart raced immediately. I looked at Killian, he looked
flabbergasted, staring back at me.

"It was all me." Axel chuckled, shaking his head. He reached
into a pocket in his coat suit. Getting out the crystal necklace, fixed
like it was before Killian broke it. *It was him.* He had been
following us since the beginning. It was he who had planned it first.

"You spelled us..." I said in realization.

"How should I explain..." He laughed, walking back and
forth, swinging the crystal necklace. "You see, I arrived in London
only for the purpose of finding Illuminators and killing vampires,
according to orders from Stellar Court and Kaan. I couldn't believe
the *resemblance* between you and Celeste when I saw you walking
around with your friend. So, I followed you, while also following
them." He looked at the duo. "It took me a long time to make that

spell and bring you two together. Just a bit of enchanting potion in the food caused Killian and you to feel drawn to each other. That was temporary of course. I just had to be close enough to do the *actual* spell that would help me control Killian for a short period of time." He half-laughed, looking at Killian. "And well dear *Clara*... you know the rest."

I couldn't believe it. I sat there shocked, trying to make sense of everything.

"I remember now, all of it." My voice shook, a tear falling from my cheek. "After Killian gave me the necklace, you and your group of witches took us to the forest..."

Axel nodded, a smile crept across his face and continued. "I took you there after Killian compelled you on my orders, to make you believe you have been hurt by him. Then, I made you forget you ever met him, while he still remembered about what he did to make the compulsion make sense... and to feel guilty. Seems to me like it worked perfectly."

"You spelled me to hurt..." Killian started. Axel shook his head, walked closer to him, and then looked at me.

"The specific spell I created for you wouldn't have worked if there wasn't an inch of attraction between you both. Killian bit you because *he* at some point wanted to," Axel said. Killian looked at Axel like he wanted to straight-up murder him and I wouldn't have stopped him. Killian thought he had hurt me by personal choice. He could only remember hurting me and compelling me to forget. But not being ordered to do so. The memories ran around my head like a cycle. The pieces came together again and again with the last memory I needed, the memory that both Killian and I had forgotten.

"I want you to bite her. Make her fear you, but don't leave her dead yet. Then forget you ever met me. Forget what I ordered you to do the past few days, including this night, and go on with your life as normal," Axel said to Killian, who stood in front of him like a statue. Then, Axel walked to me.

"Run. Feel the fear. Feel the hurt. Forget you ever met me. I will see you soon..." Axel said, touching my hair.

"Go." Axel had snapped his fingers. I ran as fast as I could, Killian following behind.

The fear I had and the humid smell as I ran that night in the forest. Killian had bitten me that night, following Axel's last order, but not as much as to leave me dead. I was standing right there like a puppet next to them as he spoke to him. The cruel way Axel ordered him to hurt me, to forget he had seen and had been bossed around by him. Axel whispered to me to forget him, to run for my life. And I had.

"You were supposed to remember everything at the ball, but of course, I didn't know you already had based on your memory powers," Axel said. That is why I remembered everything again at the ball. Because Axel was there to make me remember. I did remember and drove all my hurt towards Killian, then told him the truth of what he had done.

"You were always there," I spoke in a whisper. "At the cafe, at the library, at the ball. You sent vampires to kill Killian and Gilbert. You told Kaan who we were." *The answer to all of the mysteries was right in front of me.*

Everything fit like a puzzle. Axel wanted to kill two birds with one stone. He made Killian hurt me so I could hate vampires. Then I would have sided with him and the witches. It all made complete sense. It made sense to have the powers I had when that specific situation ignited them. That is how I remembered what Killian did. But Axel's spell was too powerful for me to really recall what he did in the forest. Everything had started because of him. And because of him, Kaan had found us.

"You are *sick*," Gilbert said, disgusted. "All of that for nothing."

"Not for nothing. I found two powerful Illuminators for Kaan to use," Axel responded. My head burned like fire. I tried to raise my head, but my neck ached. I closed my eyes, trying to breathe steadily. *Focus.*

"You couldn't have done all of this by yourself," I hypothesized, wondering if there was more to what he was saying.

"No, I didn't. I had to keep an eye on all of you." He moved closer to me again and smiled. "Someone special helped me... a lot."

I glared at him, wondering what the hell he meant by that. Then, he walked towards the double doors and opened it, standing in the doorway.

"Do you want me to tell her? Or do you want to make an entrance?" He asked someone behind the opened doors that none of us except him could see. The sound of heavy heels walking the cemented floor echoed. The closer it got, the more I could feel my heartbeat pumping, like waiting for a jump scare in a horror movie.

And it stopped beating for seconds as that *someone* appeared in the room.

"*Dani?*" That was all I could manage to say. She had a grin on her face, but not the friendly kind. A smile I had never seen her wear. The kind that an enemy wore, like Axel or Kaan. Her face filled with no care. The face of a complete stranger.

"Hi, Clara." She smirked as she walked towards me. Her flowy white and black dress moved at her pace. She was wearing the black puffy jacket I had seen her wear a few hours ago at my parents' house with Aurora.

"What did you do to her?" I asked Axel. He watched Dani without responding.

"He didn't need to do anything," Dani said. "I helped him. I *wanted* to help him. To spy on you, give him every detail of what you did, where you were, etc."

I shook my head. It couldn't be possible. Something was wrong. My *friend* couldn't have betrayed me.

"*There is a great coffee shop around here too, just in the next street. It has five stars,*" Dani said. I walked next to her, looking at my phone and checking the time.

"*Alright, send me your address once your date is over. Remember I made a reservation for dinner already. I'll probably go to the cafe and shop for presents.*"

"*Okay, I will. Don't worry.*" She smiled at me widely. "*Drink a coffee for me!*" she added, walking away from me to the other side of the street.

"*Good luck on your date!*" I waved, walking away and looking *around to find the coffee shop she talked about.*

"You convinced me to go to the coffee shop."

"I knew it would work. Coffee is such your weakness." She mocked. "It's pathetic." I looked her straight in the eyes and her hands. But she looked straight back at me, her eyes blank and hands unmoving.

"Why would you? I don't understand. I didn't do—"

"Do anything to me?" Dani interrupted. "No, you didn't. Axel offered me a lot of money. And I needed it, Clara... but you wouldn't understand since you literally have everything. A nice family, people who care about you, even Johnny and Santiago care more for you," she grunted irritated and rolled her eyes. Even though I was hurt, a hint of anger slowly increased inside me. Because how could I have been so foolish not to see it through her? How could I have not known my closest friend? I was blinded by our friendship and trusted her so easily.

"I didn't know," I said, trying to understand her. "I could have helped you, Dani."

"I didn't need pity, *especially* not from you," she shot. I looked at her, trying not to cry at the betrayal. Then I remembered the ring I had seen her wearing in London after coming from Clark's date. Now, I knew it wasn't Clark who had given it to her. Before I thought it was him, so I never asked.

"The diamond ring. I thought Clark had given it to you..."

Dani just laughed. Of course, she never liked him. She just used him to get away from me, to hide away, and work with Axel in secret.

"I would like to keep watching this, but Danielle, we need to inform Kaan," Axel interrupted. Dani only nodded, and she turned away, giving me a cold look before walking out of the room with Axel. It was me who had pushed her towards Clark too.

I had never felt so betrayed. My mind kept running in circles and I wanted it to stop. Silence rested inside the large room until I spoke.

"We have to get out of here. I have to find my sister," I mumbled, without looking at Killian or Gilbert. I blinked multiple times, trying to untie my hands and legs without bursting into tears.

"Clara..." Gilbert started to say. "Stop, you will hurt yourself."

"He's right, Clara," Killian added.

"This is all my fault. Neither of you should have been here."

"Our choice, it's not your fault," Gilbert responded.

"I don't care if I have to kill thousands of supernaturals. We will get out together," Killian affirmed. *I hope so.* I thought.

After a few minutes, Axel, Ed, and Julien walked into the room once again.

"Untie them," Axel ordered Ed and Julien. Ed went ahead to untie Gilbert, Julien untied Killian, and Axel untied me. I glared at him. He looked at me closely and stared like a psychopath.

"Don't think about trying anything, Clara dear," Axel whispered in my ear. However, it wasn't me who needed the warning. The moment Killian got untied, he started to go off on Julien, trying to bite him.

"I don't think so, Vampire," Julien said, using his Flamer

power to back Killian off. He only backed down when Gilbert shook his head at him. We got tied up again as they transferred us somewhere else in the factory. They pushed us forward to keep walking, down empty stairs and destroying hallways. "Save your energy," I whispered to Killian. When we walked closer to each other. I could see the fire in his eyes. Always ready for a fight. But he nodded anyway.

I couldn't keep track of how many left and right turns we made around the abandoned factory, especially when I intensely wondered what room Aurora was in. Until finally, Axel stopped in front of the only double doors that looked slightly cleaner than the others. He knocked twice and opened the doors gently, they creaked and echoed in the silence. Axel walked in first. Julien and Ed shoved us into the small room.

The room seemed to take my breath away, literary. There were no windows, but only candle lights, a medium table, and two armchairs. Black walls filled the entire room with only a tapestry showing a map of Kosmos hanging on the wall. The map was neatly and more accurately drawn. Unlike the other map I had taken from Lunar Castle, this one showed more buildings like the Armory and Weaponry buildings next to Stellar Castle, the small lakes in each court, and other villages in Ether and Arkadia. Kaan sat down in one of the armchairs, looking at the map closely. Then he stood up and walked close to where we stood, ordering his followers to leave the room.

"Pleasure to see you again, Ms. De Rose." Kaan smiled, once Axel disappeared out of the room.

"The feeling is not mutual," I responded. "Where's my

sister?"

"You will see her once you do what I ask..." Kaan said.

"And I won't do what you ask before I see her."

"You will. Or you won't see her at all," he threatened. His smirk faded away, looking at Killian and Gilbert. I was about to protest but decided otherwise and waited to know exactly what he wanted first.

"You must be starving, Mr. Walker," he continued, mockingly.

"I'm on a special animal diet, but I think I can cheat one day," Killian said, staring at Kaan's neck.

"You won't have much luck." Kaan laughed, looking unbothered. "Mr. Gram, your presence here is merely necessary."

"Then let him go," I demanded.

"That's not an option. Not until I get what I want," Kaan responded coldly.

"Which is what, exactly?" asked Gilbert. Kaan started to pace around the room, his black coat giving a flow of cold air.

"The *Illuminated* contains a secret. One that I've spent years figuring out. The book itself has immense power, but *you* knew that already, didn't you?" He looked at me. His pacing back and forth started to make me anxious. "That is why you were able to locate it."

"You want to take its magic?" I asked.

"You're *smart*." Kaan smiled. I rolled my eyes, and he continued, "And to get that magic, I will need an Illuminator with each of their powers." Of course, he wanted to find both me and Killian.

"Including us."

"Including you," he repeated. "Walker is not an Illuminator, but he has the counter-power of yours. Therefore, that's enough."

"What makes you think the people of Kosmos, including Illuminators and Stellar Court, will help you take that much power?"

Kaan smirked. "They will. Illuminators are already on the witches' side. We manage to convince the doubting ones and Stellar Court is well... not exactly aware of any of this." I frowned, remembering how quickly Ed's opinions changed.

"You *spelled* them," I said, looking straight at Kaan.

"*Drugged* them to be exact," he said. "Axel's plan, of course. A master in potions. I would take all credit, however, Stellar Court was already ahead with the plan."

"You let Stellar Court do it to the people of Kosmos, only so that you can later drug the Court itself."

"Surprising really. Never thought any of them, including Axel, had much potential," Kaan said as if talking to himself. I had barely eaten any food on Lunar Castle the last few hours, not until I got to Texas. Axel had poisoned the food, making Illuminators follow the Court's orders.

"But a potion can only be temporary. It messes with everyone emotionally. You can't permanently spell thousands of people," I added. *Not even with the magic he will get from the book. That would be beyond the laws of the entire universe.* It was just impossible. I didn't need to read it to know that. Something told me Kaan had a second plan. And that plan involved me and Killian. Kaan wanted me on his side. I was the only one he wanted to keep imprisoned.

But why? What other plan did he have that involved me?

"You have another plan," I thought out loud, filling the blanks. "A loophole."

Kaan stopped pacing and stood in front of me without saying anything, smiling. "You plan on using me and Killian... to erase everybody's memories after you get the power." My mind raced with thoughts. "Maybe even create and alter memories, if that's even possible. Because that's the only way you can rule Kosmos."

CHAPTER 18
CHEMICAL AND PHYSICAL
REACTION

T O GAIN AND USE SUCH POWER was dangerous. Especially when that power was used for bad motives. The whole reason why Illuminators were created was to maintain a balance between the supernatural. To make sure that magic was used only for good. And that is what I intended to preserve.

The duo and I were taken back into the large room, tied up in chairs again in the right corner. This time, the quietness had disappeared. Replaced by movement and whispered conversations. In the middle of the room was drawn a pentagram for the witches to make the spell. And the *Illuminated* sat on a podium placed in the middle of the pentagram. Illuminators surrounded it in a circle. An Illuminator with each power: four Earthkalais, four Jovian-kalais, and four Celestialkalais. Then, there was me and Killian, still tied up. Axel and Dani stood across us, guarding one of the four exits while other witches paced around the room, staying close to the remaining exits. Two witches stood behind us, making sure we didn't try anything. I recognized them from the time Killian and I ran away from the mall.

Kaan had planned all of this for years. To rule Kosmos and have everyone at his feet. He just needed the last two Celestialkalais. And he got us because I was too desperate to get answers.

"I'm not an Illuminator, but we are definitely not letting him go through with this right?" Gilbert whispered.

"Of course not. I think I have a plan," I answered. *I really hope it works.*

"Whatever, you are thinking Clara, my well-thought plan is way easier, more efficient, and less time-consuming. Just kill everyone and be done," added Killian, looking desperate. I raised my eyebrows at him.

"Save your plan as plan *Z*," Gilbert said.

The double doors to our left opened, where Kaan came in dressed in a more modern and fancier coat. It was still black colored but with silver stitching and buttons at the center front. Everybody, including the Illuminators, stopped their chatter and bowed down at the sight of Kaan. He walked with confidence to the center of the room, glancing at me as he did.

"Untie her... *and* him," he demanded to a witch behind us. I was confused about what was about to happen. I shook my hands once I was untied and the witch grabbed me by my arm quickly, probably thinking I was about to use magic or something.

"They just hurt," I explained, but he didn't let go and shoved me forward towards the podium. I slightly glanced at Gilbert and

Killian, to let them know I knew what I was about to do. Or I hoped that I did. Gilbert looked somewhat confused, while Killian looked completely furious as he was also shoved into the Illuminator circle.

"There," Kaan said, nodding across from him. We stood across from each other, the podium standing between us. In sight, I could see Killian looking around the circle. What *I* knew was that witches were going to make a spell that would somehow take the magic out of the book and into Kaan. I wasn't sure what my exact physical plan was with the spell, but Kaan was not going to get that magic. Refusing the spell with my *own* magic was an option. There was a chance that if I concentrated enough, the spell would not even start. *It's all in the mind.*

Kaan put his hand on top of the opened book. For him, the *Illuminated* must have looked blank, but I could see the cursive and old writing that explained the powers of each Illuminator.

"Your hands." He held out his hands, looking straight at me. I sighed uncomfortably and shook my head. "I thought you would deny so I brought you motivation to help you with your decision." I stood still, without moving an inch.

"Bring her," he demanded. I turned to look at the double black doors as I heard her voice.

"Let go of me!" She screamed. My sister's silhouette entered the room with a gun to her head.

"*Aurora.*"

"Clara?" Aurora frowned. Tears in her eyes fell over her cheeks. "Let go of me!" She screamed at the witches holding her, trying to get to me. I ran to her, but the moment I hit the end of the pentagram, I was pushed back by an invisible force.

"Let go of her!" I screamed at the witches, getting up. They ignored me and got ready to pull the trigger.

"Fine, I'll do it!" I said, turning back to Kaan. "Just tell them to let her go."

"Your hands first," Kaan responded. I walked back to the center, stood across from him, and grabbed his hands, they were ice-cold at the touch. *I'm going to be sick.*

He nodded at the witches. They let go of my sister but stood closely behind her.

"See? It wasn't that hard was it." Kaan winked at me, smiling.

"Start," Axel said from behind Kaan. The witches, including Kaan, started chanting a Latin spell that I didn't pay attention to. Because seconds before they started chanting, I sensed a warmth coming from the book. The warmth first touched my hands then all around me, like feeling the Sun on my entire skin but not exactly burning. *It shouldn't be this easy to get the magic.* I started focusing on it.

It isn't. A voice that was not my own responded in my mind. I was going to ask where the voice came from, but I guessed I wasn't going to receive an answer as a new vision came to mind.

I hadn't been inside Stellar Castle, but there I was. At least, mentally. I stood inside of a golden room, in the middle stood a brown dais. And floating on top of it, a 3D solar system model, exactly like an Orrery. Golden rings surrounded it, making it look more beautiful and shinier. *The Astral Orrery. It represents Kosmos magic, a witch-created symbol that only connects all witch magic,* the voice said. *Both types of magic are part of the universe, but they cannot be mixed.* The whole model moved, including the golden rings and individual planets, as each of them glowed like the drawings in the *Illuminated*. Planets. Each of them represented each Illuminator. If the spell that the witches chanted was strong enough to transfer the book's magic to Kaan, then maybe I could transfer it to something else. *Causing a chemical reaction and using my power to bring back everybody's memories and beliefs.*

You know what to do, Clara, the voice said confidently.

The witches continued chanting. It was time. I closed my eyes and tried to concentrate. Whether it was witch magic or Illuminator magic that I felt, it was magic, nonetheless. Different sides of the same coin. It couldn't be connected, but it could work together for a purpose. Power surrounded me. Like a warm, dangerous feeling. *Are you the one to secure it?* were the words written in the book after I opened it for the first time. *I am.* I thought in my head.

"Why is it not working?" Kaan said angrily. He stopped chanting, but the other witches kept going. His hands held mine too firmly; they were starting to hurt.

I glared at him. "Like you said, this is Illuminator magic. It is not for you or anyone besides an Illuminator to use." I let go of his hand, watching the book dissipate into thin air. A vision of the Orrery planets lighting up flashed in my mind. I suspected magic from the book connected with the Astral Orrery in Stellar Castle, causing a brief burst all around Kosmos. For the reason that the second I let go of Kaan, he stumbled back following in sync with every other Illuminator and witch in the room. Both types of magic, Illuminator and witch, had collided with each other.

Chemical reaction.

The Illuminators stood up slowly looking around. Their faces, their memories, and their beliefs were brought to reality. *The spell is broken.* Witch magic had slowed for a few minutes. I wanted to run to my sister, but being closer to Kaan made it easy to stop him if he tried to do anything.

"No!" Kaan screamed as he remained weakly on the floor. The spell had probably weakened him the most. The other witches stood up slowly, grunting from weakness or pain. Without hesitating, Kaan turned to the witches behind Gilbert and Killian, who was trying to untie himself.

"Kill them!" Kaan screamed.

But Killian was faster and bit one of the witches who was inches away from Gilbert. A slight of disgust crossed my mind, but it was not the time to get angry.

It was at that moment that everyone shifted and realized it was time to do something. Some of the witches tried to walk towards the Illuminators, chanting a spell that with luck didn't get to finish. The Earthkalais and Celestialkalais grabbed hold of the witches closer to them. Meanwhile, Kaan stood up looking at Axel, as if they could read each other's minds. Dani stood next to Axel semi-shocked at everything that was happening, but that didn't stop her from looking at me cold-heartedly. Kaan proceeded to walk towards the Joviankalais, the pure science order that were not sure what to do. Without nature, metal, chemicals, or creator tools around, they were pretty much defenseless.

"You underestimate us," Ed said, who stood next to a Joviankalai Arch, realized what was going on, and created a protection wall between Kaan and the Joviankalais. At the same time, Axel managed to magically aim at throwing an *Allium* syringe at Killian, who was rubbing off blood from his shirt. Being a second late, Killian managed to obliviate both Axel and Dani. Then, he fell down, watching Axel and Dani proceed to run out of the room scared and confused. Killian grunted and murmured something I wasn't able to hear. Gilbert stood next to the two weak witches close to him, watching them closely. Avoiding them from getting to Killian.

"What do we do?" Ed asked, looking at me and then at every other Illuminator in the room. I stayed quiet because I hadn't planned further ahead. What were supposed to do to the witches that followed Kaan? What were we supposed to do to Kaan? Killing them was not an option I had in mind, no matter how badly I wanted to keep balance.

"Let's take them out, there's probably more witches outside or night vampires," Julien spoke with great confidence. He looked at me, as if for approval. I nodded. Every Illuminator did too as they started moving towards the exits with the witches walking weakly and slowly in front of them until the room was only filled with five people.

Kaan laughed, the second the door closed behind them.

"It's over, Kaan," I said. He turned around to look at me. I stared him straight in the eyes and stood my ground.

"As long as magic exists, it is never really over," he said and in a flash, disappeared, entering a red portal. I looked at Gilbert confused. Then I turned to look at my sister.

"Aurora? What are you doing?" I said. She stood hypnotized,

pointing a gun at Gilbert.

"I'm supposed to kill him," she spoke like a robot.

"She's probably compelled," Gilbert said. "Axel must have convinced his vampire friends." I looked at Aurora.

"Aurora. Look at me. You don't want to hurt anyone, okay?" I shook my head and walked closer to her.

"Don't walk any closer," she demanded, then pointed the gun at me.

"No, Aurora. Stop."

"I have to kill him... and I will." She pointed the gun back at Gilbert. In a panic, I ran to her. And grabbed the gun from her hands. Instead of fighting it, she let go easily and stood still, looking at Gilbert. I proceeded to check if the gun was loaded. But it was empty.

I was too distracted, inspecting the gun to notice Kaan appearing and standing a few feet away from Gilbert.

"I do love knives," he said, throwing a dagger and disappearing back into thin air.

I wasn't fast enough to run towards Gilbert and use a protection wall. Not fast enough to stop the knife from hitting his chest, deep and close to the heart.

"Oh my god," I whispered as I approached him, dropping the empty gun. "Oh my god, Gilbert." I crouched next to him. Killian slowly sat up and moved next to Gilbert as well.

Gilbert laid awake, breathing slowly. Red-silver blood coming from his wound stained his white-colored shirt.

"My parents... figure out," he said in a whisper. Killian moved closer to him.

"I did, mate... in secret. I was going to tell you. There is no truth, everything we knew was correct," Killian said. "They loved you till the end, Gil." Gilbert's eyes watered and held a half-smile on his face.

"No, no, no... Gilbert," I cried. "Hold on, okay. Killian and I will get help." I looked at Killian. "We have to take him to the hospital quickly." But Killian did not move or speak. I looked around looking for a phone, anything to communicate with someone else.

"Killian, we have to move! An Illuminator biologist or a mind healer is just outside, they might know something." Killian shook his head, but I continued rambling. "I mean he is a vampire he can still survive, it's a *metal* knife and it doesn't have Illuminator blood," I said, grabbing Gilbert's hand.

"He's still human," Killian mumbled.

"That's why we have to take him to the hospital anyway!"

"It hit right in his heart. He has only a few minutes left."

I shook my head. I refused to believe the truth.

"Stay awake, Gilbert. Okay? Look I still haven't fully paid you for the hospital, you have to open a great bakery, and you have to teach me the recipe secrets ..."

Gilbert pressed his lips tight. "Your friendship and trust were more than enough." I closed my eyes, focusing on every happy memory I had with him, hoping that it could help him stay awake. His friendship with Killian, his best days at the bakery, and moments with Mary and William. Every one of his happiest memories went through my mind like watching someone's life before me. Like I was there all along.

I opened my eyes to see him again, but his own eyes were slowly closing. "No, stay awake. Please, you have to stay awake!"

He looked from me to Killian and smiled. "I will see on the other side," he whispered, tears running down his cheeks. His brightness slowly faded away and his grip on my hand released as he took his last breath. And he was gone.

"No, no..." I cried, lying next to him. My voice lost power. "You can't die."

"Clara..." Killian murmured. "Come on, we have to go, Goldenrose." But I didn't move, and I couldn't. I didn't want to leave Gilbert. I couldn't believe that he was gone.

Everything after that was a blur. I saw shadows in the dark, whispering. Silhouettes of people screaming, running, fighting, and disappearing into black holes in the air. Killian's words echoed in the silence as he walked me out of the abandoned building and into a car. My eyes became so heavy that I fell into a deep sleep. One that I hoped never to wake up from. But when I did, it was the most excruciating pain I could ever feel.

CHAPTER 19
PANIC ROOM

"CLARA," A FAINT VOICE SPOKE. "Clara, wake up."
I crept open my eyes, lids heavy, and sat up. Light shone inside the confined gray room. My body ached. I grunted, blinking at a nurse in front of me. "Here's the food for today. Eat well." She smiled, turning around and leaving through the dull door. The sound of the door being locked echoed through the gloomy room. A tray laid in the bed with disgusting-smelling food, soggy pancakes, oatmeal, sausages, and sour orange juice. A breakfast meal without scrambled eggs. But that was the least concerning, as my mind recollected everything. Every single detail and feelings of a dream that was not real.

"Oh my god," I whispered, shaking my head. *But it felt so real. How is it not real?*

It couldn't be possible that I had dreamt all of it.

It shouldn't be possible. Because I could still feel my eyes heavy from the crying. I could still see Killian's face with pain and hear the voice of Gilbert's last words. I could feel all of it. I could see all the memories.

But at the same time, I remembered the days I spent alone in the mental institution, daydreaming of another life. Of a life that I wished I had.

I stood up, walking back and forth. The universe crystal ball standing in the small window reflected my silhouette. "How was it all a dream? Why am I still here?"

Tears ran down my face for minutes. I sat down on the bed, replaying everything that happened in the *dream* world. That's how I called it. A world of magic and dreams.

I was such a fool to think that all of that was actually real. To believe that my family loved me, that I had some friends, and to believe that I was part of some special powerful group of magical people. At a certain point, it wasn't that surprising that everything had been a dream. Not after the years I had spent daydreaming of another life. Or the days I spent locked inside the room, having nothing to do but to just think.

An hour later, the nurse came back. I quickly wiped my face with my sleeve to conceal the crying, moving my messy hair from my eyes. I looked at her as she came in. She wasn't the same nurse I had yesterday. They usually changed shifts. Unlike the last nurse, she seemed nicer.

"You didn't eat?" she asked. I shook my head.

"I'm not that hungry." I stared at the crystal ball, the only thing I brought from the house that I was able to keep.

"They told me you didn't eat enough yesterday or the days before." I sighed, barely listening, repeating in my head the names of the planets shown in the ball in order. *Sun, Mercury, Venus... Pluto.* "I'll let it pass for right now, but you will have to eat later, okay?" I only nodded. She took the tray and placed it in the gray cart that stood in the hallway. Then, she came back to the room.

"By the way—" she continued, "—you have to come with me. You have a meeting with Dr. Credell."

I scrubbed my eyes, following the nurse out of the room. My body felt weightless, empty from both inside and outside. The hallways smelled fresh and clean. I was alone, but at least inside a somewhat clean and comfortable place. Yet that didn't make me feel any better.

Some patients walked in the hallways, talking to themselves. Others walked with tied-up hands and bodyguards behind them. Before coming to the institution, I had imagined a hospital with long white and gray hallways and the smell of sewer water. But it was the opposite. Walls in gray, white, and *beige* surrounded everything. Colors I liked turned to complete sadness. The hallways were normal, but with a lot of turns, it could be easy to get lost. Workers often cleaned the hallways and rooms. The only downside was the disgusting food and the suffocating rooms.

We made another turn around in another hallway. I could hear screams from afar. But the nurse seemed unbothered as we passed the white double doors and into another part of the building. I looked away from my reflection in the glass walkway after two seconds. Dull eyes stared back at me. I was my own stranger. The nurse finally stopped, knocked on the door with the

Dr. Credell sign and nodded at me to go inside.

I opened the door to Dr. Credell's organized office. He sat down in his chair looking at his laptop, then looked up the second he heard me walk into the room. Files stood neatly everywhere. At the desk, the file cabinet, and the bookshelf.

"Hello, Ms. De Rose." He stood up and half-smiled. "Please sit down." He pointed to the black couch by the window.

Dark green filled the thin gaps of the blinds. I walked to it and sat down, feeling the streaks of sunlight warming the skin beneath my beige pajamas. He brought his chair a few feet away from me, sat with ease, and fixed his glasses in place. I wondered how he would look without them. Or if he could even see at all.

"Alright, Ms. De Rose," he said, turning around to grab a file from his desk and opening it. "You have been here for about one month and a half."

I nodded slightly.

"Last meeting you didn't want to speak. Are you ready to do it now?"

I stayed silent.

He continued, "Look, Clara. I can't help you if you don't tell me what is going on. Your family and friends are worried."

"I'm not crazy," I responded, looking into his young eyes. But I was the only one to believe so. It had been fourteen days in confinement, forty-eight days in the asylum, and still nobody believed me.

"It will be a lot easier for you to get out if you tell the truth about what happened that day." *That day.* The day everyone decided they were done with me, the day everyone turned their backs on me over a lie. A lie that didn't even make sense at all.

"For the hundredth time, I *told* the *truth*. I didn't hurt anybody. Or had *reason* to hurt anybody. All of it is a lie. There is no reason for me to be here because I didn't do anything and I'm *not* crazy," I ranted.

Dr. Credell nodded quietly. Even him, who was a few years older than me, didn't believe me. Just as the last time I had explained. Of course, he didn't. Because everyone had told him the exact opposite.

"You've been here about two months, Clara. And I don't see any progress. Nurses say you still spend days alone, sitting down in the room or sleeping. You don't come out to talk with other patients and you don't want to eat," he continued.

"The pills make me feel tired," I said. "And I don't see the point in making friends anymore. I don't need to anyway because most are actually crazy and *I'm not*."

"Do you still see the visions?" he asked slowly.

"They are not visions, they are..."

"Daydreams?" He finished my sentence. "That is what your parents said you would say. You talk to yourself while daydreaming?"

"You don't?" I asked, smiling at the stupid question. The same question my mom had asked me a few months ago. She saw me pacing around my room, talking to myself. I had just finished a book and was daydreaming about another alternative ending. *Daydreaming... not hallucinating.*

My mind had woken up, saw the signs, and they still called me crazy. My parents and friends asked me why I suddenly wanted to be alone. Why I didn't talk or go out. *The hypocrisy.* Why I spent time sitting down thinking or reading a book. *The gaslighting.* Why I wasn't the way I was before. Before I was being brainwashed, just as I was being now.

At first, my head was filled with questions about good and evil. Confusion about my actions, my feelings, or theirs. But I realized who I was and who I thought everyone wanted me to be. I was not happy, but I was not sad either. I was just there. Following orders, being nice, solving people's problems, etc. Actions that a selfless person would do. Truthfully, it did make me happy to make people happy. But I was emotionally tired of giving and not receiving. I changed for me. When my mind opened and I saw that no matter how much effort I made, after everything I had done, everyone was slowly turning away. First my sister, my friends, then my parents. And complete loneliness came in. The sad truth is that I had always been alone. I just never saw it until months ago.

"Your family is here today," Dr. Credell said, closing the file. "Including your sister." He walked to the door.

"I'll see you in a few days, Ms. De Rose. I hope to see some great progress," he said, opening the door. I got up and headed out. The nurse waited for me outside and led me to one of the visitor rooms where my so-called, caring family waited for me.

I didn't smile when I entered the room. I would have preferred it if they didn't visit at all. It had been precisely two weeks since their last and only visit. But I was too angry at them before to speak to them. I was of course still angry but now with a mix of sadness and disappointment.

The room smelled like soap, my mom's smell. It filled the small room. My mom smiled at me and got up from the chair to give me a slight hug. She pulled away when she saw I wasn't returning it and sat back down. I sat across from my parents, trying to hold back tears. My palms ached out of pressing my nails hard on them.

"What are you doing here?" I mumbled. My mom looked at my dad, their faces almost expressionless.

"We care about you, Clara," she responded, and my dad nodded. They could've been cast as actors with the sudden sad expressions. Only for a few years, now and then, I held their care. There were times when I could see a glimmer of light in their eyes. Hope. Love. Easily faded away in seconds at the realization of their actions. Gone in the middle of the night, just like that.

I scoffed. "No, you don't. If you did, you would have believed me, that I'm not crazy. You wouldn't have chosen Aurora's word over mine."

"We don't think you are crazy," my dad said.

"Ironic, seeing as I've been in this *mental* institution for a month and a half."

"We just want you to get better, Clara," my mom replied, eyes lowering from my sight.

"Better at what exactly? Become your perfect child again? Be who you want me to be. Pretend nothing is wrong?" I half-laughed. "Seems like Aurora is doing that already."

"That's not true, Clara." She frowned. "Maybe you would like to talk to Aurora? Maybe to say sorry?"

Aurora hadn't visited me at all since I'd been to the hospital. I wasn't sure if it was because she was guilty or just didn't care about me at all. Option two seemed more believable.

"I have nothing to be sorry about," I shot back, hearing the door open and seeing her shadow walking closer.

"We will come back later and leave you two alone," my mom whispered to her. She and Dad got up to leave, their presence replaced by my older sister.

Aurora held a strained smile, her body stiff until my parents left the room. Her aspect changed into complete coldness matching Dani's facial expression, reminding me of the dream I had.

"How are you doing, sis? You're not becoming *crazier*, are you?" She mocked.

"We both know I'm not crazy. You know I didn't attack you or my boyfriend." I tried to stay calm.

"Based on facts, you are." She smiled, sitting in front of me. "And it is *my* boyfriend now, in case you don't remember."

Frankly, it didn't matter that she had taken Soran, we had been in an unsure, no progress relationship anyway. But I couldn't understand why my own sister had betrayed me. The morning before my parents arrived from vacation, I sat quietly in my room editing some photographs, reading books, and studying for college. As I read, I got hungry and headed to the kitchen for lunch. Soran and Aurora were sitting on the couch laughing.

Around those days he had broken up with me, but I rolled my eyes at him out of shock at seeing them together. After a few minutes, I was walking out of the kitchen and heard the noise of something falling in the hallway by the stairs. I walked fast towards it. Soran laid on the floor unconscious with blood coming from his shirt as Aurora cried next to him, her head also wounded. Then, she started screaming at me, telling me what I had done. It was like a blur. But I clearly remember the bloody knife on the floor. I was confused, but I shook my head, knowing I hadn't done anything wrong. I couldn't have done anything wrong. But my parents came into the house only seconds later, witnessing the aftermath. I'd been taken by the police and had endured trials until it was decided that I was insane.

Guards forcibly took me to the institution. I had no choice but to drop college and leave everything behind. Soran and my ex-friends sided with Aurora, who knows what lies she told them. I clearly remembered having seen Aurora smirk as I was taken inside the institution for the first time.

"How could you lie? To everyone: my parents, Soran, my friends? What did I ever do to you?" I asked.

She chuckled and stood up to leave. "You are not so perfect anymore, are you? Maybe, you never were..."

"Was it jealousy, then? Was it because I was who they wanted me to be?" I frowned. "And when you saw I was over the edge with it all, you took your chance to shine. Made a plan, acted as the victim, and made everyone believe I was more 'crazier' than they already thought. Congrats, sister, they should give you an Oscar for that." She stayed quiet, inspecting me like a rat lab. "Answer me!" I stood up to approach her.

"You are *pathetic*," she responded with a smirk on her face.

I couldn't hold in my anger and slapped her. The cameras started rolling. She dramatically fell to the floor and slid back to the wall far away from me.

"At least I'm not a traitor!" I stood my ground, watching her.

"Help!" she screamed to the point that my old self would have believed it. "Please, don't hurt me!" And guards quickly entered the room, taking me harshly by my arms.

"Let go of me! I didn't do anything!" I pleaded as they took me out of the room. My parents stood outside shocked. "I didn't do anything, Mom. Please you have to believe me! Check the recordings! Dad, it is the truth! I'm not crazy, she is!" They both shook their heads, turned away from me, and helped Aurora get out of the visitors' room while the guards took me back to my prison. *Room 1216.*

The walls echoed in my mind. They screamed to get out, to run, and never turn back. But I couldn't, no matter how much I wanted to. The guards screamed at me to stop fighting it, shoving me inside the loneliness. I felt the walls slowly closing me in, suffocating me.

"Please, let me out! I'm not crazy! You have to believe me!" I repeated, crying and pounding at the gray metal door. I punched it until blood appeared on my knuckles, and I could no longer feel the pain in my hands.

Within a matter of ten seconds, two nurses came in and stopped me. They tried to hold me still as they sedated me and put me in bed. I tried to fight off the sleepiness, but it was impossible. I gave in, hearing the door of the room close.

But before I could fully drift off, I saw blue light coming from my left arm and a faint warmth. Feeling weak, I slightly raised it to see the blue light slowly fading from inside my forearm. And a drawing, larger than a quarter, appeared like magic; neatly drawn with detail and hanging feathers. A second before I dozed off, I saw the black ink appear. The tattoo of a dreamcatcher.

I fell back into a deep sleep with Kaan's words echoing in my mind. *As long as magic exists, it is never really over.*

TO BE CONTINUED...

ACKNOWLEDGEMENTS

I would like to start by saying that you might be shocked about the ending, just as I was when I thought about it for the first time.

There are people who, even though they haven't read much about this book, have always been there since I started and very well know how writing means so much to me. I won't be saying full names for privacy.

I want to thank Jessica (Jessie) for literally being there since the very beginning. When I named my novel and the main characters you were there. You were the first person I showed and told my ideas to and wrote them in my draft notebook. Even though we never talked after high school, wherever you are, thank you. I miss you.

Another person I want to thank is Quinn (Charlie). I have not forgotten about you. You were there during my drafting days and the first beta reader I ever got. We got to talk about our university experiences, and I will never forget the amount of positivity you gave me. You were the first to read my drafts and helped me with my writing. Even though you didn't get to finish the story, I hope that you are finally able to read the final product. Thank you.

Jesi (a.k.a. Scarlett Downs), my friend, I cannot even find the words to begin saying thank you for literally everything. Out of everyone, you were always here in the process of writing and editing. You were the first to read and finish my manuscript.

Because of your motivation, I continued writing. I owe you so much. I will forever be grateful to you. I hope all your writing dreams become accomplished and don't forget I'm always here when you need me.

I want to thank Izzy for being there since the beginning too. You were the first person I told I was writing a book, and you were there when we received a notebook which would later turn into my 'Illuminators Drafting Notebook' in high school. Since then, you've watched me write and draft (during lunch in school) and at home whenever we called. Thank you for motivating me to keep going and always showing writing positivity. Thank you so much.

Lastly, I would like to thank all of my wonderful and chaotic siblings. You all have been there since my reading, writing diaries, and novel days. Out of all of us, I'm the only one who likes reading and writing, therefore you never read my book or a draft (I don't even think you ever will). But you all always showed positivity when I talked about accomplishing my writing goals. You were all there when I was obsessed with vampires, magic, and the universe. When I started writing diary entries and all those days I spent writing The Illuminators in the corner of my room. To my older brother, thank you for always telling me to never give up on writing. To my younger sister, thank you for listening to me rambling about all the ideas I ever had for this novel. To my little brother, who happily said he would read my novel when he was older. Thank you all so much from the bottom of my heart.

Once again, thank you so much! I love every one of you. To my siblings, if you ever decide to read my novel, I hope you love it as much as I do.

FREQUENTLY ASKED QUESTIONS

1. What inspired me to be a writer?

Like I'm sure every other writer has said, I began to write because I loved reading. I loved going to the school library to check out books because my parents wouldn't let me buy actual copies at the time. Until I managed to persuade them that reading was a valuable habit. I started reading more and writing diaries. Till then writing almost daily became a habit.

2. When did my writing journey start?

My writing journey started when I wrote in my diary every day. To be more specific I liked movies and shows like Twilight and The Vampire Diaries. I might've begun writing on diaries, either due to TVD or after watching The Adventures of Sharkboy and Lavagirl. The mix between supernaturals, magic, and dreams were topics that interested me.

3. How did The Illuminators came to be?

I knew I loved writing but never thought I would actually do it. So, The Illuminators came to me like a miracle. From a simple gifted school notebook to the sudden idea of writing a supernatural love triangle. Weirdly enough, the first thing that came into mind after my main character names was the title for the book. I wasn't sure what the story was going to be about, but I knew after the title that I wanted it to represent a battle between dichotomies (a.k.a. light and darkness).

4. Any other hobbies besides writing?

Other hobbies that I do are playing piano, photography, editing, and making videos. Playing piano interested me since I was younger

,but I didn't fully played actually bought a keyboard or played songs until listening to the Twilight soundtrack by Carter Burwell.

5. What makes this story unique?

Dichotomy makes this story unique. This series is a battle between good and bad or light and darkness. I believe readers will be able to connect with the experiences of these characters and find their own path to light. Unlike other stories, I want The Illuminators to send a message to all the people that anything in the universe is possible. That everything can be accomplished with the mind, heart, and soul. If you search for the light, you will find it.

THE ILLUMINATORS PLAYLIST

Illuminate - Wildes

Illuminated - Hurts

Ticking - TIN

Experience - Ludovico Einaudi

Daylight - David Kushner

She Remembers - Max Richter

Cosmos - Hazy

Cardigan - Taylor Swift

The Other Side - Ruelle

Mr. Sandman - SYML

Broken - OTR, Au/Ra

Jungle - Emma Louise

Lovely - Billie Eilish

Ceilings - Lizzy McAlpine

Unfair - The Neighborhood

Dream - Imagine Dragons

Mind is a Prison - Alec Benjamin

The City Holds My Heart - Ghostly Kisses

I Lost A Friend - Finneas

So Close To Magic - Aquilo

Mr. Forgettable - David Kushner

1216 - Echos

Panic Room - Au/Ra

Guadalupe Gonzalez is a Texas-based author of YA fantasy and fiction novels. She graduated in 2022 with an Associate's of Life Sciences and is graduating on 2025 for a Bachelor's of Science in Forensic Chemistry (including a minor in Forensic Science). After graduation, the goal is to publish more books and pursue a forensic chemistry career. She doesn't plan to stop writing and publishing stories anytime soon.

STAY CONNECTED WITH LU ON:

Website: www.illumiverse.store

Instagram: instagram.com/lugonzalezauthor

Youtube: www.youtube.com/@lu.theauthor